GO F@!K YOURSELF

LAWRENCE ALLAN

1st edition

First published in 2025 Copyright © 2025 Lawrence Allan All rights reserved.

ISBN: 979-8-9861761-5-4 (ebook)

ISBN: 979-8-9861761-4-7 (paperback)

Designed by Yummy Book Covers

Other Books by Lawrence Allan

Big Fat F@!k-up

Big F@!king Deal

For more information about Lawrence Allan,

check **out LawrenceAllanWrites.com**

or subscribe to his newsletter at

https://bit.ly/LAWnewsletter

*For those who have hit rock bottom
again and again...*

Go F@!k Yourself

1

—

IT WAS ONE o'clock on a Tuesday morning. "Gypsys, Tramps, and Thieves" played loudly so there was no possibility of falling asleep at the wheel as I drove east on the 10 from West Hollywood to Highland Park. Zipping around a few cars, I asked myself what the hell I was doing. And *why*? I should've been in bed.

"What. Is. This. Shit?" demanded Anton, the reason I was in the car rather than asleep. He was in his mid-twenties, broad shouldered, Black, with short, tight locs. He was in a gray sweatshirt and a leather jacket, trying to fight off the chill of L.A. in March. He wasn't the kid I remembered from three years ago.

"What?" I asked, passing a slow-moving sedan with a

dented back bumper. Even though it was winter — L.A.'s version of winter, anyway — I was sweating as I regretted my recent life choices. I really should've ignored Anton's knock on my door.

He told me he was in trouble and thought, the madman that he was, that he should come to *me* for help.

It had been over three years since we had last seen each other. That was when he had gotten into trouble with the LAPD, who were dead sure he had committed an assault during a robbery. The evidence against him was bad, and his lawyer — my mother — suggested he take the plea deal. Gordon Bixby, the in-house detective at Mom's firm and my mentor at the time, agreed. No one believed Anton's pleas of innocence except little old me, a former child star who had crashed his career with booze and pills but retained his uncanny knack for hearing lies even when they were spoken as the God's honest truth.

Of course, everyone thought I was dumb for believing in Anton. I was just a baby private detective at the time, just learning the ropes. What would I know?

"This shit." He aimed a finger at my phone, which was sitting on the dash of my Toyota. "What is it?"

"The song?" I also pointed at my phone. "It's Cher."

He looked at me blankly.

"*Cher*," I repeated. "You know... Cher. Cher? Singer. Actress. One-named *icon*?"

My eyes bugged out. "You don't *know* what you *stole*? I don't know which is more upsetting."

He shrugged again. "I was told not to ask questions, so I *didn't*."

I stuffed down the impulse to scoff — displaying my growing maturity — and instead said, "Just so *I'm* clear: You got involved in a theft without asking what it was you were stealing?"

"You sound pissed."

I clicked my tongue and wagged a finger. "Au contraire. I am *angry*." Turning away, I stepped into my kitchenette, grabbed a clean glass, and filled it with water from the sink. "You know why?" I didn't wait for an answer. "I got you out of a big mess, and here you are, into another one." I drank. "You told me you were going to get away from the shitty people."

He slumped, like the air had gone out of him. "I tried, OK?"

Anton was telling me the truth, but... "What does that even mean?"

"That means, I *tried*, OK?" His back was straight again, shoulders turned to me, his voice firm. "Not all of us have lawyer moms and movie checks coming in." He pointed to the movie memorabilia on my walls. Old posters of movies I had starred in. Photographs of me with A-listers. He took a short breath. "I got things I want to do in this world, and that means I need money. And you know? Legit people aren't fans of my résumé. I did the job tonight because I can't just keep taking from my mom and my girlfriend. I did the job because I am *trying* to make something of myself. And that means having money."

He let that hang in the air. He was — sorta, maybe — right. Which made me the asshole. I didn't like that. I took a breath. Anton had grown up a lot since I had seen him last, which had been right in this living room.

"You have a girlfriend?" They grow up so fast.

"*Jimmy.*"

I nodded. "OK. You stole… *something.*"

He licked his lips. There was more. "It might be worse, actually."

"Worse?" And did he say *might*?

"Yeah."

"What happened?" I was thirsty again.

Traffic was almost nonexistent at this time of night, so we made good time. I left the 10 and took the ramp onto the 110, heading north. The playlist moved on to "Dance Monkey" by Tones and I. Anton, lost in thought, said nothing.

Back at my place, he had laid it out. A man named Devon Philips, an old friend, had offered Anton an opportunity he couldn't refuse: five thousand dollars for driving and not asking any questions. Devon, Anton, and two other guys he didn't know met up at a large, ground-floor unit at a self-storage facility in Highland Park. Inside, Anton had been handed the keys to a white, unmarked van and told to drive the rest of them to a gallery called Objet Exotique on La Brea Avenue between Beverly Boulevard and Melrose. It specialized in old things, knickknacks and tchotchkes, especially artifacts from the East; the sort of objects rich folks like to have in their homes and tell you all about.

When they arrived at the gallery, Anton backed up to the loading dock, just as he was told. The other three popped out the back, returning twenty agonizing minutes later. As two of them pushed a black plastic box on a dolly, a two-foot cube with latches like a small shipping container, Devon finished up inside before heading to the van. Anton thought it was weird that the box was the only thing being taken, but he had agreed not to ask questions.

On the way back, Devon was in a mood to celebrate. After all, the job was pulled off and nothing had gone wrong. And it was a better haul than he could imagine. Anton was relieved. The other two were quiet and kept eyeing each other.

When they returned to the self-storage, Devon jumped out and pulled up the rolling door to the unit. Inside was a man, waiting. He was, according to Anton, "older than me." He was maybe Middle Eastern, wearing a nice, black suit and a white shirt. At his feet was a large duffel bag.

Hopping back in the van, Devon told Anton to back the

van in. Once they were parked, Anton reached for his door, but Devon told him to stay put.

He and the other two got out. Anton saw the two men exchange glances.

This is where, of course, everything started to go wrong.

I took the York Boulevard exit off the 110 and headed west into Highland Park. We were almost there.

Anton had kept an eye on things through the unmarked van's driver's-side mirror, watching as the meeting suddenly took a turn with Devon in the middle of two angry sides. When the guys came out and Devon's hands went up, Anton decided five thousand dollars wasn't worth it. He jumped out of the van and was already out of the building when he heard the gunshots.

Back at the bungalow, he had said, "I drove here as fast as I could." I made a face, and he assured me he had ditched his car away from my place. "It's all fucked up, and I don't know what to do."

Did he think *I* knew what to do? The way he was looking at me I was sure that he did. Time to burst the bubble. "I don't know what you want me to do here. I'm not a fixer, if that's what you're thinking." I looked around for my phone. "I could call my mom, we could go to the police — "

"No. No cops," he said, shaking his head. Words tumbled out of his mouth. "They're just going to arrest me, railroad me like they did last time. Except this time I *was* involved, but I'm not the mastermind, you know. You got to help me get out of this."

And there it was. Me standing there in my boxers and an old T-shirt and who knew what my hair looked like, and I was being asked to get Anton out of trouble — whatever that meant — and probably commit a felony or two in the process. All I wanted to do was say no. Instead, I mumbled, "Anton, I... I don't know if I can get you out of *this*."

He searched the room for words. Finding none, he nodded and pressed on his knees, standing up. "I thought, of all people, you could... I dunno, do something." He turned to the door.

"It's not that I don't *want* to help." Which may or may not have been true. "I just don't know if I'm the guy."

He stopped and looked at me while I wondered what exactly my problem was. He looked as lost as I felt. I licked my lips. "Since the summer..." — and what a shitty summer it had been — "I haven't had any real cases. I might be a little rusty."

I don't know why I was choosing this particular line of bullshit, but it was my way of giving Anton a reason to find someone better.

"Jimmy, I don't know anyone else who could do *anything* for me. *You're it.*"

Now *that* was a punch in the old stomach. I put up a hand. No más. "Let me change, and we'll go take a look at the situation," I said.

Ten minutes later, with me now in a midnight blue suit with a burgundy shirt and black leather shoes, having run a comb through my hair, we were on the road.

We pulled into the self-storage place. I looked up at the sign and saw that it was called U-WareHaus-It. I couldn't help but have mad respect for the branding mind that had come up with that insane spelling solely to secure a trademark.

The parking lot was empty, the concrete silver under the lights. Nothing was moving. My stomach felt tight.

"Around the back," Anton mumbled.

I followed his gaze and pulled around the building. I stopped the car along the back fence, the still-open door of the storage space in view. I wasn't ready to go in. I turned off my car and said to him, "We could still just call the cops. It would be trouble for you, but it would be the cleanest thing to do."

Anton stared at the building. He shook his head. We were going to stick to the plan, I guess. See what was there and figure it out. I got out, and he followed as I led the way to the storage unit.

The space was a car length and a half deep, about twelve feet wide. The fluorescents cast a bone-bleached glow over the space.

First thing of note: the van was gone. Anton had driven

his car back to my place. So who took the van? But then, there was a bigger issue. It was the second thing: the dead body of a Black man in the middle of the floor.

"Devon," whispered Anton. "Shit."

The man that was Devon laid on the floor near the back wall, dressed in black, sprawled in a small pool of blood. He looked like he had been in his late thirties; his hair was cut short, faded in the back. His chest was bloody, and his eyes and mouth were open. All three gaped at the ceiling. My stomach turned cold and my arms tingled. I had to remember to keep breathing.

Anton took a step closer, but I stopped him with a hand on his arm. "Go back to the car."

"What? No. That's — "

"I know who it is. The situation has moved from being shit to *really* fucked-up. Go back to the car."

"But Devon — "

I put my hands up. "There's nothing you can do. Right now, I have to make a call, and you can't be here when the cops show up."

2

—

Three Years Ago

SLUMPING IN A chair along the wall of my mother's office, I listened as people talked seriously about something. I stared at the clock, willing its hands to move faster. It was nine thirty in the morning, and I was still figuring out how people could function so early in the day. Which begged the question, why would they want to? With so many hours in the day and night to choose from, why would anyone do anything "productive" this early in the morning?

Simply put, I was a mess. Only six months sober, the longest stretch I had managed yet, I was still figuring out how to navigate reality. I just didn't know how people did it day after day.

An elbow jammed me in the ribs. I flinched as the blow snapped me out of my reverie.

The attack had come from my left and was delivered by Gordon Bixby, who sat next to me against the wall. He was a former LAPD detective who took retirement to come and work with my mom at her firm. He was in his late fifties, narrow shouldered and Black, his gray hair still rocking the police regulation cut. He always dressed professionally but unimpressively. Today was no exception: He wore a dark brown suit with a white button-down and a red tie that curved over his developing belly.

He looked at me with knitted eyebrows and lips pressed together. "Are you paying attention?" he said under his breath. His look of annoyance was familiar by now. We had been working together for months, and by working, I mean I was a pain in his ass as he tried to make a detective out of me per my mother's request. She thought it would be good if I had a steady job and, as an added bonus, someone kept me on the straight and narrow.

I nodded, assuring him I totally was as I sat up. He shook his head.

My mother, Greta Cooper, was looking at me, fingers laced together as she sat behind her desk. I guess Gordon and I hadn't been as subtle as we thought.

Her face was passive but told a whole story of disappointment. She was in her early sixties, white and her black hair was just starting to gray and, unlike Gordon, she knew how to dress to impress in her deep purple suit and cream-colored silk blouse. And she was impressive. She was a well-respected defense attorney in L.A. County who put the Cooper in Cooper and Associates, a firm that could handle everything. A one-stop shop for all your legal woes.

Two other people gawked at us as they sat in chairs before Mom's desk, a Black woman and her son. The woman arched an eyebrow as she stared. She was in her early forties, wearing dark-blue slacks, black flats, and a sleeveless white blouse. Her purse remained looped around a shoulder as it sat in her lap. Her shoulder-length hair was pulled back into a ponytail.

On her other side was her son and, as I began to recall, the whole reason I had been summoned to the office at nine in the morning. Twenty-one years old, he leaned past his mother to look at me. He was dressed in a crisp, white shirt that looked brand-new, jeans, and sneakers. A Dodgers cap covered his dyed blond hair. He glared at me, confused, with one leg bouncing in agitation.

His name drifted back into my mind. Gordon had told me all about him when he picked me up that very morning.

Anton Greene was a kid in trouble, and Cooper and Associates was there to help navigate those waters as a favor to a former client. The district attorney had filed charges, believing he had been a part of a break-in in Silver Lake during which a woman had been assaulted. The motivation? Drug money.

Mom took a breath and brought her attention back to the mother and son. "Mrs. Greene, I'm going to be frank with you. It doesn't look good."

"I know that," Mrs. Greene replied, her voice tight. "He's no saint. He's been in trouble before. But he said he didn't do this and I believe him."

Mom glanced at Gordon, who shifted in his seat. She looked back at Mrs. Greene. "I'm a mother, too," she said with the barest of gestures toward me. "And sometimes we want to believe what our kids tell us. Especially when they're in trouble."

I don't know if she ever believed *me*, but she was trying to make a point.

Anton shook his head. "I *didn't* do it."

His mother swatted his shoulder, correcting him, and Anton sat up straight. He huffed. "I didn't do it, Mrs. Cooper."

Mom wagged a finger. "It's Ms. Cooper." The divorce was long since settled and Dad had left town, but Greta Cooper had spent so much time and money on branding that she wasn't going back to her maiden name. She did, however, return to the case at hand. "There's a witness, the victim's statement and physical evidence. All of it places you at the scene of the crime."

"She's wrong or lying," he stated.

I squeaked, then slapped a hand over my mouth, hoping no one had heard me.

"Anton," Mom started. "there's money with your fingerprints on it at the crime scene."

"Why would I leave *money* if I was robbing the place?"

He made a fair point.

"I don't know, Anton. You tell me," she quietly replied.

"I don't know how those got there!" Anton insisted. "Because I wasn't *there*."

I squeaked again. Gordon glanced at me. I cleared my throat and shifted in my seat.

Mom shook her head. "I'd like to believe you, but you haven't even given me an alibi. If you weren't there, where were you?"

Anton said nothing. His mother stared at him.

Mom waved her hand in the air, annoyed. "All right. I can only help you if you help me." She looked to Mrs. Greene. "Right now, there's an opportunity. The DA doesn't want to have a trial. We don't want to have a trial. The plea agreement they've offered… it's not bad." She looked at Anton. "They want you to name the others you were there with."

Anton pursed his lips, breathing heavily through his nose. "How can I name names when I wasn't there? I don't know *who* was there!"

I squeaked again.

"Do you have something to share, James?" my mother snapped, causing three other heads to whip toward me.

I swallowed, looking at everyone while they all again stared at me. "Nope. No." I paused. "I mean..."

Mrs. Greene shook her head. "Which is it?"

Gordon looked up at the ceiling, probably hoping this would make him invisible. Or, at least, not party to my shenanigans.

"Anton's telling the truth," I managed. "He didn't do it."

Silence. Then, Mom let out an exasperated sigh. Gordon looked down at the floor, hoping it would open up and take him quickly.

Mrs. Greene looked me over, considering me seriously for the first time. "What's your name?"

She was clearly not a fan of my oeuvre.

"Jimmy Cooper."

She glanced at my mom, who nodded, admitting I belonged to her. Mrs. Greene shifted back to me, saying, "OK. So you think my son is telling the truth. How do you know?"

"How do I know?" I looked at Anton, who peeked out from behind his mom, his eyes asking me the same question.

"How do you know he didn't do it?" she said.

My mouth opened. Closed. How could I explain that I just *knew*? That I could tell when someone was lying because I was *really* good with body language — hello, acting career

— and Anton *wasn't* lying? There was no buzz in the back of my head, no sweats, no nothing. And if he wasn't *lying,* that meant he was telling the truth. He didn't know who was involved. He wasn't there. And he didn't rob that woman.

If I said all that though, I'd look like a crazy person.

"He seems like a good kid," I said, caving in.

Mom tsk'd and shook her head. "James."

Mrs. Greene snorted. "You almost had me," she said as Anton shrank back into his seat. "He is not a good kid. He's had problems with the law before, just got lucky." She looked at her son. "Looks like you've run out of luck."

I pressed on. "I can't explain it. I just know he's telling the truth."

Mrs. Greene frowned. "What do you do here? Are you a lawyer?"

Mom coughed.

"Well, I'm — "

Gordon jumped in before I could finish. "He's working under my supervision. I'm the in-house detective. I support Ms. Cooper's work."

"So you two figure who *really* did it?"

Gordon swallowed. "That's not exactly the job, Mrs. Greene. We look for evidence that might create reasonable doubt for a jury," he said, nodding toward Mom.

Mom nodded back, then said, "He's the foundation for a good defense."

Ugh. Get a room.

Mrs. Greene shook her head and pointed at me. "I want what he said."

"Excuse me?" replied Mom.

"He said my son's not guilty." She looked at me. "I want you to prove he's innocent."

I looked at Gordon.

Again, he swallowed. He hated delicate situations. "That might not be possible, ma'am. Reasonable doubt might be the best — "

"No," stated Mrs. Greene. "That's not good enough. I don't want this reasonable doubt bullshit hanging over Anton's head and future." She looked at my mom. Anton licked his bottom lip, eyes darting among everyone else in the room.

Mom took a breath. She nodded, then turned to Anton, saying, "You need to tell us everything, Anton. We can't do what your mother wants if you're not honest with us."

Anton eyed his mother and then mine. His upper lip glistened. He licked away the sweat as my mom tapped her desk.

This kid did not want to talk. I felt it viscerally in my chest, so much so I was gonna have a heart attack. It must've been either bad, though maybe not criminally bad, or embarrassing enough he didn't want to say a word about it in front of his mother.

I felt so seen.

"Greta," said Gordon in his easygoing baritone, "why don't you and Mrs. Greene get a cup of coffee?" *He* had seen Anton too.

Mom looked at him. An eyebrow twitched. The two must've had some sort of telepathic communication going because Mom put her hands on her desk and said to Mrs. Greene, "That does sound lovely. Would you like a cup? We have great coffee here."

Spoilers: We did — and still do — not.

Mom stood. "Let's let the boys chat."

Mrs. Greene glared at Anton, who did not meet her eyes. Resigned, she stood, hitching the strap of her purse higher on her shoulder. Mom smiled politely, gesturing for her client to lead the way out.

As soon as the office door began to close, Gordon took the seat vacated by Anton's mother. He put himself on the edge of the chair and lean forward. Even though he was taller, this made him eye level with Anton. "OK, son. Your mom is gone. What is it you don't want her to know?"

"You promise not to tell her?"

Gordon agreed. "You're the client, not her," he explained. "What were you doing that night you don't want her to know about?"

Anton blew air out, ready to spill the beans, when his eyes shifted to me. "What are you smiling about?"

"Smiling?" I replied. Was I smiling?

Gordon's brows furrowed.

I *was* smiling. Oh, man. That must've looked *really* bad. The thing is I was giddy. I had actually convinced them that Anton was innocent. I had changed the course of this investigation. Wow. "Just happy to be here," I said.

Anton and Gordon's heads twisted to me in disbelief.

Oops.

"Help, I mean. Happy to help."

Gordon's eyes rolled just enough to be noticed. He started over with Anton. "OK," he said, his voice calm and welcoming. "Tell us what you were up to."

Anton sighed. This was it. He had nowhere else to hide.

"I robbed a drug dealer. Then went and got high."

Gordon's shoulders sagged.

"*Damn*," I said. "That's a *terrible* alibi."

3

—

TEN MINUTES AFTER I made the call, I could hear the sirens of the squad cars headed my way as I stood in front of U-WareHaus-It. Maybe it was standard practice; maybe they couldn't help themselves; or maybe they wanted to show taxpayer money at work, but I thought it was a bit unnecessary. Devon was dead, and nothing was going to change that, no matter how fast they arrived.

Two squad cars roared into the parking lot, lighting me up with their high beams. Squinting, I nodded and waved a friendly, "Don't taze me, bro," as the uniforms stepped out of their cars. A particularly stocky white officer asked if I was the one who had called it in. Which... duh.

I smiled with the appropriate amount of gallows humor,

telling them, "Yeah, I called it in. Where are the detectives?" I looked past them, hoping to catch a glimpse of plainclothes officers heading our way.

Stocky Guy ignored my question and asked, "Where's the body?"

Taking them around the back of the building, I took a quick look at my car, which was still parked by the fence, and then onto the crime scene. We stepped into the space, and even though it was quite clear where the body was, I still felt the need to point. "There he is, officer." Then, for good measure, feeling like an extra in a CBS police procedural, I added, "Found him like that."

The men and women of the LAPD nodded in agreement. Yep, indeed, there was a body and it was in the middle of the floor.

The beefy cop turned to me and said, "All right. We'll take it from here. Why don't you step outside." It was an order rather than a question. "The detectives will be here soon; they'll have questions."

I nodded dutifully, playing along with their power trip. I knew who was coming.

A young officer followed me outside into the cold air. She stood a respectful distance from me, far enough away that it didn't appear like she was guarding me, yet close enough she could chase me down if need be.

Joke's on her. She'd catch me in four paces. I run like a

toddler.

I was antsy. It could've been the chill or the evening's adrenaline wearing off, but I couldn't keep still. I'd take a step here and there, pacing but not really. And when I'm in that headspace, I get chatty.

"Cold, huh?" I said to the cop, trying to normalize this absolutely not normal situation. "I never know what to wear this time of year, you know? You leave the house with layers on and you're too hot, but then the sun goes down and suddenly it's thirty degrees cooler, and you're asking yourself, 'Why don't I own *any* sweaters?'" I paused. "Do you own any sweaters?"

She looked at me like I was insane. Which... fair.

Something caught her attention over my shoulder, the sound of someone sighing in misery.

Then a man's voice called out, complaining, "You didn't tell me it was *him*."

I knew that voice.

"Because I didn't want to hear you complain all the way here," replied a very familiar woman's voice.

I turned around to greet Detectives Kemble and Ito.

"Detective Kemble! Well, well, well, imagine my surprise," I said with Southern Belle flair while fanning myself. Behind him, technicians lugged their equipment toward the crime scene.

"Shut up, Cooper," he growled, a finger aimed right

between my eyes. Kemble was quite the lump of a man, large, white, and solidly in his fifties. His closely cut hair was more salt than pepper, and his gray suit was strictly off the rack from Ross, a big-box department store notoriously known for their slogan: Dress for Less.

Next to him was my favorite detective in all of the LAPD, Detective Violet Ito. She was a Japanese American woman in her thirties, with shoulder-length black hair, clad as always in jeans and leather boots. She wore a black wool coat, which had been given to her this past Christmas by a certain someone in her life — me, I'm that someone — because she always feels chilly this time of year. Yeah, I'm *that* kind of considerate boyfriend.

"Are we *not* spending enough time together, Jimmy?" asked Ito, her head tilting in that adorable way that she does.

I smiled.

We had finally gotten off the will-they-won't-they merry-go-round and had been officially dating since the end of last summer. It was lucky for all parties that Violet was working the late shift. How awkward would that have been if she had been over at my place when Anton knocked? More often than not, she came over to mine because she still lived with her mom, and her mom had only recently sort of started to like me. I wasn't going to ruin that by staying over at Violet's mom's house, no matter how many times she asked.

(I'm kidding. She never asked. She thought it would be weird to have a guy over at her and her mom's house. She was looking for her own place, which would make her an oddity in the LAPD, actually living in the city she works in, but, hey, L.A. prices, y'all.)

Kemble glared at her. "*Christ*. What is *wrong* with you two? We see him at *crime scenes*. This is turning into some Jessica Fletcher shit. Isn't this suspicious?"

Ito rolled her eyes. "I don't care how badly you want to believe it. Jessica Fletcher wasn't a serial killer. *Murder, She Wrote* was a TV show with a very specific story telling device. Can you just let it go?"

A dog with a bone, Kemble persisted, "We see him all the time!"

I shook my head. "Not *all* the time."

"Hey, Jimmy! Good to see you again!" one of the techs said brightly as she passed with a wave. "Say hi to your sister for me!"

Shit. Maybe I had been at too many crimes scenes.

Ito crossed her arms, jealousy in her eyes.

"I don't know who that was," I replied.

Her lips curled. We would be talking about this moment at some point in the future.

"What happened? Why are we here?" asked Kemble, taking out his notebook. "And let's not get cute, OK?"

While cute was my bread and butter, I chose peace

instead of chaos. I did my best to recap the night's events, explaining everything from Anton's knock back at my place to Anton hearing gunshots as he fled the scene.

"Anton Greene?" said Kemble. "*That* Anton Greene?"

I had known that was coming but I wasn't going to get distracted by history. "And when I got here, I found the body, but the van was gone. The deceased's name is Devon Philips."

"Where's Anton now?" asked Ito.

So I had left out some details in my retelling, and I felt bad about that. This was the challenge of having a girlfriend who worked for the LAPD. Most of the time, I liked to think we were on the same side. Seeing justice done, right? Easy peasy. But times like these, when justice might not be letting the cops handle it? Oooof.

"Could be anywhere."

It wasn't quite a lie, but I was pretty sure I was still committing a crime. "He told me this story at my place, and then he left." That part was sort of true. "He's fearful for his life. He's in the wind. There are dangerous people involved." That part was also more or less true.

"Good reason for him to come in, Jimmy," said Ito.

"You know how it is, though: Once accused of a crime, it's hard to trust the LAPD."

Kemble's jaw clenched.

Ito sucked her teeth.

I... may have crossed a line there.

"All right," said Kemble, flipping his notebook closed. "Your client — "

"Whoa, whoa," I sputtered. "I didn't say he was my *client*. I was just helping out. Being a Good Samaritan. I found a body. That's linked to a crime. You're welcome for me doing half of your job."

Kemble grunted. "That sounds like accessory after the fact." He smiled, making his threat clear.

But I wasn't going to roll over. "Listen, I'll do you guys a favor. *If* I hear from Anton, I'll really try to convince him to turn himself in and talk with you guys. With a lawyer present, of course."

Kemble seethed and turned to Ito. "It's not my business who my partner chooses to spend time with, as questionable as that choice might be — "

"Screw you," she snapped.

"But when that person compromises cases, again and again — "

I knew where this was going. My face flushed; my stomach dropped.

" — I might have something to say. Especially with what happened last summer."

I swallowed, hoping they didn't see how much Kemble was turning my insides into a red-hot lump of shame and guilt. Last summer had been bad. Really bad. A colossal fuck-up.

I was working a kidnapping case that went sideways, and a guy named Matty Goodman died right in front of me. I literally had his blood on my hands.

Because Matty was a former child star and I'm a former child star and we were on the same case together — too long of a story to tell here — his death was a very public thing. The cherry on top was that the man responsible for it got away, which *also* became a public thing.

Dear reader, your hero was back to zero.

"All right, *enough*," Ito said to Kemble, her voice firm. "There's a crime scene. Why don't you take your ass in there."

Kemble snorted and starting walking toward Devon's body. He paused next to me, saying, "Need your girlfriend to fight your fights, huh?"

I looked up at him. "Yeah. I'm not threatened by that, Kemble."

"Eat shit, Cooper," he spat and stomped off.

I turned back and met Ito's eyes. Now she was pissed.

"You're mad," I observed.

"Let's say, Jimmy, that I'm disappointed."

I pointed to the crime scene. "He started it."

"I don't care. I have to work with him."

"So I have to put up with his bullshit?"

She put up a hand. "I don't want to argue about Kemble. He's a shit bag for bringing up this summer, but you always take his bait."

I looked away and took a breath, hoping the boiling feeling in my stomach would cool. It did. Just a bit. I nodded and pointed at my car. "I should go. You have work to do."

I walked, and she walked with me. I paused.

"You don't have to walk me to my car," I said. "It's right there. Twenty feet away. I'll be OK."

She shook her head. "I don't need people listening," she said, continuing to head toward my car with me. "I just wanted to ask if you were OK."

Sweating, I replied, "OK?"

"It's never easy seeing a body. And since Matty died, you've been a little..."

"A little what?" I asked, getting a little defensive.

About ten feet away from my Toyota, I stopped in front of her. A frown flickered across her face as she looked me up and down.

"Yes, a little down. A little off? Yeah, I know," I admitted. Sweat trickled down my neck and I scratched at it. "This isn't news."

She nodded, chewing her lip. She looked like she was going to say something more but then backed off. She sighed. "You should get some sleep. You look like shit."

"Why, Detective Ito," I said. "Are you flirting with me?"

Her lips curled into a smile. At least I got that out of her. She glanced back at the crime scene; I glanced back at my car. She moved close, her eyes closing, and she kissed me, her hands resting on my upper arms. I returned the kiss. Her lips were soft and warm, and she smelled great, like being at the beach early in the summer. I wanted this moment to last forever.

Violet pulled away. "I've got to get to work."

"Me too."

She frowned.

"Sleep, I mean."

She blinked, gave me another smile, and then she turned, heading back to the crime scene. I beeped my car open and hopped in. After I closed the door, I took a long, slow, cleansing breath, desperate to calm the fuck down.

A voice from the back whispered, "So?"

I opened my eyes and looked out at the officers roaming around. Through a gritted smile, not moving to look directly at him, I muttered, "Anton. There are cops everywhere."

He grunted. "My leg is cramping up, man."

"You'll have to stay down there until we leave."

I started my car, plugging in my phone.

Another grunt. "The back seat is filthy, by the way."

I looked in the rearview mirror, as if I could actually see him. "You know what? Next time we go to a crime scene, we'll take *your* car." I put my key into the ignition.

"Did you kiss that cop?"

"That cop is my girlfriend. You have a problem with that?"

A beat.

"If you don't see the problem with that, then I don't know what to tell you, man."

I frowned, not sure what he was getting at, and started the car. "Like a River Runs" by Bleachers played us out of the parking lot.

4

—

"AND ANTON'S NOT with you, right?" asked Erika Cooper, my sister, an all-around excellent lawyer who is always reachable by phone. She was shaking off sleep, and I could hear her coffee machine wheezing in the background.

I looked across the booth at Anton, who was busy eating a stack of pancakes. "Nope. Not with me."

He looked up, reaching for his Diet Coke. He frowned as he sipped on his straw, and I shook my head, waving away his unspoken question.

Anton and I had ended up at Norms, an all-night chain diner on La Cienega, whose swooped roof was a fine example of Googie architecture. The sun was about to rise and traffic outside was picking up. After leaving the crime scene and tossing his phone, Anton had mentioned grabbing some food. This place was on the way to mine and would be open so we made a stop.

"Jimmy," said Erika with a hint of a warning. She was testing me, of course. She was the one person who always knew when *I* was lying. It was one of those skills she had picked up years ago when her older brother — me — was in the throes of his addictions, with a career in decline. Dad had left, and Mom was focused on the firm, on keeping a roof over our heads, which left Erika to keep an eye on slippery old me. She's the hero of that story.

"I'm telling you, he's not with me."

Erika paused. "All right." She knew I knew that she knew, and it was best for all parties involved to drop it. If Erika knew where Anton was she would feel obligated to do the right thing and have him turn himself in.

"How much trouble is he in?" I asked, hoping there might be an easy way out of all this. I reached for my coffee, fighting off sleep. It had been so much easier staying up all night in my twenties. Sure, the drug abuse might've had something to do with it, but after thirty... Oooof.

Erika sighed. I could hear the spoon banging against the side of a mug. She always ruined her coffee with sugar. I shouldn't have woken her up, but this was pretty much a definition of legal emergency, and I wasn't going to call my mom. She'd be, like, so mad.

"Do you think he shot Devon?" Erika asked. "Because if he shot him…" She didn't want to finish the sentence.

I shook my head as if she could see me. "Anton didn't leave out anything important, like shooting him." I looked at him, covered the phone, and mouthed, "Did you?"

His head tilted, and his lips tightened. He shook his head no and then turned back to his pancakes.

"Well," said Erika, "he's certainly an accessory to the robbery. He drove the van. But it would go a long way toward…" She paused. "It would help with a plea deal if he could turn over whatever they stole, the rest of those involved, and whoever killed Devon."

"Oh, is that all?" I said.

Anton stopped eating and looked up at me. Here we were again, Anton facing another plea deal. This whole conversation was really uncomfortable. Here we were pondering about the life of a man who sat less than three feet away from me. He could clearly hear me when I said, "Do you think he'll do jail time?"

Anton put his fork down and looked at me, his eyes narrowing, worrying about the answer. I looked away.

Erika stopped what she was doing on the other end of the call. "Jimmy, he was involved in a robbery, and a man is dead. Of course he's going to serve some time."

I met Anton's eyes. He could see it all over my face. I offered a smile, but it was weak. I felt helpless and dumb. I looked away, back outside. The sky was a blue-gray. The sun had risen; the night was finally over.

Erika went on. "The longer he goes without turning himself in, the worse it's going to be for him. If one of the other guys turns themselves in or gets arrested? Whoever makes the first deal gets the best deal."

I gently spun my coffee cup on the Formica tabletop, taking in what she had just said and realizing what I had to do. I didn't like it. Shaking that off, I said in the most upbeat tone I could muster, "Listen, thank you. I gotta go. Things to do, you know?"

She didn't say goodbye and I didn't want to be the one to hang up.

"Jimmy?" Her voice was soft coming out of the phone.

"Yeah?"

"I'm worried about you."

I chuckled. "What do you mean?" I asked, hoping it was just about tonight.

"I mean I'm *worried*. We haven't talked in months."

OK. It wasn't just about tonight. I paused, then chose deflection. "We see each other every day at work." I looked at Anton and shrugged, hoping he was on my side. He was indifferent.

"We *see* each other, but we haven't talked. Not like this."

"Are you asking me to call you in the middle of the night?"

A frustrated sigh. "No." She paused, too. "Except for

moments like this, then yeah, of course, but... It's not about these calls, Jimmy. We haven't really *talked* since Dad disappeared back to Vegas."

Dad's visit had been a bit of a roller coaster, coinciding uncomfortably, as it did, with Matty Goodman's untimely death. For a hot second, I thought maybe he and I could reconcile, that I could forgive him for everything, but then Matty died and my newfound fortunes dried up and there went Dadt, scuttling right back to Vegas, where it turned out, he had another wife and daughter waiting for him.

Did I say daughter?

No, I meant I have a half sister.

Me and my sister. *We* have a half sister. I still hadn't wrapped my head around it. I didn't even know her name.

Erika had taken the news all too well when I burst into her office the next morning, telling her what I had just found out. She nodded as she sat behind her desk, cradling an ever present cup of coffee. She took a breath and said she was surprised but not surprised. It was all very mature of her and I felt like a total weirdo for having the reaction that I was having.

Erika in the present, on the other side of the line, took a bracing sip of coffee, then asked, "Have you been avoiding me?"

I totally had been avoiding her. It felt like the easiest thing to do, easier than showing her what a mess I really was.

"No," I said to her. "I've been busy."

It was such a transparent lie that I was actually embarrassed.

She cleared her throat. "OK, Jimmy." Her voice was flat. All business. She knew the truth. "Be careful."

"Yeah. Of course."

She hung up, and I put my phone on the table.

"Everything OK?" asked Anton.

Was everything OK? I had reluctantly tied my fortunes to helping someone well in over his head, probably working directly against the interests of my girlfriend, and had just admitted to my sister that I had been avoiding her. "Oh, yeah," I said. "Nothing to worry about." I took a very deep breath.

He nodded.

I nodded.

Anton closed his eyes and rubbed them. "I'm fucked, aren't I?"

My head moved somewhere in between nodding and shaking. This is what I didn't want to do. "You need to consider turning yourself in."

"What?" He opened his eyes. "No."

"You can't just say no."

"I just did." He picked up his fork and picked at his food.

"No, no. Seriously. The sooner you go and tell them what

you know — "

"But that's the thing. I don't *know* shit. This is what I've been telling you."

We were getting loud. Heads turned in our direction. A trio of Goths a few booths away looked over, all black eyebrows, black lipstick and spiky black hair. Even in L.A. they were considered weirdos. But in reality, they wore their hearts on their black, lacy sleeves. Maybe it was the rest of us who were the weirdos.

I waved my hand for Anton to keep his voice down. We did not need to be memorable.

I lowered my voice. "You know Devon was involved. You know where the robbery took place. You know the other guys."

"I don't *know* the other guys."

"Fine, fine. But you know most things."

Anton nodded and leaned forward to whisper, "That's all shit the LAPD already know. What the fuck do I have to offer? What am I gonna get for a plea?"

I took a breath and blew it out. He was right. This wasn't going the way I wanted it. "Not much," I admitted.

"Not much, Jimmy. That's right." His head bounced, welcoming me to the party. "I'd get to be a cooperating witness and still serve ten fucking years." He looked at his pancakes and shook his head. Appetite gone, he dropped his fork on his plate and pushed it away.

I fingered my coffee cup, trying to avoid eye contact. The Goths had gone back to their own conversation, and the space between Anton and me had become a gulf. I hated everything about this moment.

Then something clicked.

"What if we got you something to offer?"

Anton eyed me.

My left shoulder shrugged as I felt the rush of an incoming idea. "We find the rest of the guys. All of them. We recover whatever you guys took. We find out what happened in the warehouse and who shot Devon. You take all of that to the DA, and we get you the best deal possible."

As I was saying it, it sounded only vaguely insane. Maybe I could pretend to be the guy who could get Anton all of that.

He shook his head. "I got a better idea. I got friends out in Palm Desert. I'll hide out. It'll blow over."

"*Palm Desert.* Are you insane? That's the desert. It's an environment that is designed to kill you. It is gray and dry and ugly. Also, there's a *murder* connected to all this. The police aren't just going to let it go." I reached over and stole a strip of bacon. "You don't have the money to run forever." I pointed the bacon at him. "My way is how we're going to handle it."

I shoved the bacon in my mouth and chewed. Kids, this was *not* the Jimmy Cooper of the last six months. I don't know who I was in that moment, but whoever he was, he felt great. I wished I could be him forever.

Anton tapped his finger on the table, announcing a counterpoint. "How about this? We cover it up. You give me an alibi for tonight."

"No, Anton, no," I said, shaking my head. "First, I don't do cover-ups. They're wrong, and they never work. They're always worse than the crime."

He cocked an eyebrow at that. "Devon was *murdered*."

"Figure of speech," I said, backtracking. "Don't shoot the messenger. Secondly, I already told the cops what happened. What do you want? Me to go tell them I made it all up?"

"Maybe you did."

I groaned as loudly as I could get away with without causing a scene. "You are making this *impossible*. Why are you making this impossible?" Because he was young, I realized. Young and scared and not in the best frame of mind to make decisions. I wiped my bacon-greased fingers on a thin paper napkin. "I am trying to help you in the only way that I can. This is how we do it, or I'm out and you're on your own. Which would be really dumb."

Anton sat back and glared. I wondered if I had pissed him off.

"All right," he said. "Fine. We'll do it your way."

5

WE STARTED BACK at the beginning.

Over refills of coffee and Diet Coke, Anton told me what he knew about Devon while I ate Norms' California Omelette: an avocado placed on top of eggs, thus making it more Californian than your other omelets. We do that a lot here in SoCal. Avocados are our year-round pumpkin spice.

Devon Philips, somewhere in his upper thirties, had lived his whole life in L.A., mostly in and around View Park, a neighborhood south of the 10, the same one Anton and his mom lived. Anton was thirteen when he first laid eyes on Devon when he showed up fashionably late to a backyard barbecue at Anton's uncle's house.

Anton's eyes lit up as he remembered. "All the guys were

so excited to see him. You could see they all thought he was cool. He knew *everybody*. Or at least he said he did. Music people. Local politicians. Comedians." He smiled. "And he had a way with the ladies."

Devon had been charming, funny, and handsome. Who wouldn't love the guy?

He was also forever chasing the big break, that one score that would set him up for good, and success was always just around the corner, one job away. That's the story of L.A. right there.

I washed down a bite of eggs with coffee. Maybe tonight was supposed to have been one of those jobs.

Devon, according to Anton, had a special knack for finding ways into places he wasn't supposed to be. This, unsurprisingly, led to a habit of taking things that didn't belong to him. Devon never got busted for anything big, but time and time again, he'd get into trouble over something small, like taking a six-pack of beer from a 7-Eleven. "Dumb stuff," said Anton, shaking his head in disbelief. "It's like he couldn't help himself."

I nodded. Devon *couldn't* help himself. Game recognized game.

I knew this also meant that, with Devon having a record, he was going to be in the system, and if he was in the system, Ito and Kemble would be hitting his known associates very soon.

Anton paused. I guessed we had arrived at the part of the story where he got involved in Devon's work.

I made it easy for him. "How old were you when you started working with Devon?"

"Sixteen? Seventeen?" He paused again, smiled. "I remember asking Devon if I could work with him. He said, 'Oh, no. I don't work *with* people. People work *for* me.'" Anton chuckled.

That was a good line. I laughed with him.

Devon had found a use for Anton. "I was like his little chauffeur. I'd take him places so he could check them out. A few times I get to be the getaway driver." Anton grinned, thrilled by the memory.

"The getaway driver?" I said, smirking. "Big need for getaway drivers?"

Anton looked me dead in the eyes. "Yeah, man. Sometimes." He took a sip of his Diet Coke. "And I'm good. Like a real natural."

I frowned and even though I had so many questions about that, I dropped it. This wasn't an interview for a job.

"Your mom must've loved you hanging out with Devon."

Anton snorted. "She did *not* like him." He shrugged. "After a while... I didn't really have a taste for that life, you know? And then, after what happened three years ago, I thought it'd be best to keep my nose clean. I stopped taking his calls."

I looked up from my plate. "What made you take this one?"

He didn't say anything.

"Anton?"

A big sigh. "I needed the money."

Obviously, there was a story here.

"We all need money, Anton," I said as I leaned back, realizing I sounded like my mom. I didn't like that and wondered if Erika ever felt the same way. "What did you need the money for?"

"Does it matter?" He stirred his Diet Coke with a straw.

"If it brought you out of retirement, back into the life of a criminal, then yeah, it just might matter."

Another sigh. This one was filled with embarrassment. "It was for my girlfriend."

"That's *right*. You had mentioned a girlfriend." I said that a little louder than I should have.

"Yeah, I have a girlfriend, Jimmy. That isn't weird."

"No, right, it's not weird. Of course not," I said, trying to dig myself out of the hole I had just made. "I just didn't know. That's great. Congratulations."

He frowned.

I had made this weird.

"She's not my *first* girlfriend. There have been others."

I put up my hands. "Right. Message received. Is this serious? The girlfriend?"

He gave me a look that told me not only was it serious but also that I should stop pursuing this line of questioning. "She's really into fashion and anime. She started making these shirts and things, and people really dug them." Anton's voice changed, growing deeper, excited. "She's thinking maybe she should go into business for herself, you know? A little side hustle."

"She doesn't work with people; people work for her."

Anton grinned. "That's right. She's hoping to sell shit online or at conventions."

"That's awesome."

He raised a doubtful eyebrow.

"I mean it," I insisted. "It's awesome."

The eyebrow dropped. "Thanks." He shrugged. "We needed a little startup cash, so when Devon called..." Anton got real quiet and looked back at his Diet Coke.

"She doesn't know?"

"About Devon? Oh, no. Janelle would kill me."

Janelle.

"And after that," he continued, "my mom would kill me all over again."

His mom definitely would.

"Why did he call you after all this time?" I asked. "He didn't have a regular crew?"

"Crew? Shit, Jimmy. This isn't a heist movie."

"OK, fair. But I didn't want to say 'gang.'"

"Yeah, thanks for *that.*" He took a pull from his drink. "No, he did not have regulars he worked with. I guess he needed a driver."

"He didn't know any other drivers?"

"I don't know, man."

"OK. What about the other two guys. You didn't know them. Did Devon?"

He shook his head, stirring the ice in his glass. "I don't think so. These guys were younger than him, older than me. One was probably a mixed brother; the other was Black. I only met them tonight — last night — at the warehouse."

"Did they have names?"

"Well, *yeah.* Did you think we were just going to say 'Hey you' all night?"

"Maybe you guys used code names or something."

Anton leaned forward. "Not. A. Heist. Movie."

I rubbed my eyes. "OK. Not a heist movie. Got it. What were their names?"

"The brother was named Abbott. The other went by Crenshaw."

"Crenshaw? Like the boulevard?"

"Yeah."

I paused. "OK. Both went by their last names and you're telling me we're not acting out a heist movie? Because, if I'm being honest, it's very much heist movie vibes, Anton."

He said nothing.

One-named guys love the air of mystery that goes along with their distinct brand of machismo. You never heard them introduce themselves in a gruff voice with "I'm Brian. Brian Thompson. Special Forces." Nope. It's always, "Thompson, Special Forces," or some variation thereof.

I'm sure there's a whole bunch of macho men on both sides of the law who don't know their partners' first names.

"These guys were pretty serious. Intense, you know?" Anton chewed on his lip, trying to explain. "With Devon there was the thrill of doing the thing. An excitement. Yeah, there'd be a payout, but half of it was the fun of getting away with it."

I nodded, remembering that thrill. And maybe I got away with a lot more than I should've. The problem with getting away with it over and over is the thrill starts to fade.

"What made you think he didn't know them?" I asked.

Anton shrugged and shook his head. "Like, there was just this vibe of disrespect to him, you know? I'd catch an eye roll or a head shake. The two of them, they definitely knew each other."

Silence. Why did Devon hire these two? What did he need them for? They must've had some skill *he* didn't. Of course, that begged the question: what *was* the job?

I heard a gasp and a laugh from the Goth kids. One of the girls had a fork to her eye while the other hand covered it. Half -and-half dripped onto the table. Ah, the old palmed-creamer-and-fork gag to make it look like she punctured her eye. Good times. The waitress looked up from the counter, wondering if she'd have to clean up the mess, but the Goth girl was a good citizen and cleaned it up.

"Shit," said Anton, realizing something in that moment. "He called me because he trusted me."

"...because he didn't trust the other guys," I filled in.

Anton looked me in the eye. "He thought I'd have his back. That's why he brought me on board." He swallowed. "And I fucked it up."

I pushed my plate away from me. I'd finished my eggs, but I left the toast. Who needed the carbs? "It's not your fault. It isn't. Devon didn't give you the whole picture, OK? You're not responsible for what happened."

"I ran away."

"There were guns, Anton. You *should've* run away. You could've been killed."

He nodded, reluctantly. I don't think he bought what I was selling.

"We're going to do right by him," I said. "We're gonna get whoever killed him."

"Uh-huh. And how are we going to do that?"

"Great question, Anton."

It really was. I wished I had an answer for him. Sometimes I just said things to get the conversation going, hoping that I would think of something in the meantime. Some plan.

"You know what we should do?" I asked.

"What?" answered Anton.

Mercifully, something clicked. See what I mean?

"*Maybe*," I said, "we need to talk to the guy who talked to Devon about you for this job."

"Devon knew me. Why would he have talked to someone else about me?"

I held up a finger. "Devon thought you were out of the game. *Someone* told him that you needed cash. That's the Venn diagram we need to solve."

"Caesar," he said.

Apparently this Venn diagram wasn't too hard to fill in.

"César?" I clarified.

Anton shook his head. "*Caesar.* As in *Planet of the Apes.*"

"Right. Great reference."

Anton continued. "He knows Devon. I had also gone to him for a loan. Thinking maybe he'd want to invest in my girlfriend's startup, you know?"

I rubbed my face. Lack of sleep was catching up with me. "Let's go see Caesar then." I waved to the waitress, making the universal sign for our check.

Anton leaned in, worry creasing his brow. "He's not the sort of guy you just drop in on, Jimmy."

"We can't just simply walk into Mordor?"

"What?" he asked, confused.

I sighed. "Does he take appointments?"

"Are you fucking with me?"

Before I could reply, the waitress dropped the check and took my plate. "You can pay up front. How was everything?" she said, more as a reflex than out of actual curiosity.

"Excellent," I declared. "Four stars. My compliments to the chef."

She offered no response, just grabbed the rest of our plates and plodded away.

I said to Anton, "I am not fucking with you. We're going to go talk to him." I plucked the check off the table and scooted out of the booth as Anton did the same. "We're just after information. And we should go now. The police will be knocking on his door soon."

We were met at the register by the same waitress. I handed her my credit card, and she started ringing us up.

"He ain't going to talk to the police," said Anton.

The waitress looked up from the register to me and Anton.

I looked at her. "This can't be the most awkward conversation you've walked into at Norms this time of day."

"Oh, no," she replied, shaking her head with a snort. "Wil Wheaton was here once."

6

—

Three Years Ago

GORDON BIXBY AND I sat in my mother's office as Anton explained what he had actually been doing the night he was supposed to be robbing a woman in Silver Lake. He told us he was over in Arlington Heights, a neighborhood about five miles away from the crime, sneaking into the home of a dealer he used to run with. Anton wanted to get high that night, and lacking funds and a stash, he'd decided the best course of action was to rob his former employer.

"And no one saw you?" asked Gordon.

Anton raised his eyebrows. "The whole point was not to be seen."

Gordon leaned back in his chair and pulled at his ear,

thinking.

"You're not gonna tell my mom, are you?" Anton was more worried about his mom finding out about the shit that he *did* do than these charges.

Gordon snapped out of his thoughts and shook his head. "You're in enough trouble at it is, Anton."

The young man looked relieved. "You believe me?"

Gordon shifted in his seat to look at me. I couldn't believe he was checking in with me and what I thought, but I nodded. I believed Anton. I also thought he was incredibly unlucky; because getting away with one robbery wasn't going to clear him of another.

"So?" asked Anton. "What's next?"

Gordon sighed. "First, we're going to go over your story, detail by detail, to see if maybe there was a chance someone saw you. Someone we can talk to and get to corroborate your story."

Anton nodded and began again from the top. This time Gordon interrupted with questions, hoping to find something we could use. Twenty minutes later, Anton was done, and by done, I mean he was tired, cranky, and losing his mind. His story hadn't changed and Gordon didn't get anything usable. He stepped out of the office to get Anton's mother.

As we waited, Anton stared across my mother's desk and out the window. From where we were in Los Angeles, the Hollywood Hills ran from left to right with the Valley beyond. Out the other window, there was the city until it ended at the Pacific. It was a pretty stellar view.

My butt had fallen asleep, so I moved in my chair, making it creak as I did. Anton turned to me. Silence. I wondered if I should say something. I was the only one in the room representing the firm. I was, you know, the adult in the room. I should say something.

"Hey," I said.

Nailed it.

"Hey."

OK, Jimmy, offer him some support. He needs it.

I said, "This whole thing… it sucks," I said.

He nodded, agreeing.

"It's going to be OK, Anton."

"You think so?"

I guess I did. I pointed to the door. "Gordon's great. If anyone can figure this out…"

"He's not the one that believed me."

I paused. "No. He didn't. He does now, though." My head wobbled. "He's a natural skeptic, you know? But he's a big old teddy bear."

"He was a cop, wasn't he?"

"Don't hold that against him." I laughed at my joke. Anton didn't. "Yeah, seriously, though, he's great."

Anton was quiet. "You're shorter than I thought you'd

be."

"Huh?"

"I thought you'd be taller. In your movies, you look taller."

"You've seen my movies?" I smiled. It was nice being recognized for my movies rather than some dumb thing I did in public while I was drunk. "It's the camera. It adds six inches."

Anton frowned.

"It's a joke." I smiled again. "We're all short. Except for, like, Josh Hartnett and Harrison Ford. Both tall." I paused. "Vince Vaughn. Also tall. But the rest of us? Short. Which, you know, should make *them* the freaks. Not us."

He nodded, unconvinced.

But there was something lingering. Something I needed to know. "What did you think? Did you like them?"

Anton frowned in confusion.

"The movies. You said you saw them. I was just — When you tell someone you saw their movies, it's accepted behavior to tell them what you thought. Did you like them?"

"Well, yeah. They were OK."

My heart stopped. I wasn't ready for this amount of honest criticism. "Uh-huh. Well. That's what we were going for. 'OK.' It's a large target, hard to miss creatively." I laughed which sounded like a car slowly going off a cliff.

Anton stared at me, unsure how to get out of this situation with a crazed and needy actor.

Same, Anton. Same.

Luckily for us, Gordon opened the door and my mother and Mrs. Greene stepped in. Relieved to shift back to his problems, Anton looked at his mom, inspecting her face for signs that Gordon had ratted him out. He hadn't. He wouldn't. Not in this circumstance. Gordon Bixby was a man of principles. He had told Anton he wouldn't say anything, and he would stand by that.

With a brief discussion of next steps, the meeting wrapped up. Mom put a hand on Mrs. Greene's forearm, promising her we would do what we could. She pointedly did not promise any results. She ushered Mrs. Greene and Anton out of the room and into the waiting hands of her assistant, who would validate their parking and escort them to the elevators, and Mom headed back to her desk.

"So?" She sat behind it and looked expectantly at Gordon.

He stood in the middle of the room, his arms hanging loosely at his side. "His story is consistent, I'll give him that."

My eyes darted between them. "Wait. You don't believe Anton?"

Gordon sighed. "Jimmy..."

"He's telling the truth," I said.

He shook his head, saying, "I don't know that."

"I *do*."

Gordon shrugged. "If only that counted as evidence." He

looked at Mom. "His story is consistent, but there's no one to confirm it. It doesn't explain away the witness and the victim's statement or the physical evidence."

Mom looked at me for a moment. To Gordon, she asked, "Who's on the case?"

"In Robbery/Homicide? Jerry Collins is lead."

"Oof," she replied.

"Oof?" I asked. "Why oof? Is it a bad oof or a good off?"

Gordon took this one. "He's relentless in his work."

A bad oof, then, but something was left unspoken.

"OK. So that's bad for us. Got it," I said. "But, I just want to offer... there's being relentless and there's being *too* relentless — "

"James," said Mom, stopping my flow. She leaned back in her fancy leather chair. "Let's take a look at their evidence again. I don't know if we can prove him *innocent*, but maybe there's something there we can exploit. At least enough to satisfy our client and get an acquittal if it goes to trial." She paused. "Let's tread carefully."

Gordon mulled it over, then agreed. He had a complicated relationship with his past life and was clear-eyed about the institution of the LAPD, what it did right and wrong, but he had lifelong friends there. If I had to guess, he hadn't quite come to terms with being on *this* side of law and order.

"I'll start with the eyewitness, take it from there," he said.

Mom approved, and with a plan in place, we left her

office, heading down the hallway, passing the offices of the lawyers who made up the "associates" in Cooper and Associates. One such lawyer was my sister. Erika was on the phone as we passed by, so we waved to each other through the glass.

Some accused my mother of nepotism when she hired Erika. That is until they met her on the other side of a trial and got pantsed by my sister. That shut them up quick.

We continued through the lobby and wound up at another corner of the floor. Gordon's desk sat just outside of a corner office, the home of Dave, the office manager. Gordon didn't want an office. He said it would cramp his style, such as it was.

I had asked if I could have an office and Dave had given me a chair next to Gordon's desk. Typical Dave move.

I sat down, spun around, and asked Gordon, "Do you know Jerry?"

"*Detective* Collins," he corrected me. "Yes, yes, I do."

That 'yes' felt loaded with unsaid details. I waited for more.

Gordon reached into his pocket and pulled out his keys and unlocked his desk.

Tired of waiting, I said, "Anything you would like to share with the class, Gordon?"

Gordon glared at me. He looked around, then said, "Worked with him for about ten years. As his partner for a few of them."

Well. That got *juicy* fast. I shook my head, disappointed.

Instead of telling me more, he pulled out a notebook and a pen, the weapons of an in-house detective. OK, Gordon did have a gun, but he kept it locked up at home.

"A former partner, huh?" I teased. "Should I be jealous?"

Gordon stopped. "What?"

"You know, I'm your partner *now*, and he's your ex — "

"No offense, kid, but you're not my partner — "

"Offense taken," I said.

He put up a hand. I shut up. Things had taken a turn.

Gordon wasn't playing. "Can we stop with this? There's work to do." With that, he stepped past me and headed to the elevators.

"What the hell did I do?" I asked to no one.

A snort came from Dave's office.

I glanced into his office and suddenly he was interested in his spreadsheets.

7

—

WE WERE LISTENING to Sweet's "Fox on the Run," heading south on La Cienega, when we hit a red light, idling next to a recently built Whole Foods on the ground floor of an apartment building that had the area's prerequisite lack of parking. Up ahead, across Jefferson Boulevard, there was another construction site.

Green fabric walls blocked most of the work. Through the gaps I could see the deep, wide hole of something that was probably going to be another mixed-use building, a very on-trend sort of development in L.A. I frowned, trying to remember what had been there a month or two ago, but I couldn't. This city does that. Change is constant, nothing makes it into your long-term memory, and if you turn away, the present will be replaced by something new when you turn back. You start to wonder if that thing had been there or if you had just imagined it.

But the thing is, while L.A.'s present is impermanent, the past hangs over everything like a bad dream. You were only as good as your last hit. What first made you famous, that will be the first line in your obituary. Whatever people remember about you, that memory has moved from fact to myth. The past doesn't exist, yet you're trapped by it.

A car horn behind us snapped me back to reality.

"Green light," said Anton, pointing up.

I pressed the gas pedal and we moved with traffic.

Anton put his head against the passenger's-side window. His eyelids kept falling, almost closing before snapping open again. I rubbed my eyes so they wouldn't do the same thing. I had a case to work.

I guess he was my client after all.

Turning off my playlist, I switched to the radio, hoping to hear the local news. Maybe something about last night had been released. Something Anton didn't know.

The host was in the middle of running down the goings-on at city hall. The place was in the midst of another corruption scandal. Unlike everywhere else, there were only three seasons in L.A.: summer, awards, and scandal.

This year's scandal involved the L.A. County district attorney, who was up for reelection this coming fall. He had been accused of turning a blind eye to the criminal conduct of wealthy Angelinos. He denied everything, claiming it was election year fear mongering by his opponent. He went on to say that the truth would come out.

Spoilers: The truth *did* eventually come out and he would be spending years behind bars.

The host moved on.

"Over in Highland Park, the police report of a murder victim in connection with a robbery that occurred last night at Objet Exotique — "

Anton's eyes widened, and he shifted in his seat. We shared a glance.

" — a gallery on North La Brea specializing in upscale artifacts. Owner Louis LaFontaine — "

Louis, like gooey. Très classy. As it would turn out, he had a French accent to go with it.

" — said the thieves made away with a ceramic Buddha from the early Ming Dynasty, approximately four hundred years old."

"Shit," whispered Anton.

" — worth an estimated three million dollars."

My car swerved, Anton braced himself, but a honk and a curse from another car and I was back in my lane.

"Because of its historical significance, however, Mr. LaFontaine, referred to the Buddha as priceless. The police have not released information regarding the victim or their connection with the robbery until the family has been notified."

The host moved on to the next story while Anton and I took a long second to process what we had heard.

"Devon didn't do jobs this big," said Anton finally said. "This was way out of his league."

"Spill The Wine" by Eric Burdon and War played as we rolled into Ladera Heights, a neighborhood south of Baldwin Hills that had been developed in the sixties, so there were a lot of Mid-Century homes with roofs tipped at a dapper angle and lazy driveways leading to the attached garage out front. I drove down a palm-lined neighborhood street. The palm fronds looked like exploding fireworks, frozen in time and space. The sun was up and had beaten back the winter chill.

We parked in front of a single-story house with a manicured front lawn. A couple of cars passed us, going the other way, probably heading to work. A little thrill ran through me. We had gotten here before the LAPD. That thrill was quickly dashed when I realized I was talking about one-upping my own girlfriend.

Anton cleared his throat and looked at me. "There's something you should, uh, know."

I took a breath, gripped the wheel of my car, bracing

myself.

"I owe Caesar money."

Of course. No wonder Caesar had put Devon in touch with Anton. He wanted his money back.

I looked at Anton. "And how does he *feel* about you owing him money?"

"I mean… you know… Not *great*." He shrugged.

"Huh." I nodded. "We've been in the car for forty minutes. You could've told me the whole time. Back at Norms…"

"I'm telling you now."

Couldn't argue with that rock solid logic. I put on my most confident smile and stepped out of my car, heading up the walkway to the front door. As I was about to step onto the porch, the front door opened.

A thin Black man stepped out of the house wearing a light blue T-shirt, sweatpants, and leather slippers. He was in his late forties, about my height and scrappy and held a coffee mug in his right hand. His eyes narrowed as he looked me up and down. Done judging, he shifted over to Anton, who had just stepped out of my car. The man's face hardened.

"Anton," he said.

"Hey, Caesar," Anton replied, bouncing his chin.

"You got my money?"

"Uh," said Anton.

"'Uh' is *not* an answer, son," said Caesar. He turned to me. "And who the fuck are you?"

"We're here about Devon."

Caesar blinked. "I don't know any Devon."

This, of course, was a lie. We all knew it was a lie, but that didn't stop him from trying it out.

Anton cleared his throat. "He's dead, Caesar."

Caesar blinked again. His shoulders fell. "Well, fuck." Defeated, looking up and down the street, he said, "Get inside before someone sees you."

I stepped into a small living room. A leather couch with an easy chair to the left was against the large front window, facing a flat-screen TV on which two CNN talking heads discussed the world's many ongoing crises. A bowl of Cheerios sat on a coffee table in front of the couch. To my left, a dining room was on the other side of the wall, and there was a kitchen beyond that. The smell of weed hung in the air, which took me back. Dad used to enjoy a joint here and there, and when he wasn't paying attention, so would I.

Anton stood next to me while Caesar closed the door, walked past us, and stood on the other side of the coffee table.

"Nice place," I said, eager to break the tension.

"Shut up," snapped Caesar. To Anton he said, "Who is this guy?"

"He knows everything. You can trust him."

"Oh, I *can*, can I?" He looked at me. "And why is that?"

That's an awkward question with no great answer. You

can't just blurt out, "Look at me, you can trust *me*!" because that's not the guy you can trust. I wouldn't. I'd been burned by too many producers to fall for that again. So how should you answer? You could say nothing.... You could just be...

Or you could ratchet up the stakes.

I said, "The cops have already ID'ed Devon, Caesar." Sure, with a little help from me, but he didn't need to know that. " It's only a matter of time before they roll up and start asking you questions."

Caesar crossed his arm, sinewy biceps bulging as he did. He glared at Anton. "Is he threatening me?"

OK, ratcheting up the stakes was a bad idea.

Anton put his hand up. "This is Jimmy Cooper, Caesar. He's the guy that helped me out last time."

Caesar's face softened. "That was you?"

"That was me."

He thought about it. That must've been enough because he dropped his arms and gave his attention to Anton."What happened to Devon?"

Anton ran through the events of last night, giving him the highlights. Caesar would glance at me, occasionally, checking to see how I reacted, whether I was actually cool or not.

Friends, let me tell you: I was cool.

When Anton got to the punch line, Caesar muttered, "Three million dollars?"

We nodded.

"Shit," whispered Caesar. Breathing faster, he turned to the front window, looked up and down the street, and then closed the shades. "Why are you *here*? You should be in Mexico or something."

"We're here for information," I said.

"Information? I'm not going to give you information."

"We just need to know about the job."

Caesar shook his head. "That shit's confidential."

My head tilted. "Confidential? Are you Devon's lawyer?"

"Yeah, *maybe* I am."

I started to sweat. Things were not going well.

"Caesar, come on, man," Anton pleaded. "I'm in trouble."

Caesar licked his lower lip, considering. He gave a quick nod. "A week ago, he comes to me. He's got a job that came with two guys. He said it was big." He paused, shaking his head. "He didn't say it was fucking *huge*."

So Anton was right: The job had been out of Devon's league. It turned out, someone had hired him.

I asked, "What do you mean it came with two guys?"

Caesar shrugged. "Two guys were already a part of the job. He didn't get into the details, which, you know, I didn't *want* to know. Devon just said he was approached with this particular opportunity and he didn't get much choice in who he worked with. He did say they needed *him* for the job. Devon was always prone to flattery."

So Devon was the one with the special skills, not the other two.

"Who approached him with the job?" I asked.

Caesar frowned at me. "What part of 'didn't get into the details' didn't you understand?"

"OK, fine. What did he need from you?"

"He needed a driver and" — Caesar rolled his eyes over to Anton — "someone he could trust."

Anton bristled, but I ignored that. "He didn't trust the other guys?"

He looked at me. "All I know is he didn't *know* them, man. He needed someone he *knew*." He rolled his eyes back to Anton. "Or at least someone he thought he knew."

"This isn't my fault, Caesar. I'm in this shit because of you."

Caesar put a hand to his chest. "Me? Oh, no, no, no. This isn't on me." He moved closer to Anton. "You have a debt, and Devon needed someone. I just put you two together."

Anton matched his step. "You're the reason I need the money."

"You weren't working real hard to pay me back. You're off with that bitch — "

Anton moved again, and before I knew it, I had stepped between them and started screeching and flapping my arms. Anton and Caesar backed away, looking at me like I was Linda Blair from *The Exorcist*.

"What the fuck, man?" asked Caesar, genuinely concerned as my screaming slowed to a stop.

"Sorry," I said, trying to catch my breath. I wasn't really sorry. It was a tried and tested maneuver. I would do that screeching thing at the dinner table when Mom and Dad would start fighting. It freaked them out so much they would stop. "We don't have time for this. You both need to be cool. Whoever killed Devon is out there, the Buddha is out there, and we need to find them both. Maybe it'll get Anton off the hook. Or maybe onto a smaller hook. I don't know. But I need you two to stop."

They agreed and stepped back. Caesar adjusted his robe.

"He didn't say anything about who hired him?" I asked.

Caesar shook his head.

I wiped my face and sighed. I hated dead ends. They were the worst, especially this early on. Sure, I knew someone had hired Devon, but I didn't know who or why. Who steals a Buddha? And in L.A., three million dollars is nothing. Yes, yes, it's a lot of money, but when you see assholes spending five million on a street car or an actress walking down the red carpet with ten million dollars' worth of diamonds dripping down her neck and don't even get me started on some of those "healthy" smoothies in Beverly Hills, three million dollars doesn't seem like much. So either the person who had hired Devon didn't *have* three million dollars or just didn't want to *pay* three million dollars. What was so special about this Buddha anyway? And where were Crenshaw and James? Who were the dudes they met up with in the storage facility?

Another question floated to the top of my mind.

"What about the van?"

"The van?" repeated Anton.

"Yeah, Devon's van," I said. "We should find it."

Anton shook his head. "It wasn't his."

"OK. If it wasn't his, where did he get it?"

"Oh," said Caesar, like it was nothing. "He always rented cars when he was working. He wasn't going to use his, and he didn't want to have a hot car on a job." He could see the look on my face. "Hey, man. He used a stolen credit card; he wasn't a moron. He would rotate through small car rentals. Never use the same one in a row. I think this time he was going by Mike Lowery."

I paused. "Mike Lowery, as in *Bad Boys*?"

Caesar nodded. "He loved that movie."

I nodded back.

This was the closest to a lead as we had. The van had to be somewhere — unless, of course, it was at the bottom of the ocean, and I hoped that wasn't the case — and rental companies didn't like to lose their assets, which meant there was probably a GPS tracker on the van.

Caesar gave me a few ideas of where Devon might have gotten the van, and with that, we were done.

Anton was first out the door when Caesar stopped me, putting a hand on my chest. Anton looked back, but Caesar said to him, "Go to the car. I want a word with my friend Jimmy."

Anton checked in with me, and I nodded that it'd be OK.

Spoilers: I had no idea if it was going to be OK.

As Anton slow-walked to the car, I said to Caesar, "So we're friends now?"

A small shrug was his answer. "What are you getting out of all this? Because Anton does not have the money to pay you."

"I'm just trying to help."

"Uh-huh." A smile slicked its way across his face. "Something you should know about me: I can see liars. And you?" He leaned in close. "You're lying."

8

—

"AND WHO IS this?" asked Moe, a mix of sparkle and suspicion in his voice as he cradled a mug of Hibiscus tea. We had made it back to West Hollywood, driving mostly in silence as exhaustion had us by the throat. He had intercepted us on the way to my bungalow. Moe was my middled-aged — though he refused to be specific about dates and years — Mexican American next-door neighbor. He had short, graying hair, was fit as hell and moved his body with ease, even wrapped as it was now in a flowing robe.

He was my confidant in this court of bungalows, a group of six Spanish-style homes I owned and rented. Built in the late thirties, they had a bit of Old Hollywood charm with their taupe stucco walls, tiled roofs, and secrets left for books like *Hollywood Babylon*. They were the big investment I didn't manage to lose during my booze- and drug-addled years, mostly thanks to the efforts of my sister and our mom. Everyone who lived there was pretty cool. And by cool, I mean everyone kept their nose out of everyone's business.

Present company excluded.

"This is Anton," I sighed, my head fuzzy. I quickly introduced the two — "Anton, Moe. Moe, Anton." — Then put my key into the bungalow's lock.

"And where have you two been?" asked Moe.

I'm guessing Moe saw us leave late last night and now dragging our tired asses back here, midmorning. Like me, Moe is an addict in recovery, so he probably wanted to make sure I was keeping my nose clean.

Anton looked around, nervous. I followed his looks. It was around nine o'clock; people were either headed to work, with a gym bag slung over their shoulders, or to the gym, also with their gym bags. I didn't know how often Anton made his way into West Hollywood and I didn't know if this place was his vibe or not. L.A. can be bit of a smorgasbord; there's a vibe for everyone. It's easy in the city, and sometimes just safer, to just go to the places you need to go and like, where you're accepted and expected. Sometimes I forgot that because work took me all over the town.

I nodded at Anton to step inside my place. As he did, I turned to Moe and said quietly, "Be nice. He's a client, and he's scared."

"I am the epitome of kindness and class, Jimmy," Moe stated, "and I am insulted you would think otherwise." With that, he moved inside and I followed, closing the door behind us.

I almost stumbled over him as he had suddenly decided to stop moving, standing a few feet away from the couch. I could see his spine straightening, his head tipping up. He was annoyed. I looked past him and found the source of the slight.

Anton had plopped onto the couch, right in Moe's usual spot.

After lingering awkwardly in the doorway with no reaction from Anton, Moe gave in and sank down at the other end of the couch. "So..." he said as I headed to the kitchen.

"So... Anton is in trouble."

Moe looked at Anton. "Is that true? You're in trouble?"

He took a sip of tea as Anton considered his words.

I grabbed the same glass from last night, still next to the sink, and poured water from the tap. I leaned against the counter and chugged the water in two gulps. "Anton may have committed grand larceny."

Moe snapped his attention back to Anton. "*Oh?*" He sounded a little too excited by this news. Since he had gotten clean, Moe lived a life of peace and calm and, outside of his love life, my life provided some necessary stimulation.

Anton sighed. "I was involved. Yeah."

"He stole the Buddha," I offered, putting my glass down on the counter.

Moe frowned. "He stole Buddha?"

Anton shook his head, "No, no — "

"He didn't steal Buddha," I said. "He stole *a* Buddha."

Anton said to me, "Technically, I didn't steal it. I was just driving the car."

Moe shook his head "Mm. I don't think the law cares about those distinctions," he said. He looked at me. "This Buddha we're talking about, that was the one in the news? Worth millions?" He stopped. He got quiet as he spoke. "Didn't someone get killed?"

Anton rubbed his face.

I stood in the doorway of my kitchenette. "Anton, why don't you grab some sleep? You can take my room." I pointed to the hallway.

"But..." he started.

I held up a hand. "Go on. There's nothing for you to do right now."

He nodded and pushed himself off the couch and lumbered down the hall. Just as he disappeared, Moe scooted over and took his spot back. He took another sip of tea while I fell into my recliner. I had never felt so heavy in my life, and I had done more than a couple of weekend benders. But that was when I was younger. And doing drugs.

"This sounds serious, Jimmy."

"Yeah, thanks, Moe. I hadn't realized."

He pursed his lips, and I nodded, apologizing. He was only trying to help. "Did you talk to your mom about this?"

I shook my head. "I talked to my sister."

"And?"

"And what do you think she said?"

"Something smart that you will choose to ignore."

"Why do you assume it was smart? I might be ignoring it because it's terrible advice."

He shook his head. "Your sister's the smart one." He took a sip of tea.

"Does that make me the pretty one?"

He paused. "Oh, honey. Not anymore. She's really grown into her looks."

"She can't be *two* things."

Moe shook his head again. "I don't decide these things. That's left up to a higher power." He took a breath. "Setting aside what Erika suggested, what is *your* plan? Do you need my help?"

I smiled. Well, as tired as I was, it was just a bit of a lip curl. This was why I loved Moe. He had your back no matter what. He was going to go down the road with you. He was the closest thing to a big brother that I've had in my life. He's picked me up — literally, sometimes — when I couldn't stand on my own. He knows what it takes to get through the day, especially hard ones like this, and still have your head on straight. So to speak.

I closed my eyes, massaging my forehead, trying to get my tired brain to think of whether there was anything he could do…

I gasped for air. My eyes popped open, and for a second I didn't know where I was.

Moe was gone. The light in the room had shifted, and I was still in my recliner. I leaned forward, putting my arms on my thighs, taking in more air and shaking off the nausea of deep sleep. I listened for a moment, but there was no movement in the rest of the bungalow. Anton must've still been out cold. Good.

I looked at my phone. I had been asleep for an hour. Violet had called, and she had left a text.

We need to talk.

Well, that would have to wait.

Instead of calling back my girlfriend, who probably had questions about last night's crime that I wasn't ready to answer, I got up and headed to the kitchen.

I got the coffee maker going, and while it brewed, I grabbed my laptop off the counter, unplugged it, and plopped back into the recliner. I pulled out the footrest and booted up the computer. Time to get to work on my one lead: the van.

Gordon Bixby liked to remind me that private detectives were always the underdogs. We would never have the resources or the legal protections the cops had, so we had to buckle down and be methodical in our research, not to mention patient. Now, I might not be as savvy as some — I'm not replacing Sherlock Holmes any time soon — but let me tell you, you don't become a star, even a child star, without two things: ambition and tenacity. And this former child star was *tenacious*.

A quick search gave me about twenty places that would rent out the kind of van Devon had gotten for the job. I eliminated the big companies immediately. He wouldn't risk doing business with them using a stolen card. That left me about ten places to investigate, and they would all have to be visited in person. My charms worked better face to face.

My cell phone dinged. It was Moe.

Are you in trouble?

I raised an eyebrow and replied: *I hope not. Why?*

Three dots did a little dance.

I think there are cops watching your place.

9

——

I LOOKED THROUGH the blinds of my front window, careful not to disturb them.

Across the parking court of the bungalows, parallel parked on the other side of the street, two people sat in an unmarked car, which sort of made it obvious they were watching my place. Who just *sits* in a car? Thieves, who are casing a place, or cops. And these had to be cops as there wasn't anything worth robbing in these bungalows.

And somehow they had managed to find perfect parking in West Hollywood. Bastards.

I dialed a number on my cell.

Violet picked up on the first ring.

"Jimmy." Her voice was tight.

"Hey, honey. What's going on?" I asked sweetly. "Is everything OK?"

"We need to talk," she answered. "Where are you?"

I looked out the window again. "You don't know?" I asked, frowning.

"Why would I know? I don't stalk you."

She was telling the truth. Which made me wonder: Who exactly was watching me? They were giving me a total cop vibe. I had dealt with enough of them to know —

"Jimmy, are you listening?"

"Yeah."

I was not.

She sighed and repeated herself. "Things are escalating. The DA is getting personally involved. He claims it's about crime getting out of hand, but this is a fucking election season, and I think he just wants his face on something exciting."

I groaned.

"So, Jimmy, I need you to come in."

"What?" I snapped. "Come in?"

"We need to properly interview you."

I breathed out slowly.

A deep voice rumbled behind me. "What's going on?"

I turned around. Anton was just stepping into the living room, eyes blinking, adjusting to the light. I covered my phone and shook my head. Anton stopped moving and frowned, worry creeping into his face.

I put a finger to my lips and uncovered the phone.

Ito was saying, "Are you still there?"

"Yeah, yeah, of course I am."

"*Where* are you?"

"At a coffee shop."

I rolled my eyes at that stupid lie. It had just poured right out of me, and now I had no choice but to go with it.

"You know," I continued, "after the night I had, I'm just exhausted. Getting all caffeinated before I head into the office."

Why didn't I just *shut up*?

She was silent. "OK, fine." She wasn't going to ask. Probably because she didn't want to know. "All right. Kemble and I can meet you in the office. When are you going to be there?"

I looked at Anton, who looked back at me, worry turning to confusion. Why was I staring at him? Did I need something?

"You know," I replied, "in a few hours."

"OK. We'll talk soon." She paused. "Until then, just stay out of this one."

"Sure!" I said, then wondered if I sounded too chipper.

Silence. "You don't know where he is, right?"

"Nope."

"Jimmy." Her tone was no-nonsense. "Like I said, the DA is involved."

"Let's talk later." I hung up.

"Was that...?" started Anton.

"Yes, my cop girlfriend."

"Oh, fuck," he gasped. "This is bad."

I shook my head., willing myself to believe the opposite. A little optimism can go far. "It's going to be fine." I shrugged, turned back to the window, and looked through the blinds again.

"What do you mean *fine*? She's got to be suspicious."

I shrugged. "See, that's a problem for later. Right now, I'm worried about the cops outside."

"*What?*"

Anton was next to me by the window in a flash.

"Anton, just be cool," I assured him. "They're here for me."

He looked at me and rolled his eyes. "They're here for you because they think you will lead them to me."

I blinked, shrugged again. "Yeah. True." I took a breath. "So here's the plan. I have a list of places I'm going to check out. Meanwhile, you stay here."

He stepped away from me, putting a hand up. "I am *not* staying here."

"Anton, I will be leading them away — "

"If I stay here, what if they just come in?"

I wagged a finger. "Au contraire. They would need a warrant. Trust me. My mom's a lawyer."

He put his hands together, practically praying for me to

listen. "Are you kidding me? Do you *not* watch the news? Have you not been paying attention? I'm a Black man, wanted in connection with a murder and the theft of a highly valued object. So if they want to come in" — he pointed out the window — "they aren't waiting for a warrant."

I blushed, feeling stupid because he was, of course, right. I took a breath. "OK. You know what? This is *great*. A team-up. A buddy cop movie."

"A buddy *what*?" It was clear Anton was losing patience with me.

"It'll be like *48 Hrs*. You know, Nick Nolte and Eddie Murphy? It's old, but it's a classic."

Anton folded his arms. "I'm the Donkey guy from *Shrek* because I'm Black?"

I shook my head. "Well, no. I mean, *no*, because I'm Eddie Murphy in this. A wise guy, speaking from his hip."

"So I'm the *cop*?"

"You know what?" I paused, looking for something to say. I came up empty. "I didn't think you had seen the movie, soooo... let's just move on, OK?" I turned to my phone and dialed.

Moe picked up right away, saying, "How on earth did they get that parking spot? What are the chances?"

As much as I wanted to unpack those questions, I stayed on task. "That's not what's really important right now."

He huffed. "Right. What do you need?"

"Anton and I have some errands. I need a distraction."

Moe was quiet for a moment, then said, "Give me ten minutes."

"Fifteen. I need to change."

"Deal."

He hung up, and I said to Anton, "We leave in fifteen."

Anton eyed the window. "What is he going to do?"

I snorted and headed to my bedroom. "Something distracting."

Fourteen minutes later, I was at the window in my tailored, navy-blue suit, which I wore over a crisp, red button-down. My mother taught me a long time ago, when you're a public figure, you never know when someone is going to snap your pic. Better to be overdressed than under.

Of course, in this case, those someones were plainclothes police detectives. So maybe Mom's advice didn't apply here, but hey, old habits die hard.

Moe stepped out of his place in the tightest T-shirt he owned, wearing an equally tight pair of jeans, showing off the hours he put in at the gym. In his hand he carried a platter that held two mugs of coffee and what I guessed were muffins.

Anton raised an eyebrow and looked at me, unsure.

"Just be ready," I assuaged him.

I clicked my car open through the window as Moe reached the street. The Toyota's headlights flashed. Moe looked both ways and then eyed the parked car. He slunk across the road, heading right for the cops.

"What's he doing?" asked Anton.

Oh, sweet summer child. I guess I had to explain. "Flirting."

Moe leaned over into the window, obscuring us from view.

Anton's eyes narrowed, straining to see. "He's doing what — ?"

I hitched a thumb at my front door. "Let's go, let's go!"

We scrambled out of my place, staying low, heading to my car. "Back seat, back seat!" I hissed.

Anton's eyes went wide, and he opened his mouth to protest.

I shook my head. We did not have time to argue. I growled, "Back. Seat."

He grunted, shook his head, and slipped into the back as I got in the front. We slammed our doors together. He lay down across the back seat as I started the car, plugged my phone into the aux outlet, and started scrolling, looking for a song.

"Are you kidding me right now?" Anton shouted.

Shit. What was I doing? "Right, you're right!" I replied, chastened. "Shuffle. Shuffle will be fine."

I pushed 'Shuffle' and reversed out of my parking spot, maybe a little too fast.

The piano intro for Styx's "Come Sail Away" started as I

turned the car around.

I pulled up to the street. Moe glanced my way. In the front seat of the parked car, the driver's eyes widened as he spotted me. I could see his partner mouth "fuck" as he scrambled to start the car, shouting at Moe, who continued to lean against his door.

I turned right, heading south to Santa Monica Boulevard.

In my rearview mirror, the car herked and jerked out of the coveted parking spot as the driver did his best not to run over Moe's foot in the process as Moe stayed in the way.

I stomped on the accelerator, making a left onto Santa Monica as other cars blasted their horns. My little Toyota roared like a baby lion down the street.

"You can get up now," I said without looking back, pretty sure I had lost them.

Anton sat up. He leaned forward, holding a limp orange peel in his fingers. From another quick look in the rearview I could tell he had something to say. "Dude. You're filthy."

I waved a finger. "In my defense, I get hungry when I'm working cases, and I like to eat fresh fruit."

"You could still throw the peel in a bag, Jimmy, and throw that shit away later."

I put my eyes back on the road. "I need you to buckle up. I don't need us getting pulled over because you're not buckled."

Anton rolled his eyes, leaned back, and buckled up.

After the high-octane adventure that started our day, Anton and I were quickly disappointed by the car rental stores. The first couple of rental places were duds, but the third offered a possibility. It was out of the way, a little run down, and willing to look the other way. But, nope. Devon hadn't been there.

So we continued — Anton now next to me up front — on our tour of the southern part of L.A. County. That's when I got the call. Linda Ronstadt's "You're No Good" cut out, and my phone started ringing.

I glanced at the phone and saw that it was Cooper and Associates. I put a finger to my lips. Anton nodded, and I stabbed the "Answer" button.

"Hello?"

A familiar woman's voice replied. "Mr. Cooper?"

It was Nora, my assistant, who did not deserve such a mess for a boss.

"Nora!" I shouted with glee. "How are you this fine morning?"

A pause. "Mr. Cooper, your mother is wondering why the police are here to question you."

Shit. Shit, shit. *Shit.* I had forgotten what I had said to Ito. This would be just embarrassing if it had been about jaywalking or a dognapping. My girlfriend was going to be *pissed.* Pissed because at best she might think I flaked out on her and, at worse, of course is that I'm deeply involved and have been lying to her.

I was thirsty again.

"Did they... the detectives, say anything?"

Another pause. "Not to me, Mr. Cooper, no, but they have been talking with your mother."

Nora took a nervous breath. Which was all I needed to hear.

"She's right there, isn't she? In front of you?"

"Yes, Mr. Cooper."

Anton's mouth formed a perfect O, which he covered with a fist. I shot a frown at him. He mouthed, "You are in so much trouble."

Before I could say anything, a familiar voice came on the line.

"James."

"Hello, Mother."

"Where are you?"

"Uh..." I was on the 105, heading west. "I don't know. I'm all turned around."

Anton snorted.

A sigh from the phone. "James." My mother has the ability to pack so much disappointment into one word. "There are detectives in my lobby wanting to speak with you. One of them seems pretty angry. And it's not the tall one. He seems to be happy. I think he's hoping you're making trouble for yourself. Is that what you're doing?"

I didn't say anything.

The phone rumbled as she moved it from one ear to the other. "What *are* you doing, James?"

I exited the 105 and headed into Hawthorne, a small city that was party of the South Bay. Home to less than a hundred thousand people, it's become a hub for aerospace businesses.

"I'm working on… something."

She sucked her teeth. "Is this about Anton?"

Anton and I exchanged looks. Erika must've talked to Mom. She always had a hard time keeping secrets from her, and by secrets, I mean the real important stuff, like life-and-death stuff, not who finished the last piece of pie in the middle of the night.

Spoilers: It was me. It was always me, and I would do it again, too.

"*James.*"

I glanced at Anton, who was looking at me intently. Then I put my eyes back on the road. "If I *was* doing anything that I shouldn't be doing, it would be for the right reasons." As I made a turn onto an east-west main road, two words floated to the top of my brain. "Pro bono. I'm doing pro bono work. You do pro bono, don't you, Mother?"

"Stop saying 'pro bono,' James. It sounds impolite coming

out of your mouth."

"Impolite?" This woman, I swear. "The point is" — I turned left into the parking lot of SB's Car Rental and parked close to the front door — "I am helping someone who needs my help. That's what people — you know, normal people — do."

She said nothing. "This wouldn't have anything to do with what happened this past summer, would it?"

I could feel Anton looking at me, but I didn't meet his eyes. I just couldn't.

"This has nothing to do with that," I mumbled.

"Are you sure? You didn't come out of that situation looking very good."

Yeah, neither did Matty, I thought.

I realized then that somewhere in the process of trying to convince her, I had started holding my breath. Now, as I tried to pull air back into my lungs, I couldn't breathe. My chest was tight, like someone was walking on top of me. Was this a heart attack? This would be a really bad time to have one. I rubbed my forehead, trying not to think about how I was dying in Hawthorne, thinking about my hands covered in Matty's blood.

"James? Are you still there?" asked Mom.

Anton nudged me in the arm. The world came back into focus.

"I am, yeah. I am." I stared ahead, into the rental place.

Inside, leaning against the counter and staring at her

phone, was a young girl in a gray polo shirt. She was Asian American and looked like she was in her early twenties. She stared intently at the phone, scrolling with her thumb while she held her chin in her other hand.

Mom kept going. "I'm just worried that you being involved in this will continue the negative press."

My face flushed, and I found myself suddenly angry. "For me or for you?"

That put her back on her heels.

If I was being honest, it wasn't the negative press that bothered me. The press is going to press no matter what. It was the lack of big cases, the occasional funereal smiles on the street, and the general feeling of the world passing me by. That one bothered me most of all.

"James — "

I ended the call.

10

—

Three Years Ago

"WHY DON'T WE just ring the bell?" I grumbled as Gordon and I sat in his car across the street from a small home in Silver Lake, a neighborhood north of downtown where the break-in had happened. Silver Lake is a cool place to live, very walkable. New Yorkers who have transplanted to L.A. prefer to live there because they think it's as close to home as they are likely to get. But I have to say, If you're leaving New York, why are you trying to recreate it?

The home was painted dark blue with white trim and had a large bay window in front. A Prius sat in the driveway to the left of the house, which presumably led to a detached garage.

"Because I don't want him to freak out and slam the door in our faces," answered Gordon, eyes on the house. Gordon was drinking coffee, the smell of which filled the car. It was convenience store coffee with a big dose of cream and I'd guess sugar. He was a secret sugar guy. He didn't know I saw him sneak a candy bar here and there, but I did.

"So we're just going to walk up to this witness and start asking questions. Won't *that* freak him out?"

Gordon's eyes shifted to me. "I didn't say I didn't want him freaked out. I said I didn't want a door slammed in my face. That makes asking questions a lot harder."

"What if he doesn't come out?"

"He'll come out, Jimmy." He took a drink from the paper cup. "You have to be patient. Let people come to you."

I looked at the house. I was not a patient person. Patience meant being quiet and still. And quiet and still wasn't something my brain did. Because quiet was deafening and still was imprisonment.

"What if he has nowhere to go?"

"*Then* I'll knock." Gordon looked at me. "We've done this before. Why are you...?" His question hung in the air.

"Why am I what?"

He shook his head. "I don't know. I don't know what this is." He paused, looking me up and down.

"This isn't *anything*," I said.

Gordon put his eyes back on the house. "Well, *now* it is."

He took a drink of coffee, leaving that comment hanging in the air.

I sighed, exasperated. Gordon loved doing this, saying something that demanded an answer and then going silent, waiting for the other person to respond.

"It doesn't *have* to be anything," I said.

He looked at me, raising an eyebrow.

I caved. "Fine, fine. I want this to work out for Anton. I feel for the kid, you know?"

A flicker of a smile on his lips as Gordon watched the house again. "See a little bit of you in him, do you?"

"Is that wrong?"

He shook his head. "Not wrong at all." He paused. "It's not just about him, is it? You've vouched for him." His finger tapped the side of his cup. "If this goes sideways, that's on you."

I shifted in my seat. "Yeah, well, there must be something to it or you wouldn't be in the car with me." I paused. "If I didn't know better, I think you're beginning to think I've got what it takes to be a detective, Gordon."

Gordon chuckled, and then his attention snapped back to the house. A pudgy middled-aged white man was standing at the entrance with headphones wrapped over his head, holding a full, reusable grocery bag and locking the front door. He was in his forties, with sandy brown hair and was wearing a T-shirt, exercise pants, and slides with socks.

Gordon and I were out of the car before he got to the sidewalk.

"Mr. Wyler?" said Gordon.

Thomas Wyler turned around and stepped back when he saw us, surprised. "What?" he replied, a little too loud.

Gordon gestured to the headphones and increased his volume as well. "I'd like to ask you a couple of questions."

Wyler pulled the headphones back from his ears. I could hear heavy metal guitars and growling from a lead singer.

"I just want to go over what you told Detective Collins," said Gordon. "Maybe there's something more you remember."

Wyler frowned. He looked at me as I stood just a little behind Gordon. His eyebrows shot up. He'd recognized me. His eyes went back to Gordon. "Are you a cop?" He pointed at me. "Because *he's* an actor."

I blushed. It was nice of him to still think that.

"I don't understand what's going on," he said.

Gordon nodded agreeably. "Yeah, sorry. I get that." He was turning on the Easygoing Gordon Bixby Charm. "I'm not a cop. Not anymore," he said, trying to put Wyler at ease. "I'm working with Cooper and Associates." He pointed to me. "We're working on the assault that you witnessed around the corner on Redcliff?"

Wyler nodded slowly, understanding but not noticing Gordon hadn't said on whose behalf Cooper and Associates were working on the assault case.

"What do you want to know?" he asked.

"Why don't you run it through with us?" Gordon suggested. "We'll see what matches your statement, what might be new?"

Wyler agreed, turning off the music in his headphones and coming closer to us. He couldn't stop looking at me. "He's Jimmy Cooper, right?"

Dude, I was right there.

"I am. I am Jimmy Cooper," I replied.

He grinned. "Is this an actor thing? For, like, a movie?" He paused. "Are you making a comeback or something? I would love that for you."

"That's really nice. From your mouth to a studio exec's ear, you know?" I said, starting to laugh.

Gordon cleared his throat.

Right. We were here for a reason and it wasn't to build my ego.

I took a breath. "It'd be great if you could tell us about what happened that night."

It was like Wyler hadn't heard me. "I'm a screenwriter. Well, you know, aspiring. I'm an aspiring screenwriter."

Oh, *shit*. Aspiring screenwriters are the worst. Almost predatory. They will take any opportunity to pitch a script to anyone in the business. I once had an extra pitch me his script while I was in line for craft services when I was making

High School Spy. He was gone before lunch break was over.

Wyler held up the bag. It was filled with books. "I was just heading back to the library. Research for my next script."

"Uh-huh," I managed. "Good for you."

"Maybe you could read it when it's done?"

Shit, shit, shit.

"Oh, sure."

Wyler beamed.

One of the key lessons of Hollywood: No one ever says no to anything. No would mean burning the bridge to a possible success down the road. The best course of action is to be noncommittal yet apparently open.

"Mr. Wyler," said Gordon, getting us back on track. I would be in his debt for the rest of the day. "About that night?"

"Oh, right." Wyler put the books down. "Well, since I quit my job as a veterinarian — "

Oh, man, this guy... he probably made so much money. There are *so many pets* in L.A. What was he doing trying to write screenplays?

" — I haven't been getting as much exercise. As a vet, you're on your feet all day, but when you're writing, really putting in the effort..." He patted his stomach. "I've been trying to get my steps in. I go out twice a day. Write a little, walk a little, that's my mantra."

"That's great. Smart." Gordon chuckled, but I could tell he didn't mean it. He just wanted some answers from this jerk. He smiled. "You were out walking, getting in those steps, that night?"

"Uh-huh. I had a late dinner, so I was getting out late. Around eight thirty. It was dark. I was coming down Redcliff, doing my thing, listening to my jams, when I saw three guys running out of this house."

"How far away were you?"

"Oh, you know, just a couple doors down."

Gordon nodded. "You saw three guys running out of a house a couple doors away. What made you call 911?"

"Huh?"

Gordon asked again, "What made you think you needed to call 911?"

"Oh, uh." Wyler stopped to think. The cops hadn't bothered to ask what had motivated this man to call, just what he had seen. "Well, you know... these guys were running out of the house."

Gordon hmm'd. "Could be they were running late."

"Huh?"

Gordon explained it to the guy. "All you saw was them running. They could've been late for something. How do you know they were fleeing the house?"

Wyler hemmed and hawed for a second. "I don't want to speak badly about the couple that lives there, given what happened, but..."

"But?" Gordon prompted.

"Listen, Chad and Deborah — "

Deborah Holt, the victim, and her boyfriend, Chad Lane.

" — have quite the reputation on Nextdoor."

Ah, Nextdoor. The app with all the hot neighborhood "goss."

"Fighting with other neighbors. And, like, take your trash cans in, is that so hard? And these parties? We can all hear them over here. Shady people around the house all the time..."

"Shady?" asked Gordon. "What made them shady?"

"Well," started Wyler. He paused and looked back and worth between me and Gordon. "They just didn't look like they were from this neighborhood. Like they didn't fight in, you know? No judgement."

Sure sounded like a whole lot of judgement.

"This neighborhood is different. I think it's all these people leaving L.A. and turning their homes into rental properties. AirBnb has totally changing everything."

Gordon nodded like Wyler had made a good point. "What about Chad and Deborah?"

Wyler went on. "Chad, the guy's a real piece of work. Huge attitude. And she's... look, I don't really like talking about them this way."

I got that familiar little buzz in the back of my head. I think he did enjoy talking about them this way.

Gordon looked at me, rolling a finger, telling me to get

on with it.

"Right," I said, remembering my one assigned task. I pulled out my phone and opened it before handing it to Wyler. "Was this one of the men you saw?"

He looked at the picture and frowned. "Maybe. Yeah. Yeah, I think so."

Gordon said to him, "You would swear to it on the stand?"

Wyler looked at the photo one last time. "Yeah, yeah. Totally."

Gordon and I exchanged looks. My heart beat hard and my skin flushed. I took the phone back, closing it. The picture Thomas Wyler had identified as the man he saw was some other Black kid with blond hair I had found on the internet. Decidedly *not* Anton Greene.

"Is that it?" asked Wyler.

"That's it," said Gordon, smiling.

"Wow. This is so exciting!" He grinned. "It's totally going to be in my next script. Write what you know, right? Crime procedurals are a little bit out of my genre, but I'm really *inspired*."

"You know a woman was beaten up, right?" I said. I couldn't help myself; this guy was being an asshole.

Wyler's mouth started moving, but suddenly he didn't have so much to say. "Well. I know. I don't mean... it's not *good*... I'm just saying..."

Gordon let him off the hook. "You have a good day, Mr.

Wyler."

We turned and headed back toward our car.

"I'll send my script to your agent when it's done!"

I turned back and waved. "You do that!" I shot him a finger gun. I didn't have the heart to tell him I didn't have an agent anymore. Not one who returned my calls anyway.

I turned to Gordon. "Him being a screenwriter made that a little more awesome. He totally couldn't tell one Black kid from another. I can't believe that worked."

Gordon paused in the middle of the street to look at me. "It works a lot." He shook his head. "He wasn't going to be called to the stand to identify Anton anyway. The DA would know your mother would destroy him as a witness."

A car horn honked. Gordon and I waved at the Saab that had rolled up as we moved out of its way.

"If he's such a lousy witness, why are they using him to make the charges?" I said.

Gordon put his hands on his hips and stared at the ground. "Because they want to close the case. Get it off their desk. Move on to something else. Same old bullshit. It never changes." He sighed.

"What's next?" I asked.

"Next?" answered Gordon. "Next we find out more about the victims."

11

—

ANTON STARED AT me from the passenger seat after I had hung up on my mother.

"Moms, huh?" he said sympathetically.

I said nothing and got out of the car, trying to shake off the call from my mother.

He did the same, saying, "Your mom hasn't changed. Tough as ever."

I pulled off my sunglasses and asked him across the hood of my car, "How's your mom?"

He wiggled his head. "Tough as ever." Then he paused. "I need to call her."

"Let's wait on that."

Anton nodded. "Are you in trouble?"

"What? Nah," I demurred. I was in a lot more trouble than I had been in in a long time. "Not any more than usual. It'll be fine." I was just shooting off lies left and right. I nodded to the rental place. "All right, let's do this." I paused. "This time let me do the talking?"

He stopped. His head tilted. He was offended.

"At the last rental place, you wouldn't shut up with your questions," I said.

"That place was *shady*. He had to know more than he was letting on."

I rolled my eyes. "Of course he knew more than he was letting on, that place *was* shady. But he didn't know anything about Devon, OK? So just be cool."

"I'm *cool*."

I shook my head. "On second thought? Just don't say anything."

Before he could say anything, I pulled the door open and stepped in as an electric chime rang. The girl behind the counter rolled her eyes from her phone to us. She pushed herself up to standing and set her phone to the side. Her head tilted, and without passion, she asked, "How can I help you?"

Clearly, she was living her best life.

I turned on my game face, a sympathetic smile. "I'm hoping you can." I leaned an elbow on the counter, just a little bit to her left. This gave her mostly my left side, which I'd been told by managers, directors, and makeup crews was the better one. I could feel Anton behind me, staring me down with a "Show me what you got" look on his smug face. I didn't mind. I just used that energy to fuel my performance as I told the rental store clerk, "I'm afraid I've lost something."

"Oh?" she replied, stretching out the word with uncertainty.

"My wallet." I nodded, acknowledging the frustrating nature of the predicament. "I lost my wallet in a van that my friend rented from you guys. Can you believe that? So stupid. I was hoping you could help me locate it."

Anton sighed heavily. I snapped a glance at him, annoyed. This was a delicate moment. He shifted uncomfortably in response to my glare. He looked at me, then at her. "Yeah. He lost his wallet."

I smiled at the clerk, hoping to bring life back to this moment.

"OK. Uh." She turned to her right and started looking under the counter. "I don't remember anyone finding a wallet." She had her hand on a cardboard box. "When was the car turned in?"

"It was a van, actually. And here's the thing," I explained, "it hasn't been turned in. Yet."

Her hand came off the box, and she looked at us, waiting to hear more. This is where it was going to get tricky.

"See, my friend — "

"Our friend," added Anton.

She looked back and forth between us.

"Yes, *our* friend," I confirmed quickly. "He rented a van from you guys. He's the best man at our friend's wedding, and he was the one who organized a little bachelor party. Overnight trip to Vegas." I put a hand to the side of my mouth. "We're all sworn to secrecy." I chuckled.

"Uh-huh," she said.

I started to worry that this wasn't going to work.

"The thing is, we got back to town early this morning, he dropped me off at my place, and *whoops*, I realized I had left my wallet in the van. I've been trying to call him, but he's just not picking up."

She nodded slowly. Maybe this was going to be OK.

Time for the big ask. "I was hoping, if you could, you know, with the GPS, track the van down?"

She raised an eyebrow, and her head tilted again. "Why don't you just go over to his place?"

A great point. I started sweating.

"Sure, yeah, I could do that," I said. "But..."

But what, Jimmy? Think of something!

Anton poked me in the ribs. I waved him off.

"I don't know where he lives," I said to the rental store clerk.

"You don't know where your friend lives?" she asked,

monotone and unbelieving.

"Jimmy," whispered Anton.

I shook my head, going with it. "I know, unbelievable. But he just moved, and I was a terrible friend who didn't help, and I haven't been over there. In my defense, he hasn't thrown a housewarming party, you know?"

Nailed it.

She folded her arms.

Scratch that. I did not nail it.

"*Jimmy*," said Anton.

"What?" I hissed.

He nodded to the wall.

Behind the young woman was a wall of headshots. Of celebrities. Businesses in L.A. really like their wall of celebrity headshots. Presumably, they were or had been customers. The guy I get my oil change from has a wall of celebrities. My dry cleaner? Same. I scanned the wall, seeing TV and film stars from bygone decades, some forgotten, some legends. Charlotte Rae from *The Facts of Life*. Hal Linden from *Barney Miller*. Don Rickles. I began to wonder how and why so many celebrities had found their way to Hawthorne for a car rental.

Anton tapped my shoulder and pointed.

I took a short breath. In the middle of the third row was an old picture of me. In it I looked about sixteen, at the very beginning of my peak. Did I rent a car here once? I was pretty sure I hadn't, but there were a few hazy years. But *Hawthorne*?

Anton said to the girl behind the counter, "You like Jimmy Cooper?"

She looked back at the wall. "Oh, him?" She chuckled. "That's my dad's idea. He thinks more people will rent cars from us because they did."

"Did *I* rent a car here?"

She paused and looked at me. I could see the moment recognition hit. It was like a wave crashing over her. Her pupils went wide, and her jaw dropped. "Oh my god, you're Jimmy Cooper! I didn't recognize you. You're so much — "

"More mature?" I said.

"I was going to say older."

Anton barked with laughter.

I smiled through the pain.

"My dad showed us all your movies. He *loved* them. Especially *Getting to Drive*. He must've watched that a million times."

I blushed, shrugged, smiled.

"He used them to learn English when he came to America."

I nodded, then turned to Anton and said, "Well. Look at that. My filmography wasn't a waste after all." I turned back to the young woman, whose dad apparently owned this shop. "So, did I rent here?"

She made a face. "I don't know." She pointed over her

shoulder. "None of these people did. Dad got a lot of these pictures from a Mexican place that closed about ten years ago."

I nodded as the conversation grew quiet. "So about the van..."

"Um," she said, considering it. Then, her face brightened. "Sure. OK. I mean, of course." She grinned. "Dad is going to be so jealous you came by when he wasn't in." She stepped to the computer. "What was your friend's name?"

I started to sweat, worried about this moment. I looked at Anton, who shrugged.

"Mike Lowery," I said. I chewed my bottom lip, hoping she wasn't a big nineties movie buff.

She nodded. "OK, let me look."

I guess she wasn't.

She clacked at her keyboard, then paused, scanning the rental forms. "It's due today." She looked at us expectantly, as if we were responsible.

Anton took a heavy breath.

"I'm sure he'll get it here," I promised.

Anton cleared his throat and eyed me, clearly uncomfortable with my deception.

"You know what?" I added. "Can you give me the location? Of the van?"

She frowned. "You don't want the address he gave us?"

"Well, the wallet is *in* the van. And I'm sure he's with the van. So, you know. I'll find him and the van and remind him it's due today." I tapped the counter for extra emphasis.

The girl lifted a shoulder. She didn't really care. Once she knew who I was, that was enough proof that we were on the up and up. After some more clacking and a photo op, she gave us a location for the van.

12

—

OH, GOODY. THE location the rental store clerk had given us for the van was in Van Nuys, a neighborhood about forty-five minutes north of Hawthorne by way of the 405, my least favorite highways. Sure, it was wide and the best way to get to LAX, but it was no 10.

We were winding through the Sepulveda Pass, just about to head down into the Valley. "Add Up My Love" by Clairo played, and I noticed Anton sitting next to me with a smile on his face.

"What are you smiling about?" I asked.

Anton gave a slight shrug. "Just thinking about how it went back there. At the car place."

I looked at him, then back at the road, then back at him,

and frowned behind my sunglasses.

"'Follow my lead,' you said," Anton continued with a little curl to his lips. "Your lead was crashing and burning, bro."

I tsked. "You don't know that."

He chuckled. "We *both* know that."

I put my eyes back on the road, flipped on my indicator and gunned it past a slow-moving truck. "No. We don't both 'know that.'"

"Hey, man," he said in a faux conciliatory tone. "It's OK to admit you're wrong."

Maybe if I was a better person, or in a better place, I would've admitted and even *thanked* Anton for saving the situation. I was, in fact, not a better person and was, also, in fact, deeply annoyed.

Anton either ignored my displeasure or didn't pick up on it. "So," he started, looking at the traffic, "is this what you do? Talk to people, then drive around and talk to more people?"

"Oh, no. *This* is an exciting day. I'm not sitting in one place for hours on end, not talking to anyone. You'd be surprised how often I'm just sitting in front of someone's home, hoping to catch them cheating on someone."

He looked me up and down, concern on his face. "Sounds glamorous."

I wagged a finger. "And don't let anyone tell you otherwise."

Anton grinned, and I smiled.

He fell silent. When I peered over, it looked like he wanted to say something.

"What's up, Anton?"

His head wobbled. Finally, he said, "I read about what happened this summer."

I clenched my jaw. Here we go.

"I'm sorry it happened, man. It was pretty fucked up."

I swallowed, gave him some more side-eye, and then took a moment to pass another car. "Yeah, it was fucked up." I looked at him again. He nodded, and we both silently agreed to drop it.

The song changed. The Velvet Underground's "Oh! Sweet Nuthin'" started just as we slipped into the Valley, which always felt like sliding into a dream. It's flat and stretches on forever, an endless collection of two-story homes, malls, and cafes. It's designed to be idyllic, the California Dream made manifest. It's not a coincidence that one of those homes was chosen to be the exterior of the Brady Bunch house. It's so pleasant that whenever I roll in, I'm afraid I'll never leave.

Off the 405, we headed into Van Nuys, toward the location of the van. I wondered just who we were going to find when reached the location.

That's when I realized I was dragging Anton and myself into something that could go sideways very quickly. The way Anton talked about Crenshaw and Abbott, they were legit and probably dangerous.

This might come as a shock, but I'm not what one would call a fighter.

My dad tried to make me into one. Back when he was still trying to be a parental figure in my life, before I had started acting, when he was still pursuing his own dream of being an action movie star — spoilers: it didn't work out — he tried to show me some moves. Of course, they were all fake, the sort of moves a stuntman would use to *not* hurt someone. None of them involved actual contact. I, however, managed to put myself in direct contact with every fake punch and pretend kick my father threw. Frustrated by my lack of prowess and constantly having to explain to Mom why I had a black eye, he stopped teaching me.

"Anton," I said "these guys could be dangerous."

He blinked. "They *are* dangerous, Jimmy."

We were on the street and close to the address as I found a spot to park.

"OK, great," I said, desperate to keep my voice in its usual octave. "We're on the same page then. You'll hang back."

Anton sucked his teeth in disagreement. "You're going to need backup."

"Backup? This isn't a TV show."

"Just this morning you said this was *48 Hrs.*"

I snapped, "That was to describe our *roles*, not how it's

going to work." I turned off the car, and the song cut out. "You need to hang back, OK? Your mom is already going to be pissed about all of this. Can you imagine how mad she'd be if I got you killed while trying to get you out of trouble?"

I got out of the car. So did Anton.

"Anton," I warned him.

He stood to his full height and leveled a stare at me over the car's roof. "How are you going to make me get back in the car?"

"Fair point." I looked around, orientating myself.

Anton spotted the van and pointed. It was parked on the street between two buildings. It was a white Mercedes-Benz Sprinter, big and cozy with tinted passenger windows, something you might see tourists using in Hollywood. It stuck out in this neighborhood like a sore thumb. I got a nervous feeling they might've ditched it here so it *would* be noticed while they were off somewhere else.

I nodded in the direction of the van and hopefully Crenshaw and Abbott were nearby. As we walked, I rehearsed what I would say to Ito when I called her later, how I would explain what we had done and how we saved the day.

The neighborhood was all apartments, two to three stories high. They looked like they had been built in the late seventies, early eighties. I'm sure in a few years, they'll be torn down and new apartments will replace the old ones, with the new ones being twice as expensive.

No one was really on the street. A car rolled down it, but otherwise, all was quiet. I kept walking toward the van with Anton in tow.

Maybe they were here, in one of these buildings. I kept an eye out.

Standing next to the van, I peeked through the driver's-side window. Nothing to see. No trash, no empty soda cans, nothing.

I shook my head and headed toward the back of the van, dragging a finger along its body as I went. It was warm to the touch. The chill of the night had been replaced by the warmth of the day. Ah, Southern California. Another peek into the van, my face pressed up against the passenger windows, showed nothing but benches.

"Dude," said Anton. "That looks hella suspicious."

I looked around. "No one's here to be suspicious. It's fine."

He shook his head, looking away, not fully on board.

I went around to the back, which is where I found the bullet holes.

"That will not buff out."

"Oh, shit," said Anton as he joined me.

There were two of them, about six inches diagonally apart, in the left door. I leaned over and looked into one of the holes. I could see inside. The bullet had passed all the way through.

I looked up at Anton. "You're lucky you didn't get hit."

He nodded, swallowing hard.

Another look around, and I decided to try my luck. I used my sleeve and took a hold of the door handle.

"What are you doing?" Anton asked, worried.

"The detective part of being a private detective." I gave the door a pull. It opened. I blushed at my good fortune. Something was actually breaking my way. Not wanting it to change, with a final look around the street, I stepped into the back of the van. Anton followed, closing the door behind.

And that's when we found the body. The smell hit us first, hot and rotting.

Slumped against the wall of the van was a Black man in his thirties, wearing all black and combat boots and sitting in a large pool of his own blood. Probably from that really nasty gunshot wound in his leg.

"*Oh*," said Anton. He slapped his hand over his mouth and nose. Anton heaved and my stomach followed suit.

Anton looked again. "It's Abbott. Shit, shit. Abbott is dead!"

I waved for him to keep it down.

My stomach turned again.

Anton groaned and heaved.

I pointed a finger at him. Desperate, I said, "Don't do that. You'll make me throw up."

"I can't help it." Another heave. "There's a fucking body

here."

"You cannot throw up in here. This is a crime scene." I choked on the words.

He clamped his mouth closed, squeezing his lips together. He swallowed and nodded, eyes watering.

Yeah, there was a body here, but worse than that, there was no Buddha. It must have been with Crenshaw. I realized it wasn't good luck the van was unlocked. Crenshaw wanted his partner's body to be found.

I closed my eyes and took a moment to settle down. There was work to be done.

I searched the van, careful to avoid Abbott's body, careful not to leave any evidence that I had been inside. Remembering what Gordon Bixby had taught me, I was methodical, starting at the front and moving back and forth. Bixby always said, "When you don't know what you're looking for, look at everything." It was tedious work, and it was hot and gross inside the van, and it was getting harder and harder to not think about the sticky, drying blood that surrounded Abbott's body.

Anton moaned as I worked.

"Do you want to go outside?"

Eyes closed, his head jiggled from side to side. "I'm fine."

"You don't seem fine."

One of his eyes opened and caught sight of the body. He gagged. "Just stop asking."

I shook my head and turned away, refocusing on the floor of the van, where I found dirt. Maybe sand? Sandy dirt? I didn't know what a geologist would call it, and I would hardly trust *any* detective who would announce where the soil was locally sourced by looking at it. That guy would be an asshole, desperate for approval.

Bile clawed at the back of my throat. "Let's go," I managed to say, and Anton and I jumped out the back of the car.

Both of us took in big gulps of fresh air.

"Oh, fuck, oh, fuck," repeated Anton. "Oh, *shit*."

"Will you stop saying that?"

"This is two bodies in less than twelve hours, Jimmy. Two bodies. I'm allowed to curse."

I put up my hands. "Yes, but let's use our inside voice to not attract attention, OK?" I looked back at the van. "Abbott must've gotten hit in an artery during the shoot-out. That was a lot of blood."

Anton waved a hand in the air. "Can we *not* talk about the blood?" He took a deep breath in through his nose and walked in a circle on the street. "What do we do?"

"Well, we can't stay here. Crenshaw must have the Buddha somewhere..." I pointed vaguely in the direction of L.A.

Anton looked heartbroken.

"Listen, we're not done yet."

"Abbott is dead, Jimmy."

I agreed. "Yes, but — "

"But?"

"The Buddha is still out there. Crenshaw is still out there. And, presumably, whoever was going to pay for it."

Anton nodded. "Uh huh. And how do you know Crenshaw just didn't toss the Buddha and get the fuck out of town?"

I swallowed. I didn't *know*. But I had a guess. "Listen, Crenshaw must know the value of the Buddha. He and..." I nodded toward the van. "They didn't go through all this for nothing. Crenshaw is out there. He'll want to get his money."

Anton jabbed a finger in my direction. "But where is he, Jimmy?"

An old man walking a small dog turned the corner and headed our way. He was of the age that he could get away with wearing hats all the time. Today he wore a porkpie.

Anton's eyes darted to mine.

"We need to go," I said.

"But *where*?" he demanded.

I pointed at the car. "Go, get in." As he groaned and stomped toward the car, I stepped toward the man. "Hey there, friend. I think you should call the cops about this van."

Anton paused, looked in my direction, then kept on going, head turned away from the man.

The dog yapped in my direction as the man slowed. "Eh?" he replied.

I pointed at the back doors. "It's got bullet holes."

The old man peered at the back of the van. "Bullet holes. Huh." The dog sat, looking up and panting at his owner.

"Bullet holes. That means it's a crime scene," I explained. "Calling the cops would be a great idea."

He rubbed his chin. "Why don't you?"

Of course that was a great question. The truth was I wanted as little connection to having been here as possible. Me calling 911 would sort of defeat the purpose, but I wanted Abbott and the van found. Maybe the techs were smart enough to tell if it was sand or sandy dirt.

"I have to go console my friend," I said, nodding toward my car. "His girl broke up with him and you know how it is…"

Not waiting for an answer, I turned and quickly walked to my car.

As I got in, Anton said, "Now what?"

"The thing they never expect," I answered. "We go back to the scene of the crime. I started the car. Spacehog's "In the Meantime" played as we left as Anton watched the old man dig out his cellphone.

13

——

"CAN I HELP you with something?" asked the saleswoman, her hands coming together, palm over palm. She was a white brunette in her forties, a little taller than me, wearing a black pencil skirt with a lemon-yellow top. She had the perfect smile to sell unusual and unconventional objects to wealthy people: charming without saying anything definite, all to suss out the customer. Would they be easygoing or demanding? Did they know what they wanted, or were they open to (more expensive) suggestions? She would bend like a palm tree in the wind to close the sale.

I expected nothing less from a place like Objet Exotique.

Unluckily for this saleswoman, Anton and I weren't really there to shop for anything.

He was sweating profusely and trying to breathe normally as he stood next to me.

"I'm looking for something peaceful," I said to her. "An object that would demand that I center myself."

"Fuuuuuuck," whispered Anton. I looked at him and smiled. When I had told him that I wanted to coming here, I thought his spirit was going to leave his body.

The saleswoman nodded. "I have some lovely pieces. Do we have a budget we're working with?"

In other words, are you wealthy, sir, or merely middle class?

"Oh, I have a budget," I said confidently.

Remember, kids, it's easy to have a budget when you aren't actually going to buy anything.

It was now after lunch time. We had parked on La Brea Avenue, and Anton had waited in the car as I walked around a bit to see if the police were still at Objet Exotique. I wasn't sure if Ito and Kemble had been by or had sent others to the crime scene, but they were gone now. I grabbed Anton, and we headed inside.

"Perfect, Mr. Cooper," she said, relieved. "I wasn't sure, given your circumstances."

I gave another tight smile to Anton. Right. My circumstances. I was still famous, but not *rich* famous. Famous, but not the public's favorite. A potent mix.

I replied, "Well. You know." I let her fill in the gaps.

She glanced at Anton, and I could see she had questions about his extremely casual look.

I grabbed him by the arm. "My art guru. He's got great taste. Especially for feng shui," I assured her. "Don't you?"

Anton licked his bottom lip. "Oh, yeah. Feng shui. It's where it's at," he muttered.

She seemed somewhat unconvinced. I gestured for her to lead the way, and we followed her as she walked toward the back of the store. The place was deeper than it was wide, with an open floor lit by skylights in the bare rafters that gave the whole place a warm, inviting vibe. We made our way through the displays of brass work, tile work, furniture, things that couldn't possibly be chairs, and things I hoped *weren't* chairs.

Anton pulled me by the arm so we were a few paces behind her. "What the *fuck*?"

"You need to chill," I said under my breath. "They might get suspicious."

"I need — ? You're the one who brought me here."

I turned to him. "Do you think they know you drove the getaway car? They weren't here. You weren't in the store. Just be cool."

The saleswoman looked back at us, waiting.

I smiled at her. "He admires your..." I gestured to the space.

Anton swallowed and nodded.

"You guys don't have any rugs," I announced. "I thought there'd be rugs."

She paused. "No, sir. We do not have rugs. Do you *need* a rug?"

I looked at Anton. He looked at her. He shook his head.

"I guess I don't need a rug." I pointed around. "Where do all of these come from?"

"From all around the world. Indigenous cultures. What you purchase here is real, not made in a factory. It has its own soul."

"Own soul?" asked Anton.

"That's right."

Anton gave me a withering look.

I pointed at the tag hanging from a marble carving of a Ganesh statue. It was about eighteen inches tall and worth five thousand dollars. "That explains the price." I chuckled at my bon not.

The saleswoman did not. "Excuse me?" she said, as if I'd farted in the middle of her wedding ceremony.

Trying to recover, I offered, "Just a little joke. You're right. These aren't trinkets."

Her eyebrow arched. "Trinkets are for tourists. These are relics."

"They belong in a museum!" I declared with a fist in the air.

On the other side of the store, a couple of customers

turned at my outburst.

Anton sighed in embarrassment.

"It's Indiana Jones," I explained. "You know, when — "

"Yeah, Jimmy," said Anton, cutting me off. "We don't care."

Rude.

The saleswoman looked me up and down, trying to decide what the hell was going on.

Anton said, "He didn't have his morning smoothie." He looked at me. "It's thrown his whole day off." Then he leaned toward her. "You know how actors can be."

She nodded, understanding, which I took very personally. How is it that *actors* are problems?

"There's a great juice bar, up on Beverly. You should check that place out," she said to me.

I nodded, still burning. "Right after we're done here. So you were taking me to…"

Remembering, she took a half breath. "Right. So I was." She turned, and we went into a corner of the store. Here there were more religious icons carved from stone and wood. All of them were larger objects, suitable for their own corners of a home or office. Many of them would overwhelm my wee little living room. These were things to build a shrine around. Something for people with budgets.

"These are great. These would totally get me to center myself," I said brightly.

She put her hand to her chest. "I feel like my brain settles whenever I'm in this part of the gallery."

I nodded along. "I was thinking about a Buddha."

Anton took a sharp breath.

"Mm, right." She turned. "We have several lovely options right here." She gestured to a bronze Buddha, sitting cross-legged on a stone, with his classic rounded belly and a slight grin. "This one is Japanese, from the nineteenth century — "

"Actually, I have something in mind. I was looking for — well, I heard about what happened last night…" I paused. "Listen, that's sort of the Buddha I'm looking for. Maybe there's another one like it." I started making a big deal of looking around the showroom.

Her shoulders dropped, her body language clearly uncomfortable with the line of questioning.

I pressed my hands together. "Is there someone else I should talk to? Maybe Mr. LaFontaine himself?"

"Oh…" She looked almost relieved by that idea. "Well, Mr. LaFontaine is…" She fingered the fabric of her shirt, trying to think of something to say.

"He's a busy man, I know," I said, "but, this would just take a minute. And" — I leaned in — "the studio is super excited to be working with me again, and I wanted something to keep me on the right path, you know?"

"The studio?" she murmured in return.

Again, I had said the right words. It didn't matter that I

hadn't said *which* studio. If there's a studio behind you, any studio, really, that means there's money.

And that means there are people who are more than happy to take it from you.

"I'll see if he's available." With that, she scurried into the back office.

Anton turned on me. "What are you doing?"

I pulled a mock look of concern. "I'm getting a little worried. I keep explaining why we're here…"

"*Jimmy.*"

"I've asked for the manager, Anton. That's what I did. She wasn't going to be able to give us what we need. Which is information."

"Mr. Cooper?" A voice carried across the sales floor, bearing the Hollywood version of a French accent. Louis LaFontaine was in his fifties, with thinning, brown hair, which he wore slicked back across his skull. He laid his image on thick, with a dapper gray suit, buttoned up, and a magenta tie and matching pocket square. "I am Louis LaFontaine. Sorry about the state of my little shop with all of the unpleasantness last night." I glanced around. There didn't really seem to be anything out of place. He took my hand and shook it. He looked to Anton and offered his hand. "And you are?"

Anton gulped. "Gary."

I sniffed. "That's it. Gary. He just goes by one name."

"Gary," Anton repeated. "Like Cher. Madonna. The Rock."

"Yeah, Gary, I think he got it."

Louis nodded and shook Anton's hand. "I understand, sir," he said to me, "that you are interested in a ceramic Buddha?"

"Yes, I am. Very much. Something that has a lot of soul," I said, looking at the saleswoman who stood behind him. "I understand you had such a piece."

Louis took a mournful breath. "Ah. Heartbreaking."

"Can't you get another one?"

"Another one? Mr. Cooper, it was *unique*," he insisted. "Only one of them in the world." He stretched the word "world" until it just might break.

"The only one?"

Louis's head shook back and forth ever so slightly. "I really shouldn't talk about it."

Oh, but he really wanted to talk about it. He seemed like he was *dying* to talk about it. He just needed a little push.

I stepped closer. "We're not talking. I'm just listening."

His lips twitched as he took that in. Then he chuckled and gave me a wink. He waved the saleswoman away as he looked out onto the gallery floor to see if anyone would overhear and then he gestured for us to come closer. "The piece was from the early Ming dynasty. Well over four hundred years old. Its size alone, as a ceramic piece, makes it unusual, and the artistry of the piece is exceptional. The look on the

Buddha's face is serene and perfect. But it's the glazes..."

The words lingered in the air. Apparently he wanted us to ask about the glazes.

"What about them?" asked Anton.

Louis's voice became hushed. "They are made from rare earth minerals in a combination never before seen and never used again. It's believed the glazes create a unique glimmer around the Buddha."

"Like Edward in *Twilight*?"

Louis looked at me blankly.

"That's OK. I haven't seen it either," I lied.

"It is said that the glimmer reflected the spirit of the Buddha. The emperor was so moved by the work that he had the artisan who made it executed so he could never create such a work of art again."

I nodded. "OK. Yeah. I get what you mean by unique."

Louis nodded in agreement.

"How did your gallery get such a piece?"

He smirked. "If you're asking if it was ethically acquired, I assure you, it was. It came from a private collector who shall remain nameless."

"Even for a certain... extravagant... price?"

He said nothing. He wasn't going to give that up.

"Something like *that* you weren't just going to put out here with the rest of the merchandise. Was it going to auction?"

He shook his head. "Oh, no. I had an interested buyer."

"Really?" Now I was getting somewhere. "Who was that?"

He demurred. "I'm afraid that I cannot disclose."

"Did anyone else know about the Buddha?"

Louis thought for a moment. "I had an agreement with the purchaser. She — " He paused, wondering if he had given anything away by gendering his interested party. Deciding he hadn't, he continued. "She is a regular customer of mine, and when I made her aware of the piece, well! An agreement was struck immediately."

Unfortunately for Louis, he had given something away. A familiar little buzz pinged in the back of my brain, and I knew he had lied to me. Maybe there was a little too much emphasis on "immediately" or how he stood there gripping his hands. Either way, he had lied to me. Others *did* know about the Buddha.

He must've realized he had said too much. His mouth became a thin line. "Are you actually here to purchase something, Mr. Cooper?"

"Oh, yeah. Yeah, totally," I said, making a big, unconvincing deal of surveying the showroom floor.

Seeing through me, Louis said, "I think it is time for you to leave. And you as well, Gary." He nodded and turned back to his office leaving Anton and me alone with the wealthy patrons and their interior designers.

"What now?" asked Anton.

"Are you hungry?" I asked, resting a thoughtful elbow on a nearby vase. Priceless; one of a kind, I'm sure. The temptation to pull the vase over flooded my body. Imagining all of those shocked faces made it almost irresistible. I shook it off once I saw the price tag.

"I'm hungry," I said, answering my question. "Let's do lunch."

14

Three Years Ago

MOE SAT CRISSCROSS applesauce on my couch, a plate of peeled orange slices in hand, watching me circle around the living room. "Could you stop?" he said. "Maybe just for a second? You're giving me the dizzies."

My skin buzzed with excitement, and I was walking on air. "Moe, I had an unbelievably good day."

He put up a hand, moving it in a vertical circle. "I'm getting all of that, honey. I really am." He plucked a slice of fruit. "But I do need you to take it down a notch. All of the orbiting around me..."

I ground to a halt in front of the couch. "Sorry, sorry." I was breathing fast. "It's just... I was *in* the room. I've never been in the room. All the months I've been there, it's always Gordon and Mom coming out of her office and telling me what to do, but today, I did something." I took a deep breath. "I convinced Mom to change tactics. She was trying to convince this kid Anton to take a plea, and I... I just said it out loud. That he wasn't guilty and he shouldn't take the plea."

I might not have argued *that,* but...

"You should've seen Mom's face."

Moe shook his head. "I imagine she was not happy." He had met her enough times and knew the history between us to get a clear mental image.

"She was *not.* Gordon didn't say much. But Anton's mom? She was, like, pointing at me saying, 'Yes, I want what he's having.'"

Moe grinned. So did I. Since I had gotten sober, Moe and I talked more and more at the end of the day. It was a check-in that I looked forward to. He had been sober for more than two years at this point and had become my sponsor through all of this.

"So. This is the case," I said. "Proving Anton innocent."

Moe took his time nodding.

"OK, that is not the universal praise and excitement I was looking for from you," I said.

He waved a hand, holding an orange slice. "No, no, don't get me wrong." He shoved the orange slice into his mouth.

As he chewed, he said, "I haven't seen you like this in…" He paused, mid-chew. "I don't know if I've ever seen you like this."

"Really?"

"You're positively glowing."

I paused. Maybe he hadn't seen me like this. When he and I met, I was using and still heading toward rock bottom, already persona non grata in Hollywood. My habit had become a production liability, and if there's one thing Hollywood can't stand, it's production problems. Do all the drugs, drink all the drinks you want, but if you start causing production delays — and time *is* money — you will be fired. No matter how big you are.

So don't do *too many* drugs, I guess, is the lesson.

The thing is, I knew this feeling. I'd *had* this feeling, but it had just been so long that it took a moment to recognize it. I had it at the very beginning of my career when I figured how I could make people laugh, that I could make people feel. Even when things had turned bad and no one knew, I still had those moments when I felt this good. I wanted to feel this good all the time.

Of course, that's not possible, especially when shit goes down and you can't tell anyone and you're all alone, but then, there are these pills that —

"Hey," said Moe. "You OK? You sorta disappeared for a second."

"Right. Yes. I'm good."

"Yeah?" asked Moe. "You want an orange slice?"

"I'm good." I smiled.

He smiled back. "But?"

But? He was saying but, and he's smiling. I was confused.

Moe put the plate to his side. "What if you don't prove this kid's innocent?"

I frowned. My head shook. "But he *is* innocent."

He nodded, agreeing. "That's not the same thing as proving it. I need you to think about how you're going to feel if you fail. And what that might do to your sobriety, not to mention this kid's life."

I licked my lips. I didn't like any part of where this conversation had turned. First it was with Gordon telling me I had put my reputation on the line and now Moe was suggesting I had also put my sobriety in danger. This didn't feel like he had my back.

"Moe, I'm trying to tell you about a good thing that I'm doing."

He again agreed. "And it's great seeing how excited you are about this new direction — "

"Whoa, whoa." I put up both hands. "This isn't a new direction. This is just for now. In a few months, I'll ease out of being a private eye and get back to work. I'll call up some producers, you know? Get some auditions."

Moe reached for an orange slice. "Sounds like a plan."

A knock sounded.

Our heads snapped to the front door. I remembered something. Plans for that night. "Crap."

Another knock.

"It's Rachel," I said.

Moe slumped.

Rachel was my girlfriend at the time. She was an actress on the way up, and I was an actor ready for a comeback. It had only been a month since we had met at a very bougie party in Silver Lake so we hadn't put a label on it.

Moe had opinions about her and we agreed to disagree.

"There's a party. In Laurel Canyon," I explained.

"Jimmy?" said Rachel from the other side of the door, annoyed to be kept waiting.

I opened it, and there she was, wearing a red, sleeveless satin dress that ended mid-thigh. She was in her late twenties, white, with cheekbones everyone wanted and brunette hair that simply cascaded just past her shoulders. Already three inches taller than me, she stood in leather boots with four-inch chunky heels so that she now towered over me. Her arms were crossed, and I thought she was going to choke out the small clutch in her hands.

She looked me up and down. "Are you even ready?"

I wasn't. I hadn't changed from work, and I didn't even have shoes on. "No, sorry. Sorry. I was just telling Moe about this new case."

She rolled her eyes and stepped into my place, missing my attempt at a kiss.

Moe picked up his plate of oranges. "He was just telling me about — "

Rachel turned to me, ignoring my neighbor. "Hon, you need to get ready. You can tell him later."

I looked at Moe. "But I was going to tell him about the veterinarian turned screenwriter — "

"Seriously?" asked Moe, orange slice halfway to his mouth. "That's insane."

"I *know*."

Rachel put up the hand holding her clutch. "Well, now you've told him. We're already late." She handed me the keys to her car. She would rather die than roll up in mine.

"If we're already late, what's a little more late?" I said, the very thing a child star who was used to everyone waiting for him would say.

Her head tilted. She was not going to take that for an answer. Which, fair. I might have been the asshole in this situation. Rachel wanted to maximize the number of people who would see her arrive, which meant balancing arriving when a certain number of people were already there without the event settling in and no one paying attention. I got that. I just had a PR person who managed all that. But, then again, I was famous, so people *always* noticed when I arrived.

I looked at Moe. He nodded, giving in. Taking a breath, he

unfolded himself from the couch, heading to the door with his plate of orange slices. "No worries," he said. "We'll talk later." With that he was gone and I headed to the bedroom to change.

Thirty or so minutes later, we rolled up into Laurel Canyon, an enclave on the south side of the Hollywood Hills with narrow, tree-lined streets and old homes. It was cozy and felt removed with the hustle and bustle down on Sunset, especially at night. In the late sixties, early seventies, it was *the* place to be. Musicians, New Hollywood, everyone was there. While it didn't have quite the same cache now, it was a still a cool place to live.

We were there to attend a party for a friend of Rachel's named Dylan. He was celebrating booking a big job on a sitcom or something. Somehow they had managed to get a taco wagon up there and parked in front of the house. A crowd of beautiful twenty- and thirty-somethings stood around the wagon, eating, drinking, and gossiping in their going out best. I could see how everyone wanted to impress each other in different ways. Like an L.A. redux of *The Breakfast Club,* there was the most fashionable one, the funny one, and the pretty one. Oh, and my favorite, the sarcastic one who was too cool even for this school. Heads began to turn as we walked up the street. I was holding Rachel's hand and could feel her excitement at having all eyes on her.

Some of them put their heads together and began to whisper. I imagined what they were saying about me, and I didn't like what I came up with.

Rachel spotted and pointed to a couple of actor friends, who squealed and ran up to her. The three women threw their arms together, hugging while I stood awkwardly to one side. Rachel had met them in an acting class; they were nice enough. One had come from Iowa, the other from Florida, and both were trying to make it in Hollywood. They made a point of playing it cool around me, which I sort of hated but which was also a bit of a relief. They had asked questions, but I didn't have much I could offer in the form of advice. "Have your dad take you on auditions and get discovered" isn't an actionable item for most people over the age of six.

After she finished chatting with the girls with a hollow promise to talk more, Rachel pulled me deeper into the house. I held her hand, standing behind her and looking around, hoping there was someone, anyone, there that I knew. I kept seeing eyes light up with recognition of me, followed by flat smiles. They recognized me, but I didn't know them, which is a deeply weird experience. Being famous breeds one-way familiarity. Add to that my recent public embarrassments and legal troubles, and it was a pretty heady social stew.

We paused in the kitchen entryway as Rachel met someone else she knew and they dove deep into conversation. I kept a hold of her hand, floating at the end of it like a balloon.

A blond twenty-something with artificially perfect teeth leaned into view. "You're Jimmy Cooper, right?"

"Guilty."

He chuckled. "I bet you're tired of saying that, right?"

Oh. I saw what he did there. A joke at my criminal expense. I always wondered what made people think *I* would find that funny. "Oh, yeah. You know it."

I kept looking around. There *had* to be someone here I knew.

The guy stepped back into my field of vision. "I'm a big fan of your work."

"Yeah? I wasn't so sure."

The blond guy laughed, though it was clear he didn't know why.

At that moment I'd even be willing to talk to a studio exec.

"How's the rebound going?" he asked.

I really looked at him then, and his face came into sharp focus. Besides the yellow-blond hair and the white teeth, he had blue eyes that I didn't believe, a narrow nose, and plump lips. He wore a slim-fit white button-down and black skinny jeans ending in boots with a bit of a heel. He oozed well-practiced charm.

"You're an actor?" I asked, but it was really more of a statement.

He paused. "Well, *yeah*," he replied, nodding.

I nodded back. "It's going well for you?"

He smirked. "You could say that." The smirk turned into a smile.

What the hell was up with *this* guy?

Rachel turned and gasped. "Dylan! Oh, my gawd! How are you?" She stepped past me, let go of my hand, and they hugged.

My face flushed. Hot and sweaty. Dylan. The guy who just got the show. This was *his* party. Not only had I just asked if he was an actor, but I'd asked how it was going for him. Being a self-absorbed addict had made me feel stupid and out of touch. I wanted to turn into vapor and float away.

I slapped on a smile. "Congratulations on the show," I said in an effort to repair what had just happened. "Sorry, my brain is just..."

Dylan nodded, a slight smile on his face. "Sure, sure. I understand." He didn't mean it.

"A sitcom," I started. "That's a big deal. Lots of pressure."

"I'm so excited for you," added Rachel.

"Thanks, thanks." He took a breath. "I've been working toward this moment for years. It feels like quite an accomplishment."

A brown-haired guy around Dylan's age put a drink into his hand, grabbed his head, and gave his cheek a big ol' smooch. "I love you, man!" He walked away as Dylan chuckled.

Dylan took a drink, then pointed at me. "You should come on the show!"

I looked at Rachel, then back to Dylan. "On the show?"

"Yeah, like a cameo or something." He looked at Rachel. "Don't you think that would be amazing?"

Rachel squeezed my hand and looked at me with something approaching affection for the first time that evening. "It would be amazing. It would get you back in the spotlight, maybe get you more jobs."

Suddenly I was beginning to like Dylan a whole lot more. When I was a movie star, the idea of doing TV was considered a career-ending choice. But I had already ended my career, so what else did I have to lose?

"Sure, sure, sounds great!" I said.

Dylan beamed. "I'll talk to the showrunner. He knows you."

I didn't want to tell Dylan the obvious: Lots of people knew me.

"He was a producer on a couple of your movies before moving into TV. Sam Hall. He said he loved working with you."

And with that, everything went cold. Sam Hall. Yeah, I worked with him. I was fifteen. Sam Hall was a fucking monster, and if things were different, he should have been in jail instead of ... Well, he was making a lot of money for someone, so he wasn't going to go to jail. My stomach churned, and I pulled my hand away from Rachel, hoping she wouldn't notice. The room became noisy, buzzy in the wrong ways.

"Yeah, yeah," I said. "Sounds good. Great, even."

I took a deep breath through my nose. I could smell the booze in Dylan's cup. It smelled like forgetting. Like an avalanche that would bury me in darkness and silence. All the best things. "I'm gonna grab a taco. You need a taco?" I said to Dylan. Not waiting for an answer, I pointed at Rachel. "You need a taco?" I paused. "Everyone! Gets! A taco!"

Turning on my heel, I headed out. I passed the taco wagon and made a beeline for my car. I didn't want to be at a Hollywood party right now. I couldn't remember. — Were they always like this? I got to the car and realized it wasn't *my* car, it was *Rachel's* car. I wasn't about to go back into the party. I went to the taco wagon out front.

I explained to the woman inside the truck that I had to go, I forgot to give my girlfriend her car keys, and if she could give them to her when she came looking for me. I described Rachel as well as a I could. Beautiful, well-dressed, tall, brunette. I looked around the party and saw several women who also fit that description. I added, "And she'll be pissed."

Reluctantly, she took the keys and said she would give them to her. She looked me in the eyes and told me she hoped my night would get better. I hoped so too.

I walked down the hill and ordered myself a car to meet me down on Sunset. Then, I looked for an AA meeting. I needed one. I was about to fall and I was afraid no one would catch me if I did.

15

LUNCH WAS A bag of tacos I grabbed from a corner stand that we ate in my car on a side street with the windows rolled down, enjoying the weather and listening to "Midnight Train to Georgia" by Gladys Knight & the Pips. Going home seemed like a bad idea, so I liked being mobile.

"You ever wonder what a pip is?" I asked, holding a grape soda in one hand and a carne asada taco in the other. L.A. has the best tacos. Not just quality, but quantity. Don't let anyone tell you otherwise.

"No, I have never wondered what a pip is. Why would I ever wonder that?" Anton replied before taking a huge bite of his al pastor. He leaned back and chewed. The motion was deliberate and without pleasure.

I shrugged. "It's something to ponder, you know? Why the Pips and not the Awesomes? At least that would *mean* something, you know?" I took a bite.

"Because the Awesomes is a dumb name, Jimmy," he replied.

"Hey, hey. I'm not saying they should've gone with that. I'm saying, why Pips, which means what?"

"Seeds." He took another bite, finishing his taco. "Also the dots on a domino."

I shifted in my seat to get a better look at this guy. "I thought you said you never wondered what pip meant."

He returned my look. "I didn't need to wonder. My granddaddy told me when I was a kid."

I nodded and worked on my taco.

Anton looked out the window. "That guy worked hard his whole life. Worked a job. Hustled for extra money on the weekends, always trying to get ahead. Got my mom through college and everything." He paused. "Summer after high school, one morning, he dropped dead of a heart attack."

I took a moment to take that in. "I'm sorry to hear that, Anton."

He nodded. "Worked his whole life for other people, then died before he could do what he really wanted. Makes you think, you know?" He balled up the wrapper, put it in the paper bag, and pulled out another taco, saying, "Anyway, why are we talking about the Pips and not what we're going to do?"

"Because sometimes the mind needs rest," I took a drink.

"A rest? Really?"

"Yes." I nodded. "We've been on the go since this morning. Some of us aren't twenty-five anymore."

"Well, what's the plan? After you're rested, I mean?"

I chewed on a taco and decidedly said nothing.

"You don't have a plan, do you?"

"I have a plan!"

"Well then, what's the plan?"

I swallowed. "Well, clearly the biggest suspect behind the robbery is whoever else Louis talked to. We just need to figure out who that is," I said with a shrug and another bite.

"And how are you going to do that?"

"I am thinking. Of a plan."

"It doesn't look like you're thinking."

I blinked. "Because you keep talking to me about thinking and not giving me a chance *to* think."

Anton shook his head and stuffed his mouth with his second taco.

The music cut out as my phone on the dashboard holder started to ring. Both sets of eyes swiveled to look at it. I didn't recognize the number.

Anton cut his eyes at me. "You going to answer it?"

I didn't move, still staring at the phone. "I don't know who's calling."

"Man, that's why you should answer it." He looked at the phone.

I grunted.

"It's going to keep ringing," he said, his voice getting tighter. If I had to guess, he did not like unanswered calls.

"It'll go to voicemail," I countered.

"I just…" He shook his head. "No." He poked the "Answer" button.

I glared at him. What an act of betrayal.

He pointed at the phone.

"Hello?" a voice said.

I pushed the speaker button. "Hello?" I mouthed a "fuck you" to Anton.

"Jimmy Cooper," a man's voice purred.

I frowned, not recognizing the voice. "Yeah…Who is this?"

"Oh, I'm disappointed you don't remember me. I don't know if I should be insulted or not." He chuckled. "This is Jerry Collins."

As the blood ran from my face and my stomach instantly tried to reject the tacos, I said, "Detective Collins." Anton and I exchanged worried looks. We both remembered Jerry Collins. He was an asshole.

"Inspector Collins now. I'm working with the district attorney in the Bureau of Investigations. I should thank you for that."

He was working for the district attorney. Ito did say the DA was getting involved, but normally the inspector in that department got involved once charges were brought and things were heading to a trial. This was weird.

I cleared my throat. "Great, great. I'm glad you landed on your feet. Let's catch up again in another three years."

"Uh-huh," he replied. "You might be wondering why I'm calling."

I shook my head. "Nope. I haven't wondered about that at all."

"Are you involved in what happened last night?"

I looked over at Anton.

"Why would you say that, Jerry?" I replied in my friendliest of ways.

Collins grunted. "I just had the most remarkable phone call from Mr. LaFontaine that a man matching your description was at his store."

Jeez, you ask a few innocent questions, and the guy goes running to the cops. He really couldn't keep his mouth shut.

"That wasn't me," I lied.

"Huh." He scoffed. "So that man who matches your description and used your name — "

I closed my eyes as I could feel the hot water we were in getting hotter.

" — that wasn't you? Next you're going to tell me that the other person who was with you matching the description of

Anton Greene wasn't him."

Anton slid down in his seat, putting his hand over his face.

"Mr. Inspector, sir, I've been at home most of the day."

Silence. "We both know that's not true, Jimmy."

That explained who had been outside my apartment building. Not LAPD, but people from the district attorney's office.

Anton was breathing heavily now.

"So, what's going on there, Jimmy?" asked Collins.

My mouth got very dry, and my stomach dropped. I felt like I was being cornered. This was one of those times I wished I was the dangerous type, the sort of creature you don't want to corner, because then I'd come out fighting with broken pieces of glass taped to my fists. But I am not that person.

I am the kind of person who hangs up.

"What the fuck, Jimmy?" Anton snapped as soon as the call disconnected, his eyes bulging. "What the fuck are we going to do?"

I took a drink and felt the cool, fizzy grape flavor go down into my queasy stomach.

The phone rang again. I jabbed at its screen and sent the call to voicemail. Gladys started singing again.

Anton pointed at the phone. "That guy, Jimmy. He's bad news. He doesn't like me, but he hates you."

I took a breath and looked at my last taco, thinking that I had made a huge mistake. "I can't finish this. You want it?" I said offering Anton my taco.

He shook his head, wondering if I had lost my mind. I put the taco back into the to-go bag and started the car, saying, "It's time to get a lawyer."

"That was dumb, Jimmy," Erika said, shaking her head. "You've put a target on your back. There will probably be charges for you too."

We were sitting at the Farmers Market. It had been around since the 1930s with row upon row of shops selling a variety of wares, from food to hot sauces to T-shirts. It was also now a tourist destination, some being delivered by the red, double-decker hop-on hop-off buses. It doesn't hurt that it's right next to The Grove, an upscale mall, and CBS's Television City.

The Farmers Market was in between peak business hours, with the lunch crowd gone and nothing but tourists checking out the place. She and I sat near the donut place.

I fiddled with my cup of coffee. "You're right, you're right." I looked over at Anton, who was back in line for another donut. "I just fed him. What the hell?"

Erika had promptly agreed to meet me here. I wasn't sure

who might be watching the offices, and being in big crowded area felt safe.

"We just had tacos. And donuts. And he wants more?"

"He's hungry."

"Yeah. But why?"

"He's twenty-four."

I shook my head. "He's a pain in the ass. Everything is an argument."

She raised a smug eyebrow. "Huh."

I smirked in reply.

Erika set her coffee aside and spoke quietly. "This is what I was worried about when we talked this morning."

Had our phone call really been just this morning? I searched the creaky corners of my memory. Shit. It had. I took a breath and drank some coffee, like that would do the trick.

"You're not doing Anton any favors. You're actively making his situation worse."

"'Actively' implies I'm executing a plan."

She raised an eyebrow. "This isn't a joke, Jimmy."

I grunted. "Yeah, I know. I'm looking for advice. Not a lecture from Mom."

The eyebrow dropped. "OK. Right." She put her hands on the table. "My advice is for Anton to come in, talk to me and Mom. We'll figure out how he can surrender to the police."

I shook my head. "That's not going to work, Erika.

"We can handle this," she said.

Picking up my coffee, I said, "He's not going to do it." I drank. "Not after last time."

Erika waved a finger in the air. "Don't put this on *him*. You're the grown-up here."

Was I? Because that did not sound like me.

"Last time Mom pushed hard for a plea agreement. He would be in jail right now if he had listened to her."

"Jimmy, this time he *did it*."

I looked down at my coffee. "He didn't 'do it' do it. He was just *involved*."

Erika looked at me for a moment, then smiled. "I have missed this."

Frowning, I said, "Missed what?"

"*You*. Like this. Advocating for your client — "

"He's not my client."

Erika's head tilted and she crossed her arms. "Jimmy, he's totally your client." She leaned forward. "I don't know what it is about this case, but for the last six months you haven't been... you. I mean, you're doing this all wrong and probably causing more trouble, but that's you. And I have missed you."

Groaning, I looked up at the metal roof above us, praying that there was an escape hatch. "I don't know what you're talking about."

Erika tapped the side of her coffee, shaking her head. "You are such a pain in the ass," she said.

Anton sat down. "So what are we talking about?"

"Nothing," I said, hoping to change the subject.

Erika turned to him, "Anton, listen. I have said this to Jimmy, but I want to say it to you. "You're in real trouble."

He took his donut out of the small, white paper bag. It was vaguely in the shape of a dinosaur with green frosting. "Yeah, I know." He took a bite.

"See? He knows," I said.

She gave me a quick dart of her eyes, then went back to Anton. "You should come back with me to the office," she encouraged him. "Jimmy will be there. We'll go over everything. We can negotiate a surrender..."

Anton chewed.

Erika licked her bottom lip. "I can't in good conscience advise you to continue doing what you're doing."

He swallowed. "Nah." He nodded. "I'm good."

She looked at me. "You're a person of interest now, too. You know that, right?"

"I've been a person of interest for a long time." I slipped on my sunglasses.

Erika nodded, a slight smile forming.

"Can I ask you a favor?" I said. "Can you get the cops off my back?"

"Off your..." Her eyes goggled. "Are you kidding me? You're talking about your girlfriend, you know."

I knew that. I really knew that. That was a problem I

would have to solve later.

"I'm just asking for some time," I said. "A day."

She rolled her eyes. "I'll do my best to give the detectives the runaround." She looked at me, her fingers laced together, just like Mom. Erika's phone buzzed on the table. She picked it up and read a text. "Nora has been trying to reach you."

I reached into my coat pocket, pulling out my phone. I had missed a bunch of calls from my assistant, a few more from Collins and two from Ito. I excused myself from the table and dialed.

Nora picked up as I moved through the crowd. "Mr. Cooper." She sounded relieved to hear from me.

"Sorry. I was ignoring my phone."

"Of course, Mr. Cooper. I understand. Ms. Cooper filled me in on the situation. It's been a difficult day."

I rubbed my head and sidestepped some slow-moving tourists. "What's going on?"

"Well..." She paused. "I have a client for you."

I moaned. "No. Not now. Nora, I'm right in the middle of something."

"I explained that to her as discreetly as I could." Her voice hushed. "She wants you to the find the Buddha."

I stopped moving. The sound all around me dropped away, and all I could hear was my own breathing. "Say that again?"

"She wants you to find the Buddha."

16

—

WHEN THE 101 North hits Ventura Beach, it hugs the coastline, and you see the Pacific Ocean. It's blue and infinite, and I never feel more SoCal than I do when I'm driving alongside it. It was the end of the afternoon, and the sun was heading toward the horizon and we drove along the highway's curves. I cranked Miley Cyrus's "Malibu." It might have annoyed Anton, but I didn't care. I was in the mood to sing along. Nora had given me our new client's info, and given our shared interested in the stolen Buddha, it felt like things were finally going our way.

The potential client was Patricia Horne. She owned her own media empire of local TV affiliates in the Southwest, California, Arizona, and Nevada and was pushing north into

Oregon and Washington. Maybe it wasn't sexy like owning a major network, but it was extremely lucrative and powerful.

When we were leaving the Farmers Market, Anton had wondered if this was a good idea.

"Good idea?" I said as I paid for parking. "This is a *great* idea."

Anton shook his head. "We should be looking for the Buddha and the guys who took it."

As the gate lifted and I pulled out of the parking lot, I replied, "This puts us in the mix of people who want the Buddha, OK?"

"The cops are *also* looking for the Buddha. Should we mix it up with them?"

"OK, fair point," I conceded. "But, unless you have a better idea, this is what we're doing."

He did not have a better idea.

Two and a half hours later, we rolled into Montecito, California, just south of Santa Barbara. If L.A. was its own planet, Montecito was its own exclusive universe, one in which there was cultivated ease, luxury, and beautiful landscape. This was the spot of the super famous and the super wealthy.

At a stoplight, I pulled up next to an old man with a tuft of white hair on top of his head, sitting in a blood-red Corvette convertible straight out of 1975. From the look he took at my comparatively late- and base-model Toyota, you'd think

I had taken a crap on the hood of his car. I revved my engine and dared him with my chin.

He snorted.

"What are you doing?" asked Anton, his voice tense.

I revved again. My car sounded like it was powered by hamsters. "Just having some fun."

Provoked, the old man set his jaw. How dare I?

"Jesus, save me." Anton looked away.

The light turned green, and the old man peeled out, the back of his car fishtailing as he went, leaving a blue-gray haze from his tires. I laughed as I turned right, heading up and away from the ocean.

Anton shook his head. I cackled.

- ——————————— -

Anton's eyes were about to pop out of his head as we rolled up the circular driveway a few minutes later. "Holy shit."

Through the trees, carefully planted to maximize privacy, we arrived at a large, opulent, Mediterranean-style mansion, wrapped in stucco and balconies. It was two stories tall, with a large front door flanked by windows and windows and windows, for all your natural lighting needs.

"Yeah," I said as we arrived yond I threw the car into park.

"I have never seen a place like this in my life."

I pulled down my sunglasses and took a better look. I

remember being invited to homes like this for glamorous parties. A Hollywood legend's birthday. A studio chief wanting to lavish talent and the execs after a very successful third quarter. "You're gonna find these all over in these parts."

Anton looked at me.

"They grow here naturally."

He sighed. "Oh, fuck off," he said as he got out of the car.

I followed, chuckling.

At the door, we were greeted by a middle-aged woman in a gray uniform. I smiled, then told her my name and that we were expected. She nodded and ushered us into the home. Somehow there was more sunlight inside the house than outside. I guess all those windows really paid off.

She led us out onto the back veranda, which overlooked a vast garden. The woman left us with a curt bow as Anton looked around.

"This a backyard?" He turned to me. "I've seen parks smaller than this."

A couple of gardeners were hard at work, raking around newly trimmed bushes. The grass was lush and green from all the winter rains. I'm sure it was the sort of garden that gets featured in magazines read and admired by old people all across the country.

"Mr. Cooper," said a man's voice.

We turned. Standing there in a smart, black suit was a

white man in his forties, with neatly trimmed brown hair, thinning in the most dignified way possible. His arms hung easily at his sides. His expensive cologne drifted over.

The man gave us a small, tactful smile. "I'm Mr. Darling." I was about to make a dumb comment about the name, but he put up a hand. "I've heard them all before, and I doubt you'll say anything particularly original."

Ouch.

He gestured to a table. "Please."

Mr. Darling waited until we started moving, and then he followed us to the table.

As we sat, he took in Anton. "And you are?"

I began. "He's my assistant — "

"Partner," Anton corrected.

"Partner," I agreed, not eager to share billing. "Anton Greene, Mr. Darling."

"I didn't know you had a partner, Mr. Cooper," he said. "Especially one who chooses to dress so casually."

Anton smoothed out his sweatshirt and straightened his leather jacket.

"He's new. Trial basis. I'm teaching what I know. He's more like an intern. We're working on blending in right now."

Mr. Darling glanced at Anton. Satisfied, he said, "Would you two care for anything?"

"You have any snacks?" asked Anton.

"Snacks?" he replied. Mr. Darling was a serious man on serious business. Snacks were beneath him.

I put up a hand. "We're fine. I thought we would be meeting with Ms. Horne?"

He crossed his leg over his other knee and laced his fingers together in his lap. "She's finishing a phone call. I was sent ahead to lay down the ground rules."

"Ground rules?" I said, suspicious.

He brushed invisible dirt from a sleeve as he said, "Ms. Horne is a busy woman. As her lawyer — "

Ooh. She had a lawyer who made house calls. Now *that's* wealthy.

" — I am responsible for making it clear what will and won't happen. She has fifteen minutes. If she chooses not to answer something, that is her answer, and you won't ask it again. Keep your questions short and to the point; she loathes digressions."

I nodded. Sure, sure. How hard would that be?

"Agreed?" He looked to Anton and me, raising an eyebrow.

"Agreed, Mr. Darling."

I actually didn't agree. I took a more Hollywood approach to these situations. Sure, I had said yes, but I had no intention of following through on that ground rule.

Mr. Darling had barely lowered his eyebrow when a voice from within the house bellowed, "Should I call you James or Jimmy?"

I turned, noticing Mr. Darling kept his eyes on me.

Stomping onto the patio was a woman who, I assumed, was Patricia Horne. She was in her fifties, with short, white hair and a stocky body wrapped in a bright, multicolored kaftan. Her eyes were hidden behind large, square Jimmy Choo sunglasses. She was barefoot and fingered a vape pen as she plopped into the seat next to her attorney.

"Only my mother calls me James," I answered.

"Fine, good." She nodded, pursing her lips. "Jimmy it is." She looked at Anton expectantly.

"This is Mr. Greene," said Mr. Darling, answering her unspoken question. "Mr. Cooper's partner."

Patricia's lips twisted. "I didn't know you had a partner, Jimmy."

I shrugged. "I'm just as surprised as you are. And who doesn't love surprises?"

An eyebrow peeked over the sunglasses. I guessed she did not love surprises. The eyebrow sank and she moved on, settling deeper into her chair. "Thank you for coming out all this way." She managed to get an ankle on top of a knee and took a hit from the vape pen. "I'm excited to meet you, Jimmy."

The way she said it, all sharp and tense, you'd think she didn't mean it.

"Oh yeah? A fan?"

"Not of your movies, no."

Anton snorted.

She wagged a finger. "That's not about the quality of the movies. I haven't seen them. I'm not much for movies. They're just so..." She looked to Mr. Darling and then out across her dominion, looking for the right word. Finding it, she said, "Insubstantial. As an art form, I mean. As a business, as content, they're fantastic. People will watch anything so long as it's noisy and colorful."

"Huh," I managed.

She lifted her Jimmy Choos. Her eyes were deep blue. "I'm a fan of your story. You were up, you were down. Then you were up again. So many people watched it. The ratings on my stations spiked when you were in the news. Then you crashed and burned. What a twist! Fantastic! The ratings were up even more. We couldn't have planned it better."

I gave a firm smile. Never let them see you wounded.

"So I'm here about the Buddha?" I said.

"Yes, yes." She pointed at me, then took another hit from the vape pen, exhaling it. "Can you find it for me?"

I took a breath and crossed my arms. "Just to be clear, we are talking about the same Buddha that was stolen, right? The one that left a man dead?"

"Well, *yes*, Jimmy," she replied, annoyed.

"The same Buddha the police are also looking for?"

She huffed, impatient. "Is that going to be a problem?"

I leaned back. "Oh, no. No." I shrugged. "Why would that

be a problem?"

She pulled the Jimmy Choos completely off. The hand gripping the vape pen pointed a stubby finger at me. "There it is. The Jimmy Cooper sense of humor I've heard so much about." She leaned to Mr. Darling. "Sarcasm is one of his favorites."

Mr. Darling nodded in agreement.

She went on. "The Buddha was mine, Jimmy. I'd like it back."

I frowned, confused.

Mr. Darling connected the dots. "Ms. Horne is a client of Mr. LaFontaine. She was purchasing the Buddha through him. She was awaiting delivery. He isn't really a victim of the crime; she is."

"*Devon* was the victim," said Anton under his breath.

Patricia turned to him. "What did you say?"

Rather than letting him reveal too much, I redirected her. "Have you spoken with the police about this?"

Back to me, she shook her head. "I met with those detectives..." She looked to Mr. Darling for their names.

"Ito and Kemble," he supplied.

"That's right. They did not fill me with confidence."

My cheeks flushed. "I'm familiar with them."

"*Really* familiar," offered Anton.

I gave him the eye.

Patricia didn't bother to notice. She was still going on

about her Buddha being recovered. "If the police even find it, they will hold on to it for God knows how long as 'evidence' until the trial is over. I can't have that. It's far too important and valuable for them to handle. They don't *need* to hold on to the Buddha to prosecute whoever took it."

She was working herself up. Clearly, she was pissed about this Buddha thing.

"So," I summarized, "you want it now so badly that you can't wait for the police and you're willing to break the law to find it."

Mr. Darling stirred. "Ms. Horne is not suggesting *any* laws get broken. And to suggest otherwise — "

I put up a hand. "She's suggesting that I interfere with a police investigation. That's a crime."

He continued. "She simply wants you to recover her property. How you do it is your choice."

"I will, of course," she said, "make it worth your while."

I nodded. She meant it. I had learned a long time ago that when rich people want something they can't get anywhere else, they will pay through the nose for it. And you let them.

"All right. I'll look for your Buddha."

"Perfect," she said, slipping her sunglasses back on.

"I just have a few questions."

Horne's head dipped, acquiescing.

Leaning back, I said, "When did LaFontaine reach out to you about the Buddha?"

"He didn't," she said.

"Oh?" I was surprised. "I was under the impression that LaFontaine had negotiated the whole thing."

Horne set her sunglasses onto the table. "Louis likes to feel important. He's been helpful to me over the years, so I let him. I was the one who found the Buddha while on a trip to Hong Kong."

"What were you doing there?"

Horne said nothing.

I tried again. "Were you there on business?"

Mr. Darling cleared his throat. "Mr. Cooper, remember our agreement? What Ms. Horne did in China has nothing to do with the Buddha."

I looked over at Mr. Darling. He was lying to me. I didn't know if the whole trip was about the Buddha or just something to do with it. I looked back at Ms. Horne, dropping it.

"If you found it, why not bring it back yourself?" I asked.

"Moving antiquities can be tricky. Especially from one country to another," she answered.

Mr. Darling took a breath. "Mr. LaFontaine has the experience and the reputation to facilitate acquisitions of this kind."

"For a percentage," I said.

"He's a businessman," she offered. "He should be paid for his work."

"And that's *all* legal?" asked Anton.

Horne and Mr. Darling gave him the eye.

Anton went on. "Because it sounds pretty corrupt."

Horne smiled.

Mr. Darling spoke up. "I assure you, young man, everything in this transaction was perfectly legal."

I turned to Anton. "See, perfectly legal" In other words, shut up. I shifted in my chair, straightened my suit. "Do you think someone else knew about the Buddha?"

"Louis loves to talk," said Patricia, before taking a drag off the vape pen.

I nodded. "I imagine you and he travel in some rarified circles. You have any idea of who might have taken it?"

She leaned forward, seething. "If I had an idea, I wouldn't need you, would I?" She leaned back, shaking her head. "I'm wealthy, connected, and a big old lesbian. That has a tendency to make people mad. A lot of egos can't handle that."

Probably not.

I smiled. "One final question. Why me?"

Patricia frowned. "Why you?"

"That's right. Lots of detectives and security people out there. I imagine with your resources you could have anyone. There's probably some former CIA agent out there desperate for your call. So why me?"

Patricia Horne fingered the vape pen, twirling it. "Because you think outside of the box, Jimmy. You don't do things the way they're supposed to be done." She nodded, agreeing with herself. "That CIA agent desperate for my call only knows how to do things by the book." She paused. "Satisfied?"

I gave her a wry smile.

The meeting wrapped, and we were escorted to the door. The sun was touching the horizon as we got into my car.

"You didn't buy all that shit about thinking outside the box, did you?" said Anton.

I grinned. "Listen, buddy, I've had my ego stroked by the best in the world. She could learn a thing or two from the execs at Warner Brothers." I put the key in the ignition. "I don't think she called because of the way I think or a coincidence."

"You think it was Louis called her?"

I nodded. "Oh, yeah. She said he likes to talk and she sounds like a favored client." I looked back at the house. "She knows we're already looking for the Buddha. She's getting onboard our bandwagon."

Anton chewed a worried lip. "We're not handing the Buddha over to her, are we?"

I snorted. "Of course not. We're turning that thing over to the police. It's evidence in a murder."

Anton nodded, satisfied.

I started the car and pondered what was next. We were both exhausted and needed some place to hide out for a bit, but I didn't like my best option.

17

——

WE WERE GOING to my mom's.

My reasoning was this: Her house was the last place on Earth that I would like to go. They would know that. And given that LAPD and the Bureau of Investigations didn't have infinite resources, they had to make choices when it came to where they'd search. And I was betting that Greta Cooper's place wasn't going to be one of those choices.

I did not make this decision lightly. It had been years since I had been over to Mom's, not since an attempt at a family gathering for Thanksgiving went disastrously wrong. Uncle Mike was wrong to say what he said, and Mom had no right to tell *me* to shut up. RIP pumpkin pie. You served your true calling. Human rights aren't up for debate.

But family politics aside, we needed a place to crash.

The sun had fully melted into the ocean, and the temperature had dropped with it. The 101 was filled with traffic moving slowly in both directions as people made their way home. Even "Celebrity Skin" by Hole was not loud enough to quiet the worries running through my head.

"Does she know we're coming?" said Anton, interrupting my thoughts.

"Who? My mom?"

"Yeah."

I shook my head. "In my experience, it's better to ask for forgiveness than permission."

He raised an eyebrow at me. "How's that working out for you?"

"Honestly? Better than it should."

He chuckled. "You want me to drive?" he asked.

"Drive?" I shook my head. "I'm driving. Why would I want you to drive?"

He shrugged. "You've been driving all day. You look tired."

Oof. Those three words cut right to the heart even if I wasn't an actor anymore. I might not have the career, but I still had an actor's vanity.

"Besides," he said, the real reason coming out, "I feel stupid sitting here. I can drive. That's what I do. It's why Devon hired me. I'm really good at it."

I wagged a finger. "I'm good at driving. Look at me, right

now, I'm staying between the lines. I haven't hit anything."

He sighed. "You know what I mean."

"Yeah, well, we're in rush hour. Right now, we don't need your special skills."

Anton gave up and stared at the red taillights in front of us, allowing me to return to my thoughts, which swirled around Patricia Horne.

Rich people. They gave me a headache. They could be dense, petty, fickle. Their wealth protected them from consequences and gave them a sense of unearned expertise in every field. I get to say that because, for a time, I was rich.

Even with all that it was not enough to plug the wound at the very heart of my soul. And that made me crazy. I think it makes them all crazy. The same things that motivated them to success — the desire to be loved, to not hurt — are the same things that can't be solved with money. Cash and attention will never staunch that wound. But we go on like it will.

That's nuts.

So, here we were: a super wealthy person was after a rare object to soothe whatever hole she had, an object that had left one person dead and put Anton on the run. And all he had wanted was some cash to help his girlfriend start her business.

I looked at Anton, his head rested against the window, his eyes closed, asleep.

All of this sucked.

We finally got off the freeways and threaded our way through Culver City to Mom's place. Culver City was the home of Sony Pictures Studios (née MGM). If you look carefully, you can see the rainbow that told everyone that *The Wizard of Oz* was made right there; just down the street at Selznick International, *Gone With the Wind* was in front of the cameras at the same time.

Mom lived on a quiet street south of all of that Hollywood history. It was the same house I had grown up in; we'd moved there when I started getting jobs and Mom had opened her firm. It was a cream-colored two-story, with an attached garage. My bedroom was on the top and in front, which made it easy to sneak out at night, across the garage roof. Then movie star hijinks would ensue, all of which would wind up in the tabloids over the following days.

Anton and I passed it twice, just to make sure there weren't any cops watching the place. Having decided the coast was clear, we parked a few doors down, nestling my car between a couple of family-sized SUVs. The front light was on, but the living room was dark. I checked the time. Nine p.m. Not super late.

At the front door, I rang the bell and rubbed my hands together, shuffling my feet.

"Nervous?"

I looked at Anton. "Why would you say that?"

He blinked. "Because you look nervous."

"Why would I be nervous? It's my mom's house. Which I am visiting uninvited. In a state of lawlessness."

"Point taken."

The door opened.

Erika stood there, confused.

"Um, what are you doing here?" she asked.

"What are *you* doing here?" I answered.

She wasted no time on an answer. Instead, she waved us inside, looking up and down the street as we moved past her. She closed the door and leaned against it.

We stood in the entryway of my childhood home. Off to the left was a dining room, to the right a living room. A hallway, covered with curated photos that created a sense of a normal family life, led to the TV room, and the kitchen, and a carpeted stairway up to the bedrooms. On the way up were school pictures of Erika and me. About halfway up, mine turned into headshots. (I always missed school picture day until I just stopped going to school at all.)

"What are you doing here?" Erika repeated.

Before I could answer, I heard Mom's voice.

"James?"

I turned, and I was shocked by what I saw.

Mom stood in the hallway, wearing sweatpants and a hoodie. A *hoodie*.

"*What* is happening? Am *I* on drugs again?" I wondered aloud.

Mom put her fists on her hips. "James." My mother could derive so much meaning from how she said one word. It was clear where my acting talents really came from.

"What happened to your real clothes, Mother? Was there a break-in?"

She harrumphed. "After a long day at work, I like to put on something comfortable."

I shook my head. "Yes, OK, but I imagined it was you taking off the Neiman Marcus and putting on the Ann Taylor. This...? I don't even know you."

Mom gave me a classic Greta Cooper look and then shifted a softer gaze toward Anton.

"Mr. Greene, how are you?"

"I'm fine, Ms. Cooper. Good to see you again."

She nodded. "Are you hungry?"

"Starving, ma'am."

"There's Chinese in the kitchen," she said, pointing the way. "Help yourself."

He didn't need to be told twice. Hunger and a strong desire to get out of whatever this moment was were motivation enough to leave.

Erika and Mom turned their attention to me. This time, Erika put her fists on her hips. "*Why* are you here, Jimmy??

"Well, I was hoping that maybe Anton and I could spend the night."

Mom's head tilted to one side. "Are you suggesting I

should harbor fugitives?"

I put up a finger. "Ah. But we aren't fugitives. You know as well as I do that neither one of us has been charged with anything. And he's just a suspect in a crime, so… you know… *not* fugitives."

Erika looked over at our mother.

Mother looked like she was about to speak when I said, not anxious for a lecture, "I didn't know where else to go. They're watching my place. They might be watching Erika's." I gestured to my sister. "If you want us to go, we'll go. I don't want to get you into trouble. It's just…" I shook my head. Running around all day, and with more people getting involved in this case by the hour, I was exhausted. "We just need someplace to rest for a bit. Catch our breath. Then we'll go."

She pursed her lips. "Don't be ridiculous, James. You can stay as long as you need."

My cheeks flushed, and I felt my eyes water. I hadn't realized how much I needed to hear that from her.

I looked at Erika. She knew the question.

"Mom and I, we've been trying to strategize for Anton," she explained. "Especially with the DA so interested in this case."

Mom nodded. "James, I wasn't exactly thrilled you invited Detective Ito and her partner to my firm and without showing up."

Violet was pissed I hadn't shown. I had chosen chaos and ignored every call she hade made and text she had sent after not showing up. I knew it was a bad decision from both a legal and a romantic perspective, but lying to her felt like it would be even worse. Better to ask forgiveness than permission, right?

How *was* that going for me?

"I'll talk to her," I said, "but, there might be some extra twists to consider."

I filled them in on my meeting with Patricia Horne. Erika and Mom exchanged glances. Mom shook her head, worried.

"You know her?" I asked.

She nodded. "I have bumped into her from time to time. She is not to be trifled with."

"*Trifled*. Gotcha."

"James, she is a very serious woman. Lots of powerful friends. Including the district attorney."

I licked my lips. Her being friends with the district attorney begged the question: Why did she need *me* to find the Buddha?

"Noted," I said, feeling a cold, cold pit of despair open up inside me. Things were getting harder, the path forward more thornier, and I didn't like any of it. I may have been unhappy two days ago, but my life hadn't been in danger. "I'll be careful. As always."

Mom grunted, took a few steps toward the kitchen, and

then paused. "I would suggest not waiting if you want to eat something." She went on her way.

Erika turned to me. "You've been busy," she said, a flash of excitement in her eyes.

I shook my head. "Don't start with me." Something flipped inside. I was full of fight, and I didn't even know why. I just needed a fight, and I guess it was going to be with Erika. Whether she wanted it to be or not.

"What do you mean 'don't start'?'"

"I mean, with your 'I'm happy to see you like this,' or, you know, 'You're finally stepping into your light.'"

"'Stepping into your — '" She scoffed. "I would never say that. At least if you're going to put words into my mouth — "

"Whatever you'd say, I don't want to hear it."

She crossed her arms and gawked. "You're mad at me?"

"That's right, I am," I said. Yeah, I guess I was. I *was* mad at her.

"You are mad… at *me.*" She poked herself with her thumb, looking for clarity. "This is insane, Jimmy. I've only been trying to help."

"Yeah, yeah, with all your encouragement. *Thanks.*"

"Encouragement is a *good* thing. Most people like being encouraged."

I put up a hand. "Well, to be honest, it's not something I'm looking for right now."

She recrossed her arms. "You might not be looking for it,

but I'm giving it to you."

I rolled my eyes. "OK, great. Here comes Erika Cooper, ready to save the day!"

Her voiced pitched to an octave higher. "Excuse me?"

"Oh, come *on*. You're always there, ready to swoop in the moment I mess up."

"I'm your sister," she emphasized the word. "That's what family does for each other."

"You know what? Maybe you shouldn't. Maybe you shouldn't bother putting me back on my feet because I'll just fuck it all up." I was getting fired up. This was a barn burner. "You know why we haven't 'talked' in months? Because I haven't wanted to hear your Pollyanna bullshit on how I could snap out of my funk." Even as I said it, I didn't believe me. But why let that stop a good roll? "Sometimes I wonder if you hadn't 'been there' for me all those times, saving me from myself, maybe I would've hit rock bottom sooner and gotten clean."

Blood drained from Erika's face. "You don't mean that."

I swallowed. "And this case? Anton? I don't want to do this. I'm a fucking idiot. A fraud. He's going to go to *jail*."

"James!"

I turned around, taking hot, fast breaths. Who wanted some of this?

Mom and Anton stood in the hallway, looking at me like I had lost my damn mind.

Shit.

Anton, of course, had heard everything, and it was clear from his face that his heart was broken. Mom's lips were tight, her brow furrowed. She was pissed. And she was right to be so.

"I am officially done for the evening," announced Erika. She headed to the kitchen.

Mom said to Anton, "Use the phone upstairs in my office to call your mother. She'll be glad to hear from you. Keep it short and don't give her any details that might get her in trouble later."

Anton gave a quick nod and a lick of his bottom lip like he was about to say something. He decided against it and headed up the stairs.

"Anton…" I called after him.

He kept going.

Erika was back, her briefcase slung over her shoulder. "Good night, Mom," she said, blowing our mom a kiss in her direction. "See you tomorrow."

She walked past me, opened the door, and closed it behind her.

I looked at my mother, hoping she'd say something.

"You had better go eat. The kung pao chicken is getting cold."

That was something.

She stepped onto the stairs. "I have to get the guest room

ready for Anton and get you sheets for the couch."

"What about my old bedroom?" I asked.

"James," she simpered, "where do you think my home office is?"

18

—

Three Years Ago

"CAN I ASK a question?" I asked Gordon as he drove us east across town. It was a late morning after the party; Santa Monica Boulevard moved at its usual slow pace; and the sun was already bright and hot, challenging my sunglasses. I wiped imaginary crumbs off my off-white linen suit jacket, then started to inspect my lime-green button down shirt. "Not case related. Career related."

Gordon's eyes darted between me and the road. "I guess."

We bounced in silence on the street as I thought about what I wanted to ask, annoyed that Gordon refused to even listen to the *radio* when he drove.

I folded my arms, grabbing my elbows. I had been up late.

After the AA meeting, which lasted a few hours, I had gone back home, ignoring all the texts from Rachel — she was *not happy* — and knocked on Moe's door. Luckily for me, he wasn't entertaining anyone. We talked for hours about what had happened at the party, and the talk did its job. I stayed sober. I wasn't sure how much I wanted to tell Gordon. After all, I was his partner for now, and I didn't need him doubting me.

He paused at a red light. "Jimmy?"

Right. The question, not case related.

"Maybe it *is* case related."

"What?"

I nodded. "It's a case adjacent question."

"If you don't get on with it, I'll push you out of this car."

He meant it.

I took a breath. "What if we can't prove Anton innocent?"

Gordon nodded. "Still thinking about what we talked about?"

"Moe brought it up too. He's worried about the consequences if we can't prove Anton innocent." I shifted in my seat, turning toward Gordon. "We know Anton's innocent — "

"I don't know if I *know* — "

"We know."

"We *believe*."

I sighed. "Whatever." Gordon might believe, but I knew.

We were getting off topic. "We believe he's innocent. What if we can't prove it?"

The light turned green, and Gordon went with the flow of traffic.

He started chewing his bottom lip. "When I was working with the LAPD, most of my time was spent trying to prove someone guilty beyond a reasonable doubt." He took a drink of coffee. "Even working with your mom, I've never been asked to prove someone innocent. Mostly we just look for enough info to screw up the prosecution." A shrug. "Most clients are happy to get off."

"Especially the guilty ones."

Gordon chuckled. It was warm, inviting, the laugh you got from your favorite drinking buddy at your local bar. "Especially those." His laugh slowed. "Yeah, defending the guilty was a bit of a Twilight Zone if you ask me."

"'Even the guilty deserve a zealous defense,'" I said, doing my best Greta Cooper imitation.

Gordon laughed again, this time deeper, more fully. "That's good. That's real good. She know you can do that?"

"Oh, she does. It is *not* one of the things she loves about me."

After our laughter played out, I said, "I guess I'm afraid that we're not going to do it. I was confident about it, but Moe reminded me it's possible this could go wrong."

Gordon nodded. "It could. It could all go wrong."

"When it went wrong as a cop, how did you live with yourself?"

Gordon gave me a low *ooh*. "'Live with yourself' is a pretty big thing. I just went on living. Hopefully I learned something. Something I used on the next case." He paused. "You had movies that bombed — "

I hissed. "Low blow, man."

He pressed on. "You survived and made more. How did you do that?"

"I did drugs, Gordon."

He took his eyes off the road and looked at me, embarrassed to have asked the question that granted him this answer.

I shrugged, and he went back to driving the car.

"Jimmy, at the end of the day, this is a job. Sometimes we get it done, sometimes we don't, but we keep doing the work. Maybe we can do some good along the way."

Forty minutes later, we arrived back in Silver Lake and parked a block away from Chad and Deborah's house (i.e., the scene of the crime.)

This time, Gordon wasn't going to wait for someone to come out. We went right up to the door.

Deborah Holt opened the front door of her home after Gordon's second knock. We were a block over from our dear friend Thomas Wyler. The Holt-Lane residence was a single story, Spanish-style home in faded green stucco, with a large front window, and a driveway on the side that led to the garage in the back. Deborah was in her late twenties, thin and white, with a poof of auburn hair covering her head like a cloud. She wore jean shorts, a red string bikini top, and large, movie star sunglasses with dark brown lenses. Around the edges of the left side of the frame, I could see bruising.

"Yeah," she said, an arm up on the doorframe, the other on the door, ready to slam it shut.

"Deborah Holt?" asked Gordon, who already knew who she was.

"Yeah," she said again, annoyed. "But I prefer Debi. One b, one i, no e."

Noted.

Gordon nodded. "My name is Gordon Bixby, and this is my associate James Cooper — "

Ugh. *James*. Did that really sound more professional?

"We have some questions about what happened to you."

She crossed her arms over her stomach, her head tilted down. Quietly she said, "More? I thought I didn't need to talk about it anymore."

I peeked behind her, into her living room. There was a massive flat-screen behind her, with speakers set on either side. The place looked like a mess, and not the sort of a mess that's made after a ransacking. This mess was well earned and lived-in.

Gordon's voice softened. "I understand. It's just... some

following up."

Debi shook her head, not understanding. "I was told it was all taken care of."

"What do you mean?" asked Gordon. "Who told you that?"

She frowned, her eyebrows disappearing behind the sunglasses. Her body language changed. She stood taller, her arms crossed tighter. "You're not cops, are you?"

Busted. Suddenly the sun felt really hot on my back.

"No," confirmed Gordon. He didn't mind misleading people — after all, that was one of the tools he had used as a detective when he worked for the LAPD — but he wasn't a fan of out-and-out lying. That might actually get him into some trouble. "We're with the law firm of Cooper and Associates."

Debi sucked her teeth. "Uh-huh."

"We have questions."

She looked from Gordon to me. Then, over her shoulder, she shouted, "Chad!"

Chad Lane. The boyfriend. This made things easier. He was someone else we wanted to talk to. He showed up at the door wearing only a pair of jeans. Did no one in this house own a shirt? He was ten years older than Debi; his chest was also thin and covered in bad tattoos of heavy metal bands. He saw us. and his features grew hard. "Who the fuck are you two?"

"They're *lawyers*, Chad," answered Debi. "They have questions."

"Do I look like a lawyer?" I said.

Gordon put out a hand to shut me up and shook his head. "We're not lawyers."

"Not lawyers, huh?" He sniffed, eyes darting between Gordon and me. His body was practically vibrating with aggression.

Yeah, this guy was high. I recognized it. And if I had to guess, it was coke.

"Then what *are* you?"

"We just have questions. About the night Debi got hurt. One b, one i. Did I get that right?" asked Gordon. I could see what he was doing, trying to make a connection with her.

She shifted. She hadn't expected that. "Yeah. I got hurt."

"Do you want to talk about it, Debi?"

Chad stepped between us and her. "OK, you know what? This is private property. I don't want you here."

Gordon put his hands up. "That is, of course, within your rights," he said, though he didn't move. He was going to keep them talking. Smart. He was worming his way in. Sooner or later, they were going to say something that was useful to us.

"You're damn right I'm within my rights."

Gordon nodded.

"If you're not careful," Chad said, "I'm going to call the

cops."

My head buzzed. That was an empty threat. Chad wasn't going to call the cops.

"That's right," added Debi. "He's going to call the cops on you guys."

Even Debi didn't think he was actually going to call the cops. I tapped Gordon on the arm. He glanced at me and I gave him a look. He knew what it meant. Had we actually developed a shorthand? We were so adorable.

"Debi, Chad, I understand," Gordon said. "Sooner or later, though, one or both of you will have to testify about what happened."

"Testify?" Debi asked, worried.

"Don't worry, baby." Chad licked his lips. "There's not going to be a trial. The kid they arrested? He's guilty." He was lying. How would he know? "Collins told me there wouldn't be a trial."

"He did, did he?"

"Why did he say that?" I asked.

Chad's eyes widened. He realized he might have said something he shouldn't have. His lips flapped up and down, struggling to say something, anything. "He said it, because... you know... because the kid did it." That sounded convincing. "So fuck you."

He stepped back and slammed the door in our face.

Gordon and I looked at each other.

"Did that go well?" I asked.

Gordon turned without answering, heading back to the car, so I followed.

"You should know," I began, "that Chad was lying about Anton. About him being guilty."

In the middle of the street, Gordon wheeled around on me. "What? Your superpower told you that?" he snapped.

I stopped moving. "Well..." I didn't know what to say.

Gordon pointed at the house. "It's *obvious* he's lying, Jimmy! I don't need you to tell me that."

I put up a hand. "Where is this coming from?"

"*Fuck!*" he shouted to the sky. He got real quiet afterward and looked away, putting his hands on his hips. He was breathing hard, his chest moving up and down with effort. Finally, he said, "This is bad, Jimmy."

"Bad? Bad how?"

He took a deep breath. Something rolled around in his head. He looked at me. "Why is Chad lying?"

I shook my head. I didn't know.

"Part of being a detective is getting inside people's heads. What makes them tick."

"What's their motivation."

He nodded. "So why is Chad lying?"

"Because he knows who did it."

"Mm-hm." Gordon nodded. "And why would he do that?"

I blinked, looked around, thinking. "He's protecting

them."

"Or?"

A sour taste burst into my mouth. "He's afraid of them. Something worse could happen."

Gordon rubbed his eyes. "Maybe." He shrugged, shaking his head. "Maybe they got what they wanted. Maybe they're sending Chad and Debi a warning. But the thing is... it's what Collins said."

I was beginning to see why Gordon was angry. "That there wouldn't be a trial. Collins is tied up in this. He's protecting Chad with this bullshit about Anton? Why?"

Gordon shook his head. "I don't know. But whoever did it is more important to Chad and Collins than Anton."

I looked back at the house. "It needed to be kept quiet. But then the neighbor saw what was going on and called 911."

Gordon nodded. "A police report. A paper trail."

I took a breath. "And a crime needs to be solved or it just keeps going. People might ask questions."

"Collins gave them an answer."

"Anton," I said.

Gordon dug into his pocket, pulling out his car keys. He beeped the car open. "We talk to Collins."

19

I DON'T THINK you know how mad I am at you. How bad this is.

It was the first text in the morning. It was from Violet and I stared at it as I sat on the edge of the couch in Mom's living room, still in my clothes from last night. It was a seldom-used space at the front of the house designed in California casual. Big, stuffy, dusty-gray easy chairs with a matching couch bracketed a glass coffee table in between, with carefully chosen coffee table books holding it down. Large windows brought in all the light, and of course, there was the very unused fireplace.

I had slept poorly on the couch, as a familiar feeling kept bubbling up, wet and heavy. I was going to have to apologize to people for the reckless and dumb behavior I'd committed the whole day before. This time, it was made all the worse because, being sober, not only did I remember all of it, but I couldn't claim I was drunk and stupid.

Worst Wednesday morning ever.

Which wasn't true, but it felt very much so at the moment.

I stretched, and my body cracked and complained with every move. I went back to my phone and scrolled through more of the texts Violet had sent. Some of the highlights included:

Where are you? We're waiting for you at your office. Kemble is pissed.

Are you in trouble?

This is ridiculous. You're not even picking up your phone!?!

Are you with Anton? That would be bad, Jimmy. Really bad.

I began to ask myself: Should I apologize in the order of offenses or to whomever I saw first? Should I be writing it down? Instead of answering my questions — yes, I should have been writing it down, and yes, I should call Violet and explain the situation — I got up and stumbled into the kitchen.

Mom was already awake and dressed for work in a lavender blouse and a dark purple skirt. Even though she had already cleaned up last night after I awkwardly ate alone, she was cleaning again. This time it was the sink. She stood at a white enamel farmhouse sink, scrubbing it fiercely while wearing blue kitchen gloves. She loved this kitchen, having had remodeled it five years ago with white marble countertops, an island, recessed lighting, and a refrigerator that was a technological marvel. The kitchen was bright, modern, and ready for *Architectural Digest*. Its only quirk was a trippy pattern to the floor tiles if one stared too long, which Mom said you weren't meant to do anyway.

In the breakfast nook, on the round table, sat a pitcher of freshly squeezed orange juice with glasses surrounding it.

I headed to the freshly brewed coffee and grabbed a mug from the cabinet above, cell phone in hand, still considering what to do.

Without turning around, Mom said, "Good morning, James. You sleep well?"

I grunted as I poured coffee.

"Well, I hope you're feeling better," she said. "I would hate to see a replay of last night."

"You and me both, Mom. You and me both."

I leaned against the counter, ignoring my coffee for a hot second. I stared at my phone, thinking about how to reply. I mean, I *should* reply, right? While every bit of me just wanted to continue to ignore Violet's texts, wasn't I a grown-up in a grown-up relationship? And didn't that mean I should have a grown-up response? Last summer, finding ourselves in a bit of an ethical pickle, we had agreed to set some boundaries when it came to work. Basically to stay out of each other's business. But this was a little different. This wasn't an ethical pickle. This was an ethical buffet. I didn't want her to get into trouble, and I didn't want her throwing the cuffs on Anton. Or on me.

A thought popped into my head.

I typed:

It's a bad movie night.

"Bad Movie Night" was a tradition between Ito and me. Once a week, one of us could declare it was a Bad Movie Night, and we would get to choose whichever movie we wanted to watch without the other saying no or judging. I started it because I desperately wanted to rewatch 1980's *Flash Gordon,* which — spoilers — she loved, and I didn't want to have an argument about, so terms were set. Ultimately Bad Movie Night was about trust that everything would turn out fine.

I hit "Send" and stared at my phone, waiting for her response.

"Good morning, Mr. Cooper," said a cheerful woman's voice.

I looked up from the tiled floor and its trippy pattern and found Nora, my assistant — I still couldn't believe I had an assistant — standing in the doorway with a pink box of donuts with a file folder on top. She was a lanky woman in her twenties, the sort that went hiking every chance she got, dressed for work in a pastel orange pantsuit that complemented her blonde bob cut. So *SoCal*.

"Good morning, Nora. I see you brought the good stuff."

Nodding, she placed the box of donuts on the island, then hooked a bit of hair behind her ear.

Mom rinsed the sink, pulled off the gloves, draped them over the faucet, and turned around. "Thank you for coming over, Nora."

"Of course, Ms. Cooper," she said with a smile.

I don't know how Nora managed to navigate the personalities of the Cooper family and still managed to stay upbeat.

"James, get Nora a cup of coffee."

Nora turned to me. "You don't have to do that, Mr. Cooper."

Mom gave me a look over Nora's shoulder that suggested that, yes, indeed I did need to do that.

"No problem," I said, turning and grabbing another mug. I poured some coffee and then stared at the mug. My face flushed with shame as I realized I had no idea how she took it. I must've stared at it for too long.

"With milk and sugar," Nora offered.

Saving me once again. I smiled at her, fixed up her coffee, and handed it to her. She accepted it with both hands and a little bow of her head. She said to me, "I have the files you asked for," and gestured to the folders on top of the box.

I reached for the folder and opened the donut box with

the other hand. Mom attempted to hand me a plate, but I waved her off. Donuts aren't some bougie snack. They are meant to be held, never put on a plate.

Mom placed the plate, with the rest she held, next to the donut box, offering everyone a Sophie's Choice. Nora chose the plate.

Fair, given that Mom signed her checks.

Mom's eyes darted to the doorway. "Good morning, Anton."

Anton lumbered into the kitchen, waving at everyone. I wondered if he was still mad at me. His hand dropped when he and I exchanged looks, and then his eyes shifted away.

"Nora brought donuts, but would you like breakfast before that?" Mom asked. "Eggs? Cereal? I have bagels, too."

Anton shook his head. "Donuts are good." He reached in and pulled out a chocolate one with sprinkles, ignoring the plates. He looked at me, and I looked at him. His eyes refused to give up any information. He was still pissed. I guessed he was going to be my next apology.

Before I could get to it, he pointed to the folders. "What are those?"

"Oh, research on Patricia Horne," answered Nora, flipping a bit of hair over her other ear. "I'm Nora, Jimmy's assistant."

They nodded their hellos, and Anton picked up Patricia's file. "Do you always do this much research on a client?"

"Nora is thorough," said Mom.

Nora blushed. "Ms. Horne has quite the résumé, shall we say. She turned her family's ownership of a few local stations into a vast network, building a vast fortune in telecommunications. May I?" She took the file from Anton's hand. Opening it, she said, "She also serves on multiple boards, both corporate and charity" — she pointed to a printout of an article in the *L.A. Times* — "one of which might be applicable. She serves on the advisory board of the Doheny Antiquities Museum."

I nodded. That might explain her interest in the Buddha. The Doheny Antiquities Museum was on the Westside, having been founded and funded by the Doheny family ages ago with their oil money. Dad would take me and Erika when we were kids when it was hot outside and he had no idea what to do with us. He would sit while Erika dragged me from one broken clay pot to another.

Nora continued. "Lately, she has dabbling more publicly in politics, having set up a PAC and using it to support candidates and other particular causes." She shuffled through some pages. "She recently went on a trip with the district attorney to China to discuss investments by Chinese billionaires in Los Angeles." She looked up, saying, "There's been concern lately that some of those investments might lead to money laundering."

"And with the district attorney running for reelection," I filled in the blanks, "it looks good for him to be tough on white-collar crime, especially since he's been accused of turning his back on it. So he went right to the source."

I rubbed the side of my head. Maybe that's why the district attorney was so interested in this case. He was helping a friend out. Then why did she need me?

My phone shook. I looked down. Ito had responded.

I can give you 24 hours. Then you need to come in.

Not ideal.

I took a breath and looked up. Everyone was looking at me. "Right." I nodded. "We need to go back...*again*, to the scene of the crime."

20

—

IN THE CAR, heading east on Venice Boulevard, I ruminated on what to say to Anton about last night, about what an idiot I had been, and if he would accept my apologies. So far, I had come up with nothing.

He sat, watching the road and ignoring the throat clearing I was doing in hopes that maybe he would start the conversation. Nora had brought him a change of clothes from Target. Needless to say, he wasn't thrilled with the red polo shirt and jeans. "I look like an employee," he had said.

"Better employee than man on the run," I had said.

He had not laughed, the mood did not lighten, but he wore the clothes and covered the polo with a hoodie.

After twenty minutes of silence between us, I realized I

was going to have to step up and be a grown up. Besides, I had just turned left onto La Brea, heading north, and we were going to be at Objet Exotique in about fifteen minutes. So, you know, I would only have to apologize for that long.

I reached over and turned down "I Don't Feel Like Dancin'" by Scissor Sisters. Anton looked at me, our eyes meeting. He raised an eyebrow, and I looked away, back at the road.

"Hey," I started boldly. "About what I said last night."

Anton shook his head, looked forward, and crossed his arms.

This was already going great.

"I might've said somethings."

"Might've?"

My face flushed. I was really doing a bang-up job of apologizing. "OK. Right. I said some things last night." I paused. "Things that I didn't..."

"Didn't really mean? That it?" he said.

I snatched a look at him. I didn't want to lie. He deserved the truth.

"No...no." I paused. This was miserable. And embarrassing. But my public flogging had to be done. "At the time, I meant it."

His eyes darted to me. He hadn't expected that. "You think I'm going to jail?"

"I mean... I don't *know*. To be fair, I called myself a *fraud*."

I nodded quickly, trying to get him on board with my point. "Which means, in *context*, that I'm going to be the reason you're going to go to jail. That I'm going to fail you."

Anton looked away, over at the sidewalk. Kids were lined up in front of a store, a line that stretched down the block. This happened on La Brea more times than should be normal. I always wanted to stop and ask the kids, "What are you waiting for?"

But then again, I'd be disappointed if the answer was "shoes."

"Anton, the truth is I was tired and mad about this situation. I wanted to hurt Erika."

"That's fucked up, man," he said, still watching the sidewalk roll by. "Hurting your own sister."

"Well, yeah. It is. I know that. But knowing doesn't always stop me from saying something stupid." I rubbed my forehead. "You just got caught in the cross fire."

He didn't like that, and I didn't blame him.

"What did she do?"

"Huh?"

We stopped at a red light behind three cars. The song switched to "Do It Again" by The Beach Boys. (Hey, I ain't no snob. They got bangers, kids.)

"What did she do to you?" he repeated.

I tapped the wheel, sort of in rhythm. What *had* she done? As a way to get out of this conversation, I offered, "It's a little hard to explain."

He shook his head. "Try me."

As far as apology experiences went, this one wasn't my worst. The worst was when I spilled a glass of red wine — and I didn't even like red wine — all over the back of America's Dad, Tom Hanks. We were at some charity event to raise money for the Screen Actors Guild Fund, and I was bombed out of my mind. I was horrified as I watched this red stain seep into his jacket. I immediately started to apologize, and of course, *of course*, he was so *nice* about it that it just made it worse. Like, Tom, couldn't you have just punched me instead? It would've been better.

Green light.

"OK, so..." I started. "She put me in this position where, you know, I failed, and she should've known better."

He looked at me, not getting it.

I sighed. "I mean, by putting me out there, as this detective who would solve things, that was just a setup for failure, you know? She should've known better."

He raised an eyebrow. "She should've known better than to believe you'd succeed?"

"You don't get it, Anton. Matty Goodman died because of me."

He was quiet.

"Are you saying, Jimmy, it's her fault that guy died?"

My face flushed. "No, *no*. It's... that's not what I'm trying to say. It's not her *fault*. It's mine. But… listen, this wasn't supposed to be about me and her. It's about me and you." I looked at him. "I apologize, Anton," I snapped.

"OK."

"Do you accept my apology?" I said with another snap.

"Yeah."

"Great. Good. We're done here."

He opened his mouth to say something.

I shook my head. "Done, I said."

He looked away, mumbling, "OK, *whatever*." He shook his head, not looking at me.

The best apology I'd ever given was to my sister. After I had gotten sober, by way of making amends, I admitted I had sold some of her jewelry to get drugs. She said she knew and had forgiven me already. I cried. She cried. We hugged it out. But that was in the past. I owed her a new apology.

We were coming up on the gallery, and in a case of it-only-happens-in-the-movies, there was a parking spot just out front. I swerved into it and parked. I stepped out, walked around the back, and fed the meter. Even though I had grown up in L.A., I still loathed paying for parking. Except valet — that was a necessary evil. But meters… ugh. I hoped fifteen minutes would be enough.

Louis LaFontaine spotted us the moment we stepped into the gallery.

I may not run fast, but I can walk like a New Yorker when

the moment arises. I intercepted him just as he was about to disappear into his office.

"Louis, my old friend," I enthused.

He aimed a finger with a signet ring wrapped tightly around it at my face. "I don't know what you are doing here, but if you don't leave — "

Anton stepped closer to him, using every bit of his height and breadth to block the door. "We have some questions."

Louis swallowed. "Great. Wonderful. You have questions. I'm not going to answer them." He didn't sound exactly sure of himself.

I decided to push a little. "That's fine, Louis. I do wonder what the police will think when they find out you were blabbing about the statue, though."

He sputtered before saying, "I did no such thing!"

That buzz in the back of my head. It was a lie. He totally blabbed.

Anton answered for him. "They might think he was involved, Jimmy."

I nodded in agreement.

Louis's head snapped to him. "I am *not* involved," he maintained.

No lies detected. Still, he didn't know that I knew he was telling the truth. "But, Louis, dear sweet Louis, they won't know that until they thoroughly investigate." I looked around the store. "And I'm sure everything here is totally legit. Just as legit as you."

Louis flushed, breaking out into a sweat. He pulled out a handkerchief and dabbed his hands. "Let's talk in my office," he said, looking back out onto the customers in the showroom. He led the way.

His office was small and immaculate, with tasteful selections of Art Deco hanging in the windowless space. He sat behind his desk, a closed laptop in front of him. Anton sat in the only other chair, leaving me to stand.

"What is it that you want to know?" he asked, eager to get this over with. Sitting in his office gave him back some of his confidence. Good for him.

"Patricia Horne has hired me — "

"Us," said Anton.

I sighed. "Yes, hired us to find the Buddha."

Louis leaned back in his chair, trying to look comfortable. "Yes, well, I'm not surprised. I had told her that you had been here, asking questions."

I nodded.

He shifted again. "I had to. Someone asking about it? How did I know if you were involved or not?"

"Did you call her before or after you called the police on us?"

"After, of course." Louis licked his lips.

That was a lie. His first call was to Patricia. After all, she was the money. The order of the phone calls didn't matter much. She knew we had been there. Collins knew we had been there. And, probably, Ito and Kemble.

"Who else did you tell about the statue?" asked Anton.

Louis shot him a withering look. "Sir, I am a *professional.*"

Anton shook his head. "That's not, like, you know, answering the question."

Louis swallowed, but I didn't think he was going to answer. Time to change tactics.

"You like money, don't you, Louis?"

His eyes darted to mine. "How do you mean?" he said, fiddling with his handkerchief.

"You're a successful businessman, yes?"

"Yes, very much so. I feel that I fulfill a specific niche in this town." A slight smile, a bit of pride in his answer.

I nodded. "You know, if I had to bet what you like more than money?" I paused. "I think you like attention."

He scoffed at the idea with a wave of his handkerchief.

"Louis, come on," I said. "Game recognizes game. Sure, you make money, but it's also about *who* you get to hobnob with. That thrill when certain eyes are on you." I smiled encouragingly. "Sure, selling an expensive statue is great, but what makes it even greater is when it's sold to an Academy Award-winning director."

He blushed.

I went on. "And getting into those circles, it takes cultivation. Of knowledge. Of style. Of a brand. Everything about you screams, 'Look at me.'" I leaned forward, going in for the kill, whispering, "Is your name even Louis?"

He got very quiet. No one likes their secrets being poked, prodded out into the open.

Anton asked again, "Who else did you talk to about the statue?"

Louis LaFontaine squared up in his seat. "This can't leave the room," he said, his accent flattening into something Midwestern.

Anton's eyes bulged at the reveal.

I wasn't all that shook. The accent was generic French. It wasn't Inspector Clouseau bad, but… And if a customer had picked up on it, they didn't care. Louis LaFontaine was a delightful creation and in L.A. you get to reinvent yourself and people are delighted to join in. There was a guy in Beverly Hills decades ago who claimed to be a member of the royal Romanov (sometimes spelled Romanoff) family. He even opened a restaurant trading on the name, Romanoff's . It was open for decades and everyone knew his story was bullshit. But they enjoyed the experience.

Louis continued. "I was at a fundraiser about two weeks ago. I may have mentioned to those gathered that something… very special was coming into the store."

Two weeks ago would put it in the timeline for Devon getting his ducks in order to rob the place.

"Who was there, Louis?"

"Guys. Come on," he whined.

Anton shook his head. "We need names."

Louis continued to protest. "They are potential clients or past clients!"

"And you're concerned they won't keep working with you if you link them to a robbery," I said. "What was the fundraiser?"

"The Botanical Fund. Richard Rivers was raising money to reforest parts of Brazil."

"Richard Rivers?" asked Anton. "The music producer?"

"Oh, yes. He's a regular customer of mine. Very much into the work."

Anton looked up at me. "Devon always claimed he knew Richard Rivers."

21

———

"RICHARD RIVERS," SAID Mr. Darling over the phone, taste testing the name. "Yes, he and Ms. Horne are familiar with each other."

"Familiar" did a lot of heavy lifting in that sentence.

"Does that mean what I think it means?"

Mr. Darling, ever the lawyer, replied, "What do you think it means?"

Anton and I were sitting in my car on La Brea and we were fifteen minutes past the expired time. The red light on the meter blinked at me menacingly. Regardless, I spoke slowly, "Can you describe their relationship? Please."

Mr. Darling huffed for a second. "To be clear, there is no *relationship —* "

Lawyers.

"But I would say there is…" He paused, choosing his next word carefully. "Friction between the two of them."

"Friction, huh?"

"Yes, Mr. Cooper."

Anton looked at me.

"Do you think he's behind the theft?" asked Mr. Darling.

I rubbed my forehead. "I don't know about that yet. It's just a lead."

"If it turns into more of a lead, please let me know."

I told him I would and poked the red button, ending the call.

Anton frowned. "Richard Rivers?" he said sourly. He didn't like the idea of this man being involved. "*He* can't be involved in this."

Richard Rivers had gone in early on hip-hop, being one of the first white producers to take an interest and break it into Middle America. He was one of the people responsible for skinny white kids suddenly rapping in mall parking lots. He had been one of those skinny kids. Story goes that he was a student at USC as West Coast hip-hop was just starting out. Having been a punk, what was more punk for a white kid than hip-hop? He started recording and producing — maybe that's how he entered Devon's orbit — and after a few years he started his own label, then got a distribution deal at a major label. He started branching out as a producer and really hit it *big* when he started resurrecting artists who had fallen into irrelevance.

What was left after big?

Becoming legendary.

Richard Rivers had moved into the territory of being a living legend of the music industry and was now crossing over into cultural influence. No longer the outsider in a hoodie, he was now a mala-bead-wearing, barefoot guru who still made hit records but who also produced podcasts interviewing Very Important People, with an award-winning book or two on the side.

"I don't know, Anton," I said. "He knew Devon. Knew about the Buddha. We gotta talk to him."

That was where Nora came in. Richard Rivers was, obviously, an important man. And important people don't do anything for themselves. They have assistants. It's very possible their assistants have assistants. They depend on assistants to get anything done in their busy, important lives.

Through her own network of assistants, Nora had tracked him down. Richard Rivers was having a lunch meeting in Beverly Hills.

So we headed west.

Here's the thing about Beverly Hills, the thing they don't put in the tourist literature: The streets are fantastic. You cross over from L.A. into Beverly Hills, and the pavement becomes smooth and easy. There's not a pothole to be found. One moment you're bouncing and swerving in your car, and then... nothing. You're drunk on air. I don't know if the city hires road goblins to fix the streets at night or what...but whatever they're doing is working.

We rolled into the city as the Pet Shop Boys sang "All The Young Dudes," and we witnessed the classic ostentatious displays of wealth: pearl necklaces and clutches, expensive shirts and suits, sophisticated dresses. There was no shabby chic here, my friends. That's for the weirdos in Hollywood.

We pulled up to a restaurant off Rodeo Drive. It was a sushi place and — obviously — upscale. Anton had shifted away from unhappiness and was getting excited. Meeting a celebrity does that.

"Anton, thirty minutes ago we found out Richard Rivers might be involved in a crime."

He tried to reconcile that with his excitement to be in the same space, breathing the same air, as an idol. "Yeah, but... he's still, you know... *him.*"

The red-vested valet stepped away from the umbrellaed stand and came around the front of my car. Reaching for the door, he paused. He looked back and forth at my blue Toyota, which, yeah, maybe wasn't the typical set of wheels for this place. I opened the door, stepped out, and said, "Hey there, friend," giving him a warm smile in the process.

He smiled in return. It was automatic.

"It's a classic," I said, speaking of the car. "Everyone is gonna want one soon."

He nodded. "I understand, sir. I also still have great affection for my first car."

My face flushed as Anton laughed. I pointed to the entrance. "I'm going inside," I told him, taking the pink ticket from the valet before he slipped into my car.

Anton stepped up next to me. "Have you considered a more, you know, stylish car? Something cool?"

"Cool sticks out."

He looked at me. "You stick out."

"Yes, I do, but *not* when I'm sitting in my car. I have been doing this PI thing for more than a hot second. I think I know how to do it."

Anton shrugged.

We stepped into the restaurant. The place had been designed to maximize peace and tranquility, with natural light and bare wood. It was a mixture of traditional Japanese design and American convenience. While the tables were low and the seating was on the floor, the seats had backs rather than just being cushions. The skylights above filled the ceiling, creating the feeling that we were still outside. Next to the door was a pagoda-shaped water fountain. That felt a little on the nose.

Anton glowered at the place. It wasn't his vibe.

An elegant young man in a crisp white shirt and black

pants floated over to us. He spoke in hushed tones as if we were at a meditation retreat. "Good afternoon, gentlemen." His eyes flicked between the two of us, wondering, if, indeed, we were gentleman. "Do you have a reservation?"

I matched his tone. "We don't. Is that going to be a problem?"

He hummed and said, "I'm afraid so, sir. We do not accept walk-ins."

The restaurant was mostly empty. Guess we had just missed the lunch rush.

"Oh, I see," I said, looking around.

Found him. Richard Rivers was in the corner, chatting with a young woman whose back was to us. He sat cross-legged, an arm over the chair next to him. He was in his late sixties, with short, gray-white hair swept up and back with a big, bushy beard. He wore a loose-fitting, white-linen button down, with the sleeves rolled up. Richard held a cup of sake, a smile on his face that legendary people get to have; it held a sort of bemused charm but was unreachable.

"It's OK," I said to the maître d. "I see a friend."

He followed my look over to Richard's table. "You're *his* friend?" he asked, like I was lying to him.

"Totally," I replied. I tapped Anton on the arm, and we headed toward the corner before giving the maître d' a chance to ask another question. I opened my arms wide as I got closer. "Richard, my man!" I said in a big, boisterous, overly friendly way. "Weird to bump into you here."

The young woman turned around. She was maybe in her early twenties or even her late teens, though it was hard to tell with her makeup. She was Latina, in very good shape, and dressed in a tight T-shirt and jeans, with the intention of showing as many curves as possible. Her eyebrows went up in confusion at my exclamation.

Richard craned his neck around her. Familiarity flashed across his eyes, but so did uncertainty. Where did he know me from?

Ah, fame. So very fleeting.

The woman checked in with Richard, who decided he didn't know me. "Sorry, friend, but we're in the middle of something here," he said.

I plopped down next to Richard, trying to figure out how to sit comfortably on the mat and catching flashbacks to the third grade when I couldn't sit still in the reading circle and got sent to the principal's office again and again. I gestured with great magnanimity for Anton to take the empty seat next to the woman. He didn't move. I pointed again, and he slowly sat down, uncomfortably giving a brief smile to the woman, who was still wondering what was going on.

Richard's eyes burned into me. "Hey, man. You're starting to piss me off."

"He does that," said Anton.

Richard shot him a look. "Do I know *you*?"

Anton shut up as the real Richard Rivers began to reveal himself.

The maître d' approached the table. "Is there a problem, Mr. Rivers?" His voice was still calm, centered, but he was ready to take action if need be.

Richard pointed at me, beyond ready to get my ass tossed, when I said, "Richard, I get the sense you don't have enough peace in your life."

That threw him. "What?"

I followed his confusion with, "Have you considered the wisdom of the Buddha?"

OK, I knew I was laying it on thick, but I didn't want us getting thrown out.

Richard lowered his finger. His eyes narrowed, deep in thought. After a long moment, he looked up at the maître d' and said, "It's fine." He nodded to him. "Thank you for asking, but there's not a problem."

The man nodded and left as quietly as he had appeared.

Richard, without looking at her, said to the woman, "Give us a few minutes."

"But, Richard — "

His eyes darted to her. "Give us a few minutes, hon. Then we'll talk about your album."

The woman glared at me with the heat of a thousand suns as she stood up and stomped away, hitting Anton in the shoulder with her tiny bag. My stomach churned as I watched Richard watch her move away.

"Is she any good?" I asked.

He adjusted the beads on his wrist. "Who gives a shit?" he said, putting down his cup of sake. "What about the Buddha?"

Anton looked at me, surprised by the dissonance between who he thought Richard Rivers was and the reality before him. Friends, sometimes meeting your heroes can be very hard.

"What do you know?" Rivers asked, his voice low.

I pointed to his glass of water. "Did you drink from that? I'm thirsty."

He shook his head no.

I snatched the glass and took a drink. "I've heard you might be interested in a certain Buddha. One that was stolen the other night?"

"Who told you that?"

"Is it true?"

Recognition flashed across his face again. "How do I know you?"

"Jimmy. Cooper. Jimmy Cooper," I replied.

The lights went on behind his eyes. "*Cooper*? Sweet Jesus. I remember you. The actor turned detective." He chuckled, shaking his head in disbelief. "What the fuck happened to you?" He took a sip of his sake. "I mean... a detective? Fuck. You could be making porn, Jimmy. Probably better money and more fun. Everyone's got a kink. I'm sure there's someone hot for a former child star."

Ouch. He was really going for the jugular. Good thing I have an overly large sense of self most days.

Richard looked at Anton. "You got a story?"

Anton blinked. He wasn't ready for this much assholery.

"Riveting," Richard said into the silence. He turned back to me. "So. You're not the police." He looked Anton up and down. "You're definitely not a cop." He turned back to me. "Why are *you* asking about the Buddha?"

"Like I said, I heard that you were interested in it."

He leaned back. "From Louis LaFontaine?"

"To his credit, he didn't mention you *specifically*."

"He is the paragon of confidentiality," Rivers replied sarcastically. "Did he tell you about the Buddha?"

"I hear the glazes are one of a kind."

Rivers snorted. "It's not just the glazes. It's all of it. It's said that one glimpse of the work provides an overwhelming connection with the world. With the *universe*."

"Huh," said Anton, not convinced.

Rivers glared at Anton. I stepped in, saying, "How much does a connection with the universe cost?"

"It wasn't for sale," he replied.

"No?"

He shook his head. "He said Patricia Horne was buying it."

The way he said her name, you would think he didn't like her.

"That *bitch*."

Oh, yeah. He didn't like her.

Rivers continued, saying "He refused any sort of negotiation. That little shit is more afraid of her than me. Though I think Louis gets a perverse pleasure out of dangling rare objects in front of us."

"That doesn't sound like the Louis I know," I said, tongue firmly in cheek. "He seems like such a straight shooter."

Rivers set his jaw. "What's your interest in the statue?"

Anton said, "We've been hired to find it."

Rivers looked at him as I shook my head. I was hoping to avoid telling Rivers that bit of information.

Rivers asked him. "Who hired you?"

Anton shook his head. "We're asking the questions here."

I tried to wave him off, gently moving my hand. He was risking this whole interview.

"Are you?" answered Rivers.

Anton nodded. "When was the last time you spoke to Devon Phillips?"

He leaned forward. "Is it *Horne*? Did she send you to harass me?"

"Devon Phillips," snapped Anton. "Did you hire him to steal the Buddha?"

Rivers pulled back. "We're *done* here," he said. His eye

caught something.

I followed it.

Walking toward the table was a man in his early forties, could've been Middle Eastern. He had a neatly trimmed beard and wore a well-fitted dark blue suit and a white shirt with its collar open. Seeing us, he frowned.

"Everything OK, Mr. Rivers?" His voice was deep and professional.

Rivers shook his head. "These two are leaving. Make sure they find their way out."

Anton turned to look. His shoulders dropped. He looked at me, but his eyes kept darting back to the man, like there was something he really wanted me to know.

The new guy directed us away from the table. "It's time to go," he said with a tone that meant there would be no arguments.

As we stood and walked around the man, Anton looked away from him and started mumbling to me, "Jimmy... *Jimmy.*"

"Anton, not now."

"Jimmy..."

"*Anton.*"

Almost to the maître d stand, I paused at the young woman, who was scrolling through her phone. "You don't have to deal with his shit, you know," I said, pointing back at Rivers, who was in a deep conversation with the bearded guy. "He's a creepy old man. An asshole. You don't have to do it this way."

Her head twisted like I had just said the craziest thing. "He's going to make me a *star*."

I nodded. "I hope he does."

Outside, as I was reaching into my pocket for the valet ticket, Anton repeated my name, "*Jimmy.*"

I turned to him. "Anton, what were you thinking? You can't just *ask* them the question. You can't just accuse them —"

"Jimmy."

"They will *lie*. They will *shut down*. They will not offer any clues or leads. We don't know if Richard Rivers is a part of this or not — "

"*Jimmy.*"

"*What?*"

Anton cautiously pointed back to the restaurant. "The guy that came to the table."

I turned to look, but Anton pulled me back. "Don't do *that*." He shook his head. "It's the guy from the *garage*. The one that brought the money."

I paused, desperate to look "You're sure?"

"Super," he said.

I nodded. My heart thumped.

"OK. That's... a lead," I said. "And now we know."

Anton nodded. "You're welcome."

"Don't get cocky."

I walked to the valet. Before handing him my ticket, I said, "That guy that just came in, did he drop off his car?"

"Yes, sir."

I pulled out sixty bucks.

"Can you tell me the license plate number for sixty bucks?"

22

———

Three Years Ago

I WAS NOT impressed with the cafe Jerry Collins chose as neutral ground. It sort of sucked. The place was near MacArthur Park and had seen better days. Only two other tables had customers. The staff were indifferent. The red tile floor was grungy where it met the wall and the art had gone unchanged for decades — pictures of matadors and hot rods — which no longer matched the cuisine: generic American breakfast, lunch and dinner. And our table wobbled.

It was the perfect place to have a clandestine meeting with a presumably dirty cop.

Gordon and I did the bare minimum to blend in. We both ordered coffee, which we both promptly ignored.

Sitting across from us, like he was the fucking king of this dump, an arm slung over one of the chairs, was Detective Jerry Collins.

Collins was in his fifties, so his thick, black hair couldn't be real. And he had these eyebrows that curved upward in the middle, giving him resting empathy face. He wore a nicer suit than I had ever seen on Gordon. His thumb fiddled with the gold class ring on his right hand while he held a cinnamon roll in the other. Unsurprisingly, there was no wedding ring. Maybe he was divorced. Maybe he was married to the job. Maybe he was a douche who liked to play the field and thought a ring would slow him down.

He nodded in my direction.

"He's like your sidekick or something?" he asked Gordon, voice smooth and dripping.

What an asshole.

Gordon shook his head. "He's *not* my sidekick. He's my..." He looked at me. I had no idea what he was going to say. He looked across the table. "I'm training him."

Collins chuckled. "Word going around is you got stuck with him because your boss lady keeps your balls in a jar on her desk." He laughed at his own joke. I could smell the cinnamon on his breath.

I moved to say something, specifically how dumb and *overworked* that insult was. Like low-hanging fruit, dude. Gordon touched my leg under the table, though, and I stopped. He had told me to keep quiet during the meeting. I complained I wasn't going to sit there like a child and just let the grown-ups talk. He suggested that was exactly what I should do and that Collins would try and provoke me because that was his MO.

I argued I would handle it like a professional. Gordon told me to just shut up.

Collins put down the cinnamon roll and wiped his fingers with a paper napkin. He grabbed his mug of coffee and took a drink, keeping an eye on me. "So," he said, once he'd put it down, "we have a problem."

"We do," answered Gordon.

Collins fiddled with his mug. He said to me, "He ever talk about his time in the LAPD?" I shook my head. "Gordo here, he was a monster. In all the best ways."

Did he just say *Gordo*?

"He was a badass. I once saw him tackle a suspect after chasing him for three blocks."

I pointed at Gordon. "*He* ran for three blocks?" I heard it straight from Jerry's mouth, and there were no lies detected. I just couldn't believe it.

Gordon looked at me. I could see it in his eyes. This was not the time to scurry down memory lane.

"Whatever happened to *that* cop?" asked Collins, staring at my partner.

Gordon leaned back, crossed his arms over his stomach.

"I learned that maybe I don't need to tackle people. That I could be smart about it rather than just throw my body at a problem. But I was always smarter than you."

Collins's grin was full of anger. "Sure, Gordo. Sure."

Gordo.

Collins took a breath. "We have a problem," he said again.

"Yes, we do," Gordon agreed.

"But it doesn't *have* to be a problem." He shrugged. "This is a stinker of a case. Why are you even bothering? Greta needs the money or something? Too many deadbeat clients? " He shook his head.

My face flushed. I really, really wanted to say something. The man was talking about my mother.

Gordon leaned forward, laying his fists on the table. "If it's such a stinker, why are you meeting with me?"

Collins blinked. "I'm trying to help out an old friend."

"An old friend, huh?"

Collins looked at Gordon. "That's right. A friend. With a word of friendly advice."

"We were partners, Jerry. Not friends."

Collins nodded and looked at me. "See the kind of man you're working with? Not friends? I spent more time with him than with my ex-wife."

Ex-wife. Yeah, of course.

"Not friends, that hurts," he said.

Gordon just stared at Collins. "What's your connection

to Chad Lane and Deborah Holt? Why are you covering for them?"

"Uh-uh. No." He shook his head, sighing, and picked up his coffee. "They're the *victims*, Gordo."

"Stop calling me that."

Collins toasted with his mug and took a drink. "They're the victims here," he insisted. "That's how I know them."

My head buzzed. It was, of course, a lie. I moved to call him out. Again, Gordon put a hand on my leg, so I closed my mouth, grinding my teeth.

"You know if there's a connection," warned Gordon, "I'll find out. I was always the better detective."

Collins chuckled. "Yeah, sure you were," he said sarcastically.

Gordon nodded. "And Anton Greene? How do you know him?"

"No connection other than that he's the one that I arrested, Gordon," he snapped.

No buzz. He wasn't lying. Gordon looked at me. I shook my head. There was just a bit of disappointment in Gordon's eyes, but it was gone before he turned back to Collins.

"I don't know what to tell you. I got a witness statement. I got a victim statement. There's *cash* at the scene with his fingerprints on it." Collins shifted in his seat. "I'm getting a little pissed off here. I guess I'm just not understanding what's going on. I'm not sure who *you* are anymore."

"This the 'help' you were talking about?" Gordon deadpanned.

"This is going to blow up in your face if you keep digging." Leaning forward, Collins replied, "Gordon, just get this kid to plea. He'll serve a little time. That's it. It's in everyone's best interests."

"Not Anton's," I said.

Gordon gave me an eye; Jerry raised an eyebrow at me.

"Anton is going to go to jail for *something* someday," he avowed. "He's a bad kid, heading in a bad direction. This might be the best thing for him. Make a man out of him."

"Best?" growled Gordon.

"Yeah, scare him straight. Maybe on the inside he'll learn a fucking skill."

Like a python snatching at a rodent, Gordon's arm reached across the table. Collins moved back, but Gordon got a hold of the collar of his suit. Both men stood, and I scooted away as Gordon's chair fell back to the ground. He reached out with his other arm. Collins smacked it away and reached for Gordon.

Soon, they were old men locked in a scuffle.

"Hey, hey, hey! Back down now!" a voice shouted.

A new guy had just joined us. He was thick headed, thick bodied, and stuffed into a cheap, gray tweed suit coat. He was holding up his badge.

Gordon caught sight of it and let go, stepping back.

Collins did the same, smoothing out his lapel.

"You all right?" the new man asked Collins.

Collins smoothed out his mane of hair. "I'm fine. It's just a friendly disagreement. Isn't that right, Gordo?"

Gordo was breathing heavily as my eyes moved between him and Collins.

"That's right, Jer."

Jerry nodded. "This is my partner, Kemble. Kemble, meet a bunch of losers."

Kemble? Why did that name sound familiar?

Collins nodded toward Gordon. "This is my old partner, Gordon Bixby. He's turned his back on his brothers in blue to work for the opposition, and this one" — he pointed at me — "he's a fallen movie star. A drunk and a pill popper working for his mommy."

Kemble chuckled.

"As you saw, they threatened an officer of the law because they have a shit bag client."

Gordon didn't say anything. I was thinking of a million replies, but none of them were quite right.

"Typical," said Kemble.

Collins pointed at Gordon. "Drop this case, all right? All will be forgiven." He turned to Kemble. "We're done here." He walked past him, heading out.

Kemble gave us a final glare before turning around and lumbering after his partner.

"Kemble?" asked Gordon.

Kemble stopped, turned. Collins stopped, too, with his hand on the door.

"Are you a good cop?"

Kemble's face twitched. "What's that supposed to mean?" He looked at his partner, who only had eyes for Gordon.

"If you're a good cop, I'd watch your back."

Kemble licked his lips. The gears turned. If he said he was a good cop, would that be betraying his partner? And if he said he wasn't, then wouldn't he be an asshole? What was he gonna say?

"Fuck off, Bixby."

That was a choice.

Collins pushed the door open, and Kemble followed him out.

I looked at Gordon. "Well, *I* didn't say anything."

Gordon gave me the eye.

Something clicked. "Kemble."

Gordon shook his head, shrugged. "What about him?"

"I've heard that name before. I've *read* that name before. In Anton's files. A year ago, Kemble *arrested* Anton."

23

———

IT TURNS OUT sixty bucks was enough to get the license plate number of the bearded guy's car. Armed with that information, Anton and I left the Japanese restaurant and headed to the library to a get a name. The place was spacious, with high ceilings, vaguely in a Spanish style, and had computers that could get me to the internet for free. Anton and I sat next to each other on hard wooden chair, staring at the information on the screen at the Beverly Hills Library.

"Assim Amini," I said, trying the name in my mouth, hoping I didn't sound like an asshole.

Anton waved a finger at it. "That's totally the guy from the warehouse."

A throat cleared behind us. We turned to look. A thin woman with greying hair clothing a couple of paperbacks put a finger to her lips. My face flushed. Not sure if she had any authority or was just a pesky patron, I nodded politely rather than risk escalating the situation.

According to Amini's LinkedIn, he had been Rivers's head of security — or fixer, more likely — for about five years, having worked his way up through various firms after leaving the army. He was an L.A. native and his family was still here.

Looking for more information, I pulled out my phone and logged onto a variety of social medias. Not as myself. Oh, no. Jimmy Cooper does *not* belong to any social media platform or have a handle. I did once. However, after I made the mistake of commenting on a YouTube video that I had been featured it, I decided it was a mistake. The clip was from TMZ where, shall we say, I wasn't on my best behavior. I explained in the comment section that the video was taken out of context — which wasn't entirely true — and the replies I got were anything but supportive.

For me, the internet was best traveled anonymously.

That said, work required I be on it and have a profile. People left all kinds of information out there for everyone to see. My handle of cho!ce was Gail, a twenty-something white woman, a part-time songwriter, and a dog mom.

Men were more than happy to accept a friend request

from her, which opened up more and more circles of people.

"That's fucked up," Anton whispering, shaking his head and leaning back in his chair.

"Listen, I don't make men act the way they do," I explained. "But I will take advantage of it." I paused and looked at him. "I don't catfish with it, OK?"

"Sure, man. Sure."

I continued to look at him, trying to unpack his answer. Maybe he was still mad at me. I couldn't dwell on it. My deal with Ito was ticking down.

Finding Amini's Instagram, I started scrolling backwards in time. The guy was handsome, in his thirties, and guessing from the pictures of different women in their twenties, presumably happily single. Also included were pictures of him were variously celebrities in the music industry. All in all, he was presenting a very happy, successful life.

What are you looking for?" ask Anton.

"Connections. Surprises. Honestly, I don't know." I shrugged. "When I find it, I'll know."

I kept scrolling and scrolling. I could feel Anton's boredom grow into frustration. For him, sitting here didn't feel like anything. For me, it was the opposite. I was diving deep into Assim's life. I could see his desires, his aspirations, and the things that he loved. One could also make assumptions about the things he didn't like about his life. What he chose to *not* show were just as revealing.

Anton suddenly moved. "Wait. Stop. That one," he said pointing at a picture.

It was Assim and a Black man raising a toast with rocks glasses. By the looks of both, they had been having a good time and had put away more than one drink already.

"That's Crenshaw."

"You're sure?"

"One hundred percent."

My body buzzed at the connection. That, right there, that was what we were looking for.

Crenshaw's arm was slung around Amini's shoulder. He was light skinned, had the right amount of stubble to look cool. Where Assim wore a grey suit, Crenshaw rocked out in a tight, heather green T-shirt.

"They knew each other," said Anton.

I nodded. "Maybe it went like this. Rivers found out about the Buddha, turned to Amini, and he turned to Crenshaw."

"Why him?"

I tapped on the image, hoping Crenshaw had been tagged in the picture. No such luck.

I went back to scrolling, looking for more pictures of Assim and Crenshaw, as Anton returned to his frustration. I went back far enough I was in Assim's military days and that's when I found Crenshaw again.

It was a picture of them and other members of their unit in fatigues. I guess they were in their barracks, all grins and smiles, looking like kids.

"Because, Anton, Crenshaw had skills most people don't have."

Tapping on the picture, most of them were tagged this time.

And Crenshaw wasn't Crenshaw. Clicking on his handle, turns out his name was Malcolm Vaughn.

I turned to Anton. "Fake name. *Now* can we call it a heist film?"

His head shook slightly, like he hadn't heard me. "Go back."

I took us back to the group of soldiers. "That's Abbott." He pointed to the guy on the very edge of the frame.

Sure enough, it was. I tapped on the screen to see if he had been one of the ones tagged. He wasn't. Shit.

"They all served together," I said, leaning back. "And they look like friends."

"They didn't the other night."

Which begged the question why not?

I tapped on the picture again and all of the tags reappeared. There were three other soldiers besides our people of interest. One hadn't posted anything in two years. The other two did. One lived in Wisconsin. The other lived in San Pedro.

San Pedro sits on the South Bay, at the end of the 110, connected to the rest of L.A. by a narrow bit of land. Most people would look at the map and think, "Gosh, that can't really be a part of Los Angeles, can it?" Friends, it can and it is. Back at the very beginning of the 20th Century the Big City absorbed the Small Port City to have access to what became the Port of Los Angeles. And in order to do that, it all had to be connected.

It was still a working class neighborhood, though that was beginning to change.

Moe had grown up there and didn't have much to say about it. When he came out, he escaped to the brighter lights and prettier men of West Hollywood. He seldom went back, really only going for holidays or when his mother guilted him.

We hit the 110 in silence. I moved us through traffic and wondered if the rest of the day was going to be a silent war between the two of us.

About an hour into the drive, just south of USC, the playlist moved to "Last Night a DJ Saved My Life" by Indeep. The beat started, followed by a baseline. Then a very eighties guitar fell into the groove. Anton's head started bouncing. So did mine. Two women sang about how a song had saved their lives and Anton and I moved in the car. We started to laugh.

Maybe we'd be OK.

Forty minutes later we were rolling into San Pedro. Nora had found and texted me the address of a small, white house on a sharp hill. The white metal fence was at an angel while the house sat flat. In the distance, you could see the ocean. The front yard was small and all patio.

We walked through the gate and I knocked on the heavy screen door.

A girl no more than four in a dress, holding a Barbie by the foot appeared. She was more silhouette than person through the door.

"Hi, there," I said.

"Hi," she squeaked. She shoved some errant hair away from her face.

"Sarah!" barked a man's voice.

The girl darted away from the door, back into the house, replaced by a man, heading to the door.

"Can I help you?" The man's voice was deep and suspicious of us. He was tall, with a buzzed head, wearing a white T-shirt and cargo shorts.

I slapped on a smile, hoping to make this as easy as possible for everyone involved. "We're looking for Michael Ortiz."

"Uh huh. What's this about?" He was still suspicious, now with a little bit of worry. And he didn't answer the question.

I pressed ahead. "It's about Assim Amini and Malcolm Vaughn. Have you heard from them lately?"

The man's head tilted slightly.

"Is everything OK?" he asked.

Anton replied, "They might be in trouble."

The man took this in, looking back and forth between us. "Oh, shit. Yeah, yeah, I'm Michael Ortiz." He opened the door and stepped outside. The door sprung closed with a thunk. He was taller than me, but shorter than Anton. He looked older than his picture from Assim's Insta, but still had a lingering baby face. He had TCB tattooed on his right forearm along with a lightning bolt. An Elvis fan. He said, "People call me Mickey."

"I'm Jimmy, this is Anton," I said.

Anton and Mickey bumped fists and nodded at each other. I thought about it, but the moment passed.

"Are they all right?" he asked, suspicion turning to worry.

"That's... complicated," I answered.

"They might be in trouble," said Anton.

Mickey took a step closer. "Trouble? What kind of trouble?" I could hear his concern for his former army buddies.

"Let's just say legal for now," I said.

"What does that mean?" Mickey asked.

"When was the last time you saw either one of them?"

He looked at Anton then slowly back to me. He was weighing his words carefully. Maybe he didn't want to get himself in trouble. Or them in more.

"Mickey, how well do you know them? Assim and Malcom?"

Mickey crossed his arms. "We went to Hell together and back. You learn a lot about people."

I nodded. He was building a case to protect his friends, which I got. I would do the same. "They're involved in a theft."

"And a murder," added Anton.

Mickey's head started shaking. "What? What do you mean? Involved? Like how?"

Oh, boy. I rubbed my jaw, nervous how he was going to take the news. "They were a part of a robbery. A man's been killed. Malcolm is on the run. We'd like to find him."

Mickey was still, just breathing slowly.

"Another one of your friends is dead too," said Anton quietly.

I pulled my phone from my pocket. I showed Mickey the picture of his unit from Assim's Instagram. I pointed to the man I knew as Abbott. "What's his name?"

"Isiah," answered Mickey. "Isiah Jackson." He let out a breath of air and wiped the sweat from the top of his head. "He's dead?"

I nodded.

"What happened?" Mickey asked, putting his hands on his hips.

He was silent as I explained what happened, never taking

his eyes off of me. I met them and told him what we knew and a little of what we guessed. We told him about the Buddha and how Rivers wanted it. That Amini must have reached out to Vaughn and Jackson — those names would take some getting used to — and then someone added Devon to the team. I told him what happened in the warehouse, the shootout and finding Jackson in the van.

Mickey said nothing. I could see him chewing his bottom lip. I could feel his heart breaking for a friend that had gone to Hell with him and survived it.

Anton broke the tension. "It's true, man. I was there."

The former soldier's eyes went to Anton. "There?" Suspicion returned to his eyes.

I took a chance. "Anton was the driver. He's in trouble and I'm trying to get him out."

"I was just driving. Just getting paid. And its all just spun out of control."

Nodding, I said, "We're just looking for help. Anything."

Mickey rubbed his forehead. He said, "Assim called me yesterday. Asking if I had heard from Jackson or Mal." He took in a sharp breath. "He played like he was just trying to reconnect." Mickey shook his head at the memory. He took a breath and explained, "Assim was always the guy who had something going on. Some plate spinning somewhere. I knew he had my back, but I don't know if I ever really knew him. We're both from SoCal, but different worlds, man."

"What do you mean?"

"His family was well off. Mine worked at the port, you know? I did the army so I could pay for an education. Amini did it to build a resume."

I nodded. "What about Vaughn and Jackson? What can you tell me about them?"

Mickey shrugged. "They were good guys. Tough. Detailed." He paused, thinking. "Those two were tight. Jackson was a couple of years younger. Vaughn looked out for him like he was his little brother, you know?"

I glanced at Anton.

"They were funny together. East Coast meets West Coast. Jackson was from up in Inglewood."

Anton snorted. "I'm not far from there."

"Right on."

I asked Mickey, "Why would they get involved in a robbery?"

He shrugged. "They were not the criminal type, you know? When I knew they, they were good soldiers. How much did they steal?"

I shook my head. "Not a how much. A what. A priceless artifact. Worth a few million dollars."

"Holy shit," said Mickey. He shook his head. "I mean, if you want a motive, there's that one. We didn't come out rich. And with the way things are? I'd be thrilled if I got a dollar with every 'Thank you for your service.'" Mickey licked his lips. "I get why something like that would be tempting."

I rubbed my head, trying to make sense of something. "Assim liked Malcolm and Isiah?"

"Yeah."

"And they liked him?"

"Sure," said Mickey.

Anton knew where I was taking this. He asked, "So why did the deal fall through?"

"Shit, man, I don't know," answered Mickey, taking a step back. He was starting to end his involvement in all this. "You'd have to ask them."

Still a little shocked about what happened to his friends, Mickey turned around and reached for the screen door. With a hand on it, he paused.

"You know Isiah had a sister, right?"

24

OF COURSE, ITO and Kemble would get to Isiah's sister before we did.

We saw them standing outside of her home talking just as we turned the corner onto her street. Quickly, I swerved and parked on the street, three houses away.

I wondered how long it had taken them to get Isiah Jackson's military records. One check of his fingerprints, probably, and they'd pop up on the computer. And unless Crenshaw — nope, *Vaughn* — was careful and cleaned down the van of his fingerprints, they'd have his records too.

Would that lead them to Amini? Ortiz? Maybe eventually.

"What do we do?" whispered Anton as if they might hear us.

Mickey had done me and Anton a favor and called Isiah's sister, Seraphina. He explained who we were and she agreed that we could come over.

Ito had her back to us as she talked to Kemble. Wearing a reddish-brown leather jacket, blue jeans, and her favorite boots, she had her hands on her hips, revealing her sidearm. Kemble wore his classic herringbone suit coat that might have fit him better ten years ago, with his badge hanging from his neck. He nodded along as she talked and he flipped through his notebook.

What had Seraphina told them? What did she know?

Gripping my steering wheel, I started to worry. I imagined that they had told her that Isiah was dead and had died while committing a felony. They would ask if she knew what he had been up to and whether or not she had heard from him recently. What if she had answers? What if they knew something we didn't? The only thing that *might* keep Anton out of jail is if we're the first to solve it all. And here she was, just swooping in —

"You OK, man?" Anton asked.

I took a breath. Get some perspective, Jimmy. This wasn't a competition. This wasn't a treasure hunt. This was important. I nodded to him.

"What are we going to do?" he asked again.

Ito and Kemble stepped apart, their post-witness interview confab done. She walked around the front of their car, heading to the driver's side as Kemble reached for the passenger's side door. Ito's step slowed. She stopped and her head turned in our direction.

Instinctively, we ducked down and then peeked up to see if she had spotted us.

She was looking in our direction, probably recognizing the car.

Nothing happened. The world stopped moving. I could hear Anton's heart pounding. Or maybe it was mine.

Ito's eyes moved away. She turned back and got into the car. I heard it start up and I risked putting my head up to see more. Rather than pulling away and passing us, Ito turned the car around and headed away, out of the neighborhood.

Bad Movie Night was still in effect, and maybe she didn't want to risk Kemble spotting us.

Anton and I sat back up. Another silence.

"We're not even ten minutes from my mom's house," said Anton. He got real quiet. "It would be so easy to go home."

Seraphina lived in Inglewood, a city south of L.A. Next to LAX, it's the home of SoFi Stadium, The Forum — former home of the Lakers and where I got to see the one and only Prince perform — and, of course, the iconic Randy's Donuts with the giant donut on top.

"Yeah," I said. All of this running around was taking a toll.

"My mom has got to be so mad right now," he said. He looked at me. "Do you think your girlfriend talked to her?"

He paused. "Or Collins?"

I didn't answer. I didn't know.

He took a breath. "I hope it was your girlfriend. For a cop, she seems nice."

I nodded. "She's pretty cool." I paused. "Listen, you'll be home soon. We're going to get this figured out."

Anton said nothing. He looked over at Seraphina's home. It was an American Craftsman with its low roof and large front porch. "Do we go over there now? Or give her some time? The cops just talked to her." He shook his head. "This sucks."

"Yeah. It does." I took a breath, remembering something Gordon would say in moments like this. "It will not suck less by waiting."

I got out of the car. Anton reluctantly did the same.

A couple of moments later, we knocked on the door.

It opened before I had even pulled my hand back.

Seraphina Jackson stood there, hand on the door. She was in her late thirties and Isiah's older sister. I could see the resemblance around the eyes. Hers were red and wet. She was about my height, wearing a black tank top over faded overalls. Her hair in braids that fell past her shoulders, held together by a scrunchie.

"You Jimmy?" she said to me.

"I am."

"Then you must be Anton." Her voice was low and tired.

She waved us in and closed the door behind us. We stood in the entryway as she scrutinized us. Behind her was a living room and stairs leading up. Finally, she said, "Mickey thinks I should talk to you."

"We'd appreciate that. It's just a few questions. Then we'll get out of your way."

Seraphina put her hand up. I shut up.

"I don't care what you want."

I swallowed. "OK. I get that. What is that you want?" I asked. I learned a long time ago, when you want something it's always good to find out what the other person wants. Sometimes you aren't so far apart.

"I want this gone, Jimmy. Out of my life. Can you do that?" Head down, she closed her eyes, crossed her arms, and took a step back, trying to collect herself. Her head came back up. "I told Isiah, I did not want cops coming to my door asking about him."

I nodded. "I'm sorry that happened."

Seraphina wiped her eyes, taking a breath. "Can you make it go away?" she said. It was a challenge, not a request.

The same thing that Anton wanted yesterday morning. Just make this horrible thing disappear.

"I don't know if I can do that," I answered.

"I didn't tell the cops anything. I wasn't sure if they would come back later and charge me with, I don't know..." She searched for the words. "Criminal conspiracy or something.

I cannot be dragged into this *bullshit*. I have a fourteen year old daughter to worry about. Her medical bills are burning through what I got. And now this?"

My heart cracked. She didn't ask for this. She was just as much of a victim in all this as Devon. More, really. This is happening *to* her.

"I don't want to be *involved*," she said, her voice wavering.

I nodded.

Anton said, "You don't have to be. We won't tell anyone we were here. Definitely not the cops. Promise."

Seraphina looked at me.

"We'll totally keep you out of this," I said.

She took a deep breath.

"What happened?" I asked.

Seraphina wiped her face. She explained to us that when Isiah came back, he had struggled to make ends meet. He'd work here and there, but the jobs wouldn't last. Seraphina's daughter was ill and she could only do so much for her brother. "He was struggling, but I couldn't do anything for him. I told him to go to the VA, but he wouldn't."

That first step to getting help was always the hardest.

"A couple of weeks ago, he was over here telling me about how he and an old army buddy are going to rob some place. I went through the roof." Her voice began to rise, tighten. "What the hell was *wrong* with him? He'd just get so quiet as I..." She paused. Seraphina's voice became quiet. "I was so mad at him."

"You didn't know what was going to happen."

"I damn well know that," she snapped. "I can still be mad at him. Calls me last week, telling me that all of *my* money troubles are going to be solved. Says this job, it's worth more than they thought. Malcolm told him they were going to get *more.*"

Malcolm or Isiah must've realized how valuable the Buddha was and decided to renegotiate. With the Buddha in hand, they must have thought they held all the cards. That is, until someone started shooting.

"Do you know where we can find Malcom? Has he reached out?"

Seraphina shook her head. "But I have a way to call him."

She dug into a pocket of her overalls and pulled out a flip phone, small and gray. I hadn't seen one in forever.

"Isiah gave it to me." She dropped it into my hand. "Told me to call on this if I hadn't heard from him in a while. It meant something had gone wrong."

I looked at Anton. He was looking down at the ground.

"Isiah had always been good at being prepared." She nodded at the phone. "There's only one number."

I thanked her for her time. She didn't say anything else, just moved to the door and opened it. We took the hint and stepped outside. The door was closed before we reached the first step.

Anton looked at me like I had some words of wisdom.

I tried to think of something, but nothing came out. I offered him a weak nod. I didn't know if Seraphina was going to be OK or not. All I could do was keep her out of this as best as I could.

Back in the car, I flipped open the phone and toggled my way to the contacts. Sure enough, there was only one number. I dialed it.

It rang two times and I looked at Anton who stared at me. On the third ring, someone picked up.

A deep voice asked, "Seraphina?"

I looked away from Anton and leaned into my seat. "Not quite, no."

Silence.

"She gave me the phone," I said.

I could hear someone breathing.

"I'm not a cop, if that means anything."

The phone disconnected. Anton's eyes glared at me and his head shook. "Did he just hang up?"

I put up a hand, trying to get him not to worry as I started to worry. I dialed again. It connected on the second ring.

"Malcolm? Don't hang up."

Silence. I thought I heard a chair creak as he sat down.

"Is this Malcolm?"

A beat.

"Who *is* this?" asked the deep voice.

I swallowed. "I'm someone that might be able to help you out. I hear you have a certain object of interest."

The voice said, "Maybe I do."

I took a breath. "My name is Jimmy Cooper. I work for someone who would like to take that item off your hand. For a good price."

The silence stretched on.

"Three million dollars."

I cleared my throat. "Before we go on, I'd like to know who I'm negotiating with." Oh, shit *I* was negotiating. I hated this call. "Is this Malcom Vaughn?"

"It is."

My heart thumped with excitement. We were closer.

"Three million?" I said. "I don't know if my employer can do three million."

Anton frowned at me, mouthing "What the fuck?"

I put up my hand, trying to calm him. "What about two?" I didn't want Malcolm to get suspicious. I needed him to believe me. And saying no would be the best way to do that. "Two million dollars is a lot of money for one man."

A beat. "It's not just for me."

He was still planning on giving Seraphina Isiah's cut. I didn't want to tell him but she *really* didn't want his money.

"Uh huh," I replied. "That's not my problem."

"It is if you want the Buddha."

"That particular item is hot and rare. That makes it very

difficult to find another buyer."

Malcolm chuckled slowly. "Maybe I just get rid of it. Donate it to a Salvation Army. They'll put it on the shelf. Somebody will pay five bucks for it."

My face began to sweat. He sounded like he meant it. "You didn't go through all this to come out empty handed."

"I did not." He paused. "Two million."

Did I just talk him *down* by a million dollars? Maybe I missed my true calling.

"Cash," he added.

"Cash?"

"You think I have a fucking bank account?" he said. "Cash. Tonight."

I shook my head. "I don't know about tonight. That's a lot of money to raise in that amount of time, Vaughn."

"It'll be three tomorrow. You'll be hearing from me." He said and then hung up.

Anton looked at me. "Did you agree to two million dollars? In cash?"

I slipped the phone into my pocket. "Really drove a hard bargain, didn't I?"

Anton shook his head. "That's *still* a lot of money. Where are we going to get it?"

I frowned at him. "Relax. We're working for billionaires."

25

———

"THAT'S *ABSURD*. I'm not going to give you that money," said Mr. Darling over the speaker phone.

That wasn't exactly what I wanted to hear, especially since we were heading to his office in Beverly Hills.

I tried again. "Ms. Horne was going to pay Louis Lafontaine three million dollars. This seems quite a bargain."

"Well, Mr. Cooper," he replied, "the situation was changed. I can't in good conscience recommend my client pay for stolen merchandise. That would be illegal."

Anton gave me the eye. I shook my head and shrugged. I didn't know what was going on either.

"I was hired to find the Buddha, *Mr. Darling*," I replied.

Two could play at the Mister game.

"That's correct."

I continued, "And Ms. Horne wanted me to deliver the Buddha to her."

"That seems a fair description of your job, yes."

I rubbed my forehead. I hated how stubborn this jerk was being. "This does seem to be a pretty direct way to get the Buddha."

The plan, of course, wasn't to give the Buddha right to Ms. Horne. She could have it after all the police and the district attorney were done with Rivers, Amini and Vaughn. At the moment, I just needed the money.

"Mr. Cooper, frankly, I don't like repeating myself. I am not going to buy stolen items. I'm not going to allow my client to *accept* stolen items."

I grunted. I stopped at a red light. I had had enough. "How am I supposed to get it?"

"Are you insisting I do your job for you?" he replied as if I was the intern.

That comment disagreed with me. "Well, I suppose I could call the police," I suggested. "Everyone gets arrested, maybe even your client and we can let the police sort it out."

Anton didn't like that idea. His eyes almost popped out of his skull. I waved at him to relax.

Unfortunately for us, Mr. Darling didn't take the bait. "While I'm very well aware of your *personal* relationship with the LAPD, I don't think you'll call anyone. After all, we both know your mentee, your partner, Anton Greene is wanted in connection with the theft. Naughty, naughty, Mr. Cooper. Trying to pull the wool over our eyes."

The light turned green.

Well, *shit*. I didn't like the idea of he and Patricia Horne knowing who Anton was. I didn't know what they might do with that information. Probably use it against me. Like right now.

A car behind us honked. I waved to them and started moving.

"I guess I'll get creative then," I said and hung up before he could give a smarmy response.

"So..." started Anton, "where are you going to get that kind of money?"

I shrugged. "I said we'll get creative. So, we're going to get creative."

An hour later we were in the Valley.

"This money isn't even *real*," said Anton, shaking his head as he held a bundle of hundred-dollar bills. "Like... what the *fuck* are we going to do?"

"It's creative," I replied. "It *could* work."

We stood in the detached garage of an old friend in Magnolia Park.

"How is *this* going to work?" said Anton, now shaking the bundle of hundreds. "These don't even have Franklin's face on them."

My old friend snorted, then said, "Kid, it's illegal to make fake money." Mandy was in her late sixties. She'd greeted us at her front door in a faded tie-dye T-shirt and olive-green cargo shorts, looking a bit like a demented Mrs. Claus with her white-as-snow mullet. She pointed at the bundles. "That's actually me on them." She looked at me. "In my younger days." She chuckled. "Jimmy Smits thought it was funny as hell."

I chuckled too. I couldn't help myself. I had always liked Mandy.

Her garage served as general storage for props she had made over the course of her career that she either kept or lifted when a production was done and everyone was looking the other way.

"Why are you two laughing?" demanded Anton. "This is fucking crazy."

Mandy made a face. "They look real enough," she said. I could tell she didn't like the quality of her work being questioned.

Our call to Mr. Darling had left us with nothing. But if anything, I am a man swimming with ideas. A new plan floated up. And this one needed *props*.

Mandy was an old prop master who had handled a bunch

of network cop shows, lawyer shows and hospital dramas. We had met later in our respective careers. In Hollywood, every one before and behind the camera virtually have the same arc. Some bend short. Some bend long. All of them bend toward the low-budget movie.

"Real enough?" said Anton, less than satisfied.

I put a hand on Mandy's shoulder, trying to cool the situation.

It was about seven years ago when we found ourselves working on a heist picture called *A Sundae in the Valley*. I played a guy named Tommy Sundae, a down on his luck thief with a heart of gold, desperate for cash for his girlfriend's surgery. He puts together a crew to knock over a marijuana dispensary. I was woefully miscast, but the producers needed a "star" to get financing. At that point, my habits were costing the big studios money, so my options for work were limited.

"Yeah, Anton," I replied. "It's not real money. It's good enough for what we need."

Mandy shook her head. "This is what I got. Take it or leave it."

"We'll take it," I said before Anton could object. He tossed the bundles on the rest of the stash, and Mandy shrugged in reply and went inside her house to look for a bag big enough to carry all of the fake money.

Anton stepped in closer as I inspected a shelf full of prop

knives and swords. "Vaughn is — "

I frowned. "Vaughn?"

He sighed. "*Vaughn.*"

"Right. Vaughn." I nodded. "Crenshaw was just a really good name. Memorable."

Anton rolled his eyes. "He is going to take one look at the cash and it'll be over."

I shrugged. "It's going to be dark. He's not going to notice." I picked up a Bowie knife and fingered the rubber blade, bending it.

"What if he *does*?"

"It's touching that you're worried." I tossed the blade back on the shelf, where it landed with a thud. "But this negativity is really bringing me down."

"My *negativity*?"

"You keep pointing out problems, but I don't hear any solutions." I paused. "Do you have two million dollars in cash lying around?"

Anton didn't.

"Well," he said, "you can't go alone. That's just dumb."

That was a good point.

"And you should go armed," he insisted.

"Armed?"

"Yeah, Jimmy. Armed. You know, with a gun."

My face squished. I wasn't much for guns.

"Did someone say guns?" Mandy was back with two big

duffel bags. She dropped the bags and pulled a ring of keys on a necklace from under her T-shirt. She walked to a corner of the garage and unlocked a large, gray metal cabinet. She opened it, revealing a collection of pistols, rifles and semiautomatics.

"Yeah, *that's* what I'm talking about," said Anton, with glee in his voice. He nodded as he got closer to the cabinet.

I cleared my throat. "You realize those are fake guns, right? At most they fire blanks."

Anton turned. "Really?" he said, disappointed.

I turned to Mandy. "Can you throw in a couple of pistols?" Anton wasn't wrong about showing up armed. At least, looking like I was armed.

"Sure, why not?" Mandy answered like she was throwing in floor mats for a car sale. She chose a set of pistols and packed them in the bags with the money. Twenty minutes later, Anton and I dropped the heavy loads into the trunk of my car. Anton nodded to Mandy and got in.

Mandy studied me. "You're looking good, Jimmy."

I paused.

"But you doing OK?" she asked. Her eyes were kind and caring, her rough hands sitting on her hips.

I took a long breath and thought that question through. Most times when you're asked how you're doing, people want to hear that you're fine or good, or at least you make a joke about still surviving. But Mandy here, she'd seen me at some really bad times. She had a daughter who barely survived her own addictions. She was now sober, working up in Portland, and had become a mom herself. So, when Mandy asked, I felt like I really needed to tell her the truth.

"Can't say things have been great, Mandy, but I'm…" I glanced over at Anton sitting in my car. "I don't know what I'm doing. That kid is in trouble and I told him I'd help him. And there's this woman who has a daughter to take care of, and I told her I'd help her. I just keep picking up people and telling them I'd help them. I don't know how to do that. So why am I doing that? What is wrong with me?"

She nodded and gave me a great big bear hug. "Nothing's wrong with you. You're doing the right thing." She let go, putting her hands on my shoulders. "You don't know how much good you have put into the world, Jimmy. You don't know how you're going to help them, but you're doing what you can."

"I could be making it worse."

"Could be." She smiled.

I smiled. "You're the best."

"So are you."

I headed to the car.

"Hey," she said after me. "Am I getting any of this back?"

"I don't know. Do you need it back?"

26

———

Three Years Ago

ANTON STILL LIVED with his mom in View Park, in a postwar home, typical of this part of the neighborhood. We had driven right over after our little conversation with Collins and his partner, Kemble. Gordon ran the bell as I stood next to him, bouncing on the balls of my feet. An electronic tone ding-donged.

"Stop doing that," said Gordon, annoyed but still staring at the door.

"Can't help it. I'm nervous. I've never had to explain to someone that they're the target of a police conspiracy."

Gordon gave me a side look. "Yeah."

"Have you?"

"No." He turned back to the door and rang the bell again. "Really?"

"It's never come up, Jimmy."

The front door jerked open about a foot. Anton stood, blocking our view of the inside. He had a T-shirt on with a rapper's face I didn't recognize, jeans, and Nike slides with white socks. "Hey."

"We need to talk," said Gordon matter-of-factly.

Anton paused. He didn't like the sound of that.

I said, "This would be less weird if we came in."

That snapped him out of it. Anton opened the door wider and stepped back, allowing us in. There wasn't much to the entryway. Dining room to our right, a living room to our left, and the rest of the house in front of us.

"Is your mom home, son?" asked Gordon.

Anton shook his head. "She's at work at the hospital. Not off for another few hours. Something wrong? Should I call her?"

"Oh, you have no idea," I said quietly.

Gordon glared at me.

"Right, right. Don't alarm the client," I said. That was one of the first lessons Gordon tried to instill. Clearly, I was still working on it. I was just so excited, in all the wrong ways.

"Jesus, Jimmy," Gordon mumbled, shaking his head in disappointment.

I put up my hands, trying to slow down this car crash. "It

might not be *that* bad. In some ways, it's good."

"*Jimmy,*" said Gordon, rubbing his head. "Let me handle this."

I looked at Anton and could feel his spirit leaving his body. Gordon gestured to the living room. "Let's sit down."

Anton nodded but didn't move.

"Jimmy, get him a glass of water."

He pointed down the hallway. I huffed, a little resentful that *I* had to get the water but did as I was told and headed to the back of the house. The kitchen was on the corner of the house. A small kitchen table held a cereal bowl with a spoon in it. I could see the last bits of milk. I picked it up and put it in the sink, running some water over it and then I opened the fridge, looking for the bottled water. Which, yeah, my bad, they didn't have any. It took a couple of tries to find the right cabinet with the glasses. I snagged one off the shelf and filled it with water from the tap.

Back in the living room, Anton sat on a worn, dark blue leather recliner. He looked small in it. Gordon sat on the edge of a couch that had lovely floral pattern. I handed Anton the glass and sat next to Gordon.

The living room was well curated with memories. There were pictures of Anton at a variety of ages on the walls and in frames on the side tables. In one, Mrs. Greene embraced Anton as a toddler. In another, a twelve-year-old Anton with the biggest grin stood before an older couple I assumed were his grandparents, everyone wearing their Sunday best. Mrs. Greene and the grandparents stood with Anton as he wore his high school graduation robes, looking embarrassed as his mother kissed him on a cheek. She looked so proud of him, her only child.

Anton drank half of the glass.

"Better?" asked Gordon.

He nodded.

Gordon nodded in return. "Good. First of all, we believe you."

We? I had always believed Anton, but I guess Gordon was representing the firm.

"You had nothing to do with the break-in or the assault."

Anton took a deep breath, looking relieved. "OK. Cool, cool. But...?"

"But," started Gordon, "the reason I believe you is because I'm fairly certain you're being set up."

Anton blinked. "Oh. Shit. Set up?"

"Framed," I said.

Anton looked at me. "Yeah, I know that, man. Thanks." He asked Gordon, "Why me?"

Gordon shook his head. "I don't know yet."

"Do you know *why* this is happening?"

Gordon shook his head.

Anton's hand shook as he drank the rest of the glass of water. He put it down on the coffee table in front of him. "So you know fuck all?" He set his jaw. "I'm going to go to jail."

I could feel Anton's chest tightening. His breath was shallow, and his hands became fists. I wasn't sure who he wanted to hit, and I bet he didn't know either. He just needed to hit something. I scooted back on the couch, just in case.

Gordon put up a hand. "Let's not get ahead of ourselves, OK? Their case is weaker than they want us to believe. That's why there's the pressure for you to take the plea. I just need you to hold on."

Anton's eyes flicked to mine. I nodded. Anton agreed.

Gordon took out his phone, unlocked it. "Do you recognize either of these people?" He handed it to Anton, who looked at the DMV pictures of Chad Lane and Debi Holt. He rolled his eyes, shook his head. "I've already said it. To the cops. To Ms. Cooper. I don't *know* those people. I've never, ever seen them." He handed the phone back.

"That's fine, that's just fine," said Gordon. He slid the photos aside, bringing up a new one on his phone. "What about him?" He showed Anton a picture of Jerry Collins.

"That's the asshole who arrested me."

"You ever see him before?"

"First time I ever saw him was when he came through that door," he said, pointing to the front door.

Gordon nodded and slid the photo away, bringing up a new one, this one of Kemble. It was not flattering. I can't imagine that dude ever took a good photo. He had no good angles.

Anton look again. "Yeah, man. That's the first guy's partner."

"You ever see him before?"

He looked again, leaning forward. Getting frustrated, he shook his head and said, "I don't know. Maybe? He's an old white guy. A fucking cop."

"It's important," I said.

"What do you want from me?" said Anton. "I'll say whatever."

Gordon shook his head. "I don't want you to say whatever. I want you to tell me the truth."

"Anton," I said, "this is Detective Kemble. He arrested you a couple of years ago."

Anton stopped. He blinked. "He...? Give me the phone." Gordon handed it to him. He peered at it. "Maybe, yeah...?"

"No. Definitely. I read the report," I said.

"And you remember that guy's name?" asked Anton.

I nodded. "I have a tendency to memorize things I've read. Useful when you're handed new pages right before you're supposed to shoot a scene and Spielberg's not just going to wait."

Gordon and Anton stared at me. Truth be told, I had never worked for Spielberg. The closest I ever got was working on a film he was credited as "Executive Producer," and that was because he owned the underlying IP. Credits, man.

"It doesn't matter. The point is, he arrested you. Which means he also searched you."

Anton's face fell. "I remember that guy. It was, like, six months ago. Me and some friend, we were having a good night. Feeling good, you know what I mean?"

Gordon and I both knew what he meant.

"It was getting late, we wanted to crash, and a friend offered his place. We headed over there, but the cops got the street blocked off. Their squad cars are lit up, the stupid yellow tape. They tell us to turn around. We're like, 'We just wanna go home.'" Anton shook his head, shrugging, like it shouldn't have been a big deal. "One of the cops, *he* calls over that detective." He pointed at Gordon's phone. "He gets all upset. 'It's a crime scene,' he says to us. Like, all of L.A. is a crime scene at one point or another. We just wanted to go home. That asshole decides to arrest us."

"He searched you," said Gordon, confirming.

"Yeah, he searched us. Took everything out of our pockets. Bagged all our shit up. Booked us and everything. Had to let us go because the charges were shit."

"You got everything back?" I asked.

Anton shook his head slowly. "Nah, man. They kept my money. Some bullshit because they found some weed on us, so they could keep the cash. It might be 'drug money' or something. Bullshit."

I looked at Gordon. "That's where the evidence came from. Right out of the evidence locker."

Gordon's jaw muscles twitched. He took a breath. "You said this happened six months ago. What'd your hair look like?"

Anton touched his hair. I could see the beginnings of black roots in the blond. "Just like this," he said. A lot like what the witness had seen.

Gordon and I assured Anton that everything would be OK, and we left him. I didn't think Anton was exactly assured, but I guess we had places to go. As we stepped outside, I slipped on my sunglasses and followed Gordon to the car. "So Collins and Kemble planted the evidence. Kemble's the one who pinned Anton for it?"

Gordon beeped the car open.

"What do we do?" I asked.

"We keep our eyes open; someone's going to make a stupid mistake."

27

MOE STEPPED OUT of the changing room, dressed head to toe in black. Black suit, black shirt, and a black tie. I leaned against the wall, admiring its perfect fit. I hated him for it.

"How do I look?" he asked.

"You look great," I replied without enthusiasm.

He held his hands up to his chest. He was annoyed. "That doesn't sound like I look great."

I rolled my eyes and pushed myself away from the wall. "Moe, we're not walking a red carpet here. We're going to exchange fake money for stolen goods." I took a breath. "You just need to look the part of my bodyguard."

He spread his arms. "That doesn't mean I can't look *good*." He wagged a finger. "Just because I'm muscle doesn't mean I can't dress well."

Vaughn had texted as we were heading back over the hills. He had set a time and place for the exchange. It would be up in the Hollywood Hills at eleven. Anton was right, I couldn't go alone. The bags alone were too heavy for one person to carry. I explained to Anton I couldn't use him because Vaughn would recognize him. I called Moe and he was game. A little too game, as it turned out. He suggested we meet at the Beverly Center, a mall just on the east side of Beverly Hills that sits atop a parking garage. You can't miss it.

I took a breath. "Fine. It's *perfect*. Better?"

"You *could* do more."

I put my hands on my hips. "Do we really have to do that?"

He clasped his hands together at his waist. He set his jaw.

I nodded. "OK. Yeah. You look tough. Real tough."

He sparkled then, saying, "I do, don't I? Sometimes you have to butch it up to survive. And you *never* forget how to wear the beard, you know what I mean?"

I think I did.

Moe turned to the mirror again, straightening his jacket, flicking off imaginary lint from the sleeve. "If Tommy from my senior year of high school could see me now." He grinned.

"This is serious, Moe."

I was still debating if this was a great idea. Even though he had agreed to it, with all of the caveats of injury and even death, I wasn't thrilled. I did not want my best friend to get killed. Thinking about it, a little pit opened in my stomach.

He turned to me. "I know, honey. And I'm good. I have your back." The smile returned. "Besides, this is the most exciting thing I've done since I went on a double date with Alan Cumming." He paused. "You did *not* hear that from me."

"Like always, Moe, I will take your secrets to the grave."

He pointed at me. "Very good. Should I have a name?"

I shook my head. "You do not need a name. I know you have my back, but, you don't have to do come with me."

"I do, though." He paused. "What about José?"

I shook my head again. "You *don't*. And I'm *not* going to call you José."

He waved his finger. "It's not up for discussion. I'm going. *And* are you telling me that this client/bodyguard relationship is so toxic you don't even use my name?"

"OK, fine," I said. "Choose a name. Just not José. That feels cliché and a bit racist."

"My *uncle's* name is José."

Well, *shit*. "Fine. That's your name. But I'm not going to say it."

That settled, Moe popped back into the changing room. Moments later he was out in his light coral sweater and gray slacks. We headed to the registers. Moe looked at me as I paid for the suit, the shirt and the tie. Once they were folded and bagged, Moe thanked the young woman behind the counter. On the way out, he said "Now I need shoes."

"I'm not buying you shoes," I said as I headed to the elevator banks.

Following, Moe looked at me, eyebrows raised. "Jimmy. José needs new shoes."

"He does not." I looked down. "Those are fine."

"These are *loafers*."

"And they are great."

Moe shook his head. "They are great, but they are brown. They can't go with a black suit, Jimmy."

Of course, yeah, he was right. Brown shoes, black suit. Gross. Nevertheless... "Moe, I don't know if they're still watching my place. You took a chance coming here. We're not going back and I'm not buying shoes. Can we just stop with the games and take this seriously?"

Moe thought about it while I pushed the elevator button.

"You're right, Jimmy. José will just have to be a fashion disaster." The elevator door opened. "It should be fine. Just as long as I don't have to do any running."

We stepped inside and I pressed the button to go up a level to the Starbucks where we had left Anton.

"There won't be any running," I said. "Probably. Maybe. The plan is to *not* have any running."

The doors opened, and the Starbucks was right there. Anton was inside, sitting in the furthest corner from the entrance, nursing a cup of coffee. He spotted us and started standing up. I waved for him to sit down. He did, looking around.

"Everything OK?" I asked as I sat down.

He nodded, giving a slight shrug. "Yeah, yeah. It feels weird to be so public when the cops are looking for you." Anton nodded toward Moe. "You good?"

"I'm great."

"What's the plan?" Anton asked as he looked at the shopping bag now in Moe's lap.

Moe looked at me. "You didn't talk to him about it?"

Anton gave me the eye. "Talk to me about *what*?"

I shifted in my seat. It wasn't my plan to talk to Anton about it *now*. I had planned on talking to him when he couldn't really object. "First, we're going to take you back to my mom's place. Then, Moe and I are going to meet with Vaughn."

Anton's eyes shifted back and forth between us. "No, you're not."

"Anton," I started to explain.

He shook his head. "No, no. Uh-huh. You're going to need me. We're a team."

I nodded. "Anton, I'm trying to keep you safe. We're literally going to be with a person who has participated in the deaths of two men" — I checked my watch — "like forty-eight hours ago. So can we just skip this back-and-forth. I've already had one with him." I pointed to Moe.

"Not cute," said Moe.

"I'm not trying to be cute," I said. "I'm trying to make a point."

"You can keep your points," Anton said. "Because I'm going."

I closed my eyes and shook my head. "You'll stay in the car?"

Anton frowned. "Well, *yeah*. Vaughn'll probably shoot me if he sees me."

28

THAT NIGHT, WE wound up into the Hollywood Hills listening to ELO's "Can't Get It Out of My Head." As I drove, I ran through the possibilities of what might happen, from the best — Vaughn is super nice and the exchange is just like ordering a latte at my favorite coffee shop, easy peasy — to the worst — Vaughn shoots me and Moe, keeps the Buddha *and* the money. Hah, jokes on him.

We passed the location, a home under heavy renovation. It looked like the owners had gutted the place, down to the studs. The lot was wrapped with a chain-link fence with green fabric to discourage the very thing we were going to do. The place was dark, lit by the ambient light around us. I parked the car to the side of the narrow street and turned it off. I took a breath and said to Moe, "You ready?"

He straightened his tie and put on his "beard," toughening up and dropping some grit in his voice. "Ready."

I pulled my keys out of the ignition and turned to face Anton in the back seat. "If we're not back in ten minutes, call the police, and get the hell out of here."

"I don't have a phone. I threw it away."

I nodded, remembering that little detail. "I'll leave mine." I handed him my phone.

"And I'll need your keys."

I looked at him.

"How am I gonna get out of here without them? Run?" he said.

I sheepishly handed him the keys. "Ten minutes."

Anton agreed.

Moe and I stepped out of the car and headed to the back. I popped the trunk. Inside were two very large, very heavy bags.

Moe reached in and unzipped one of them. He took a breath. "Wow."

"What?" I looked at him and then the bag.

"I've never seen so much cash."

"It's not real, Moe."

He looked at me. "Well, yeah. But still. It's a lot of money."

I reached into the trunk and zipped the bag closed. "Can we go now?"

"Touchy." He grinned. "It's probably why you never use my name."

I shook my head and grabbed a bag with a grunt. Moe lugged the other one out of the car. I dropped mine on the ground and shut the trunk, then we headed downhill to the house.

I took a look back at my car and Anton. He gave me a thumbs up.

We found the gate halfway down the fence. Vaughn had done us a solid and unlocked it, leaving the chain hanging to make it look like it was still closed to trespassing, which we promptly did.

We headed up a gravel path to what would become the house's front door. By the width of it, it looked like it was going to be one of those classy double doors. The home looked like it was going to have an open floor plan, or maybe that was just its current lack of walls. Off to the right, through the exterior wall, I could see the most amazing view of L.A. I paused to get a look. It's magical. The city was made of stars and stretched out forever.

I could see why someone would want to live in this house.

"You're prompt. I like that," said a voice in the darkness.

It sounded like it had come from the back of the house. I strained to see.

"I was taught the importance of being on time," I said, taking a step forward.

Moe stopped me. I glanced at him. He was taking his role a little too seriously.

"Out back. By the pool," said the voice.

We passed through the house and stepped outside. Construction materials were piled around an empty pool well. And there he was, standing on the other side of the pool — the man I assumed was Vaughn. He was dressed in a gray hoodie with black pants and black boots. A backpack was slung from his shoulder.

I took a breath. This was one of the moments we had been working toward.

"Fancy seeing you here," I said, maybe a little too cheerfully for this particular context.

Vaughn frowned. His eyes twitched to Moe.

"Who's this?"

I dropped my bag at my feet. "Oh, this is my... he's my man. My... guy."

"José," said Moe, his voice gravelly.

"Right. He's my guard. The guy that looks out for me in these kinds of situations." I shut up. My nerves were getting the best of me. I smiled. Then I stopped smiling. Why did I smile?

Vaughn inspected me, looking me up and down. "This is the money?"

I pointed at the bags. "Yep. It is the money," I assured him. Moe put his on the ground. "Is that the Buddha?"

He nodded.

No one moved. This wasn't how I had thought it was going to go. In all the ways I had thought how this was going to go, awkward silence was not one of them.

I started to sweat. My mouth felt dry. My heart thumped in my chest. I started thinking about last summer, how *that* exchange had gone wrong and here I had dragged Moe into this.

"Are you listening?" said Vaughn.

"Huh?"

"I said bring the money over here."

That would be a bad idea. I didn't need him looking that carefully at it. Even without light, there was enough natural light that he'd see Franklin was missing from the bills.

When I didn't comply, Vaughn reached behind his back and pulled a gun.

This was not the first time I had a gun pointed at me. It comes with the trade, and yet it remains terrifying. It's my least favorite part of the work. Zero out of five stars. Would not recommend. Thumbs down.

I put up my hands. Moe did as well, revealing one of Mandy's pistols in his waistband.

Vaughn pulled back the hammer of his gun.

"OK, right. No need to escalate the situation," I said, licking my lips, trying to get my mouth to stop feeling so dry. "We got the money, you have the Buddha. Let's just make the exchange."

Vaughn moved around the pool, keeping an eye on both Moe and me.

"You do have it, right?" I asked.

Vaughn stopped. "Yeah, I fucking have it. That's why we're here."

"OK, OK," I replied. "I was just checking you *have* it. You were there when it was stolen?"

His eyes locked in on me.

"I just want to know that it's the genuine article. I'll be in a lot of trouble if I bring back a fake."

Vaughn took a moment. "Yeah. I was there. It's the real thing."

"Great," I said.

He raised an eyebrow. "Are we doing this thing?"

"Oh yeah." I pointed at the bags. "We're doing the thing."

He had taken another step closer when I said, "You were there when the man got shot?"

Vaughn stopped.

"I'm just curious what happened."

He tightened his grip on his pistol. "You're curious?"

There wasn't much in my mouth to swallow, but somehow I managed it. "Yeah," I said. "Morbid curiosity."

Vaughn shook his head. "I don't have time for your curiosity." He took a step.

"It's not mine. It's my boss's."

He took this in. "I don't give a shit." He waved his gun. "Step away from the bags."

"Can I put my hands down?" I asked. "I'm tired of holding them up."

Vaughn nodded. I put my hands down. Moe started to move. "Not you, tough guy. I want your hands far from your weapon," he said, pointing his gun at him.

A look of satisfaction shimmered over Moe's face at being called tough.

"I'm just looking for some information," I said. "Like, what happened? I got some sense. You wanted more. Guns came out. And then…"

The gun moved back to me. "What the fuck? Are you like a cop or something?"

"No, no, no," I said.

"Not cops," growled Moe.

I rolled my head to him and gave him the eye. I turned back to Vaughn. "Must be hard, losing a partner."

That threw him. The gun dipped a little. Was it guilt? Maybe. I decided to push a little harder; after all, the truth needed to come out. "Whose idea was it to ask for more?"

Vaughn swallowed. Now his mouth was dry.

"Seraphina told me that you both found out it was worth much more than you were told. That you were being underpaid."

Vaughn licked his lips, trying to figure out what to do.

Probably he was debating whether or not to answer my questions or just shoot me. He had been a soldier, that's a little different than being a murderer.

"Did things get out of hand?" I asked. "When you tried to renegotiate?"

"I'm just here for the money."

I shrugged. "Two million dollars, that should buy a little bit of information."

Vaughn walked the rest of the way around the pool. He stood about five feet away from me. Close enough that he would not miss and far enough away I couldn't grab his gun. "Yeah. Things got out of hand when we asked for what's fair."

I nodded.

"Who shot first?"

Devon must've stood in between the two groups. He was in the crossfire.

Vaughn paused. "I did."

But that was a lie. He was *lying* to me. Why would he lie?

He pulled the backpack off his shoulder and set it on the ground. "I'm done. Here's your Buddha."

Vaughn really was done answering my questions. Nothing left but to collect the Buddha and then call Ito. I walked forward slowly, reached down and unzipped the bag. Inside, wrapped in bubble wrap, was the Buddha, about a foot high and nine or so inches wide. I re-zipped the backpack and picked it up. It was about five pounds. And all of it worth millions.

"Thanks," I said. "Nice doing business with you." I nodded to Moe to head back.

We started walking back into the house. I heard Vaughn move to the bags.

I took a breath. I turned to Moe. "Remember when I said there would be no running. I was wrong. Run."

Vaughn shouted, "What the *fuck is this*?"

Moe and I were running through what was going to be a fine living room when the gunshots started. The wood studs splintered around us.

We were through the nonexistent doors as Vaughn got off a few more rounds. At the gate, Moe went through first and I followed, looping the chain through the chain-link fence behind, hoping that would slow Vaughn down.

Vaughn cursed as he followed us down through the house and down the path.

As we ran up the street, I could hear the chain-link fence rattle.

Breathing hard, getting closer to the car, I dug in my pants for my keys. Where were my keys? Where were —

Anton sat in the driver's seat.

I got to the window. "What are you doing?" I shouted. I could hear music. And it was loud. "Don't Leave Me This Way." Thelma Houston. Great song.

"What's going on?" asked Anton, concerned as he turned down the music.

Moe jumped into the passenger seat.

Another gunshot answered his question.

"Oh, *shit*!" shouted Anton.

"Yeah, shit!" I said. "Get out of my seat!"

"Get *in*," demanded Anton, pointing to the back. He started the car.

"Jimmy!" said Moe. "*Get in the car.*"

I was about to point out the fact that Anton was in *my* seat when a bullet ricocheted off the blacktop near my feet.

"Fuck, fuck, fuck!" I grabbed the back door and hopped in. "Go!"

Anton stomped on the gas, cranked the wheel, turning the car around, and headed back toward the house. Vaughn was walking toward us, gun raised. He got off another round before diving out of the way of my speeding Toyota.

29

———

I BRACED MYSELF in the back seat. I pushed one hand into the ceiling while the other pressed against the back of the driver's seat. Eyes wide, I tried to keep breathing as Anton raced the car down the narrow road. My car's engine whined as he took the curves, barely avoiding parked cars.

If I wasn't in fear for my life and car, I would've been impressed. "You don't have to prove anything!" I shouted.

Anton gripped the wheel and dropped into his shoulders. Down North Gower Street, we were at the bottom of the Hills, coming onto the intersection with Franklin Avenue. My car blew through the stoplight, and Anton took a hard right. I slammed against the door, Moe yelped, and my poor little car screamed through the horns and cars screeching to a halt.

I looked back. I didn't see anyone.

"OK, OK, slow down! There's no one behind us!"

I grabbed the seat belt and fastened in.

There was a gunshot.

Correction: A pickup truck screeched through the intersection, making a right and falling into place behind us.

"I mean faster! Go faster!" I shouted and held onto the backpack like it was my unbuckled child.

Agreeing, Moe pointed frantically down the street.

Franklin Avenue went under the 101 as Anton spent more time in the wrong lane than in the right one. I glanced back. The truck was getting closer. An arm stuck out of its window, holding a pistol.

A couple more rounds were fired in our direction.

My back window shattered.

"Holy fuck!" I screamed.

Anton made a left onto Cahuenga Boulevard, just missing a Mini Cooper that was pulling into the intersection. I was thrown against the belt as the backpack wanted to fly out of my hands. "Shit, shit, shit."

Car chases are the worst.

I looked out the driver's side and saw the Capital Records Building, like a stack of records, perfectly framed. I sat up, brushing glass off of myself and peeked out the back.

The truck felt like it was getting closer, and — did I hear police sirens?

We crossed over Hollywood Boulevard at one of its more boring intersections. Besides the obligatory souvenir shop, there was a Popeye's and a place that would sell you a New York style slice of pizza. Even the Walk of Fame wasn't super exciting. The kids weren't demanding to see Rex Harrison's and George Cukor's stars, you know?

And even though it was a Thursday night, traffic was picking up for the clubbers and bar goers. Anton weaved, dipping in and out of oncoming traffic. He really *was* good at this. If I had any doubts before, I finally got why Devon used him as a driver. Moe kept yelping from his front-row seat, and I kept breathing in through my nose and out through my mouth.

I heard a roar and glanced back. The truck lurched at us, ramming my car, throwing it forward. I gripped the bag and my seat belt snapped tight, but Anton kept us on the road. The sirens were closer now.

As we approached Sunset, Moe covered his eyes. A red light was waiting for us, and traffic was moving east and west on Sunset. Anton took a deep breath. Even though I was buckled in, I braced myself.

Cars jammed on their brakes as Anton wove through, missing everything.

Vaughn chose chaos, clipping a Hyundai and spinning

it as he followed in hot pursuit, sending glass and metal flying into the air. His truck kept on going. Police cars finally showed up, making their way carefully through the intersection.

"Anton," I said, breathing quickly.

"I see them!" he said, glancing into the rearview mirror. We took a sharp right and I was pulled to the left as we barely missed some oncoming traffic.

"We can't keep doing this!" I shouted.

Moe agreed. Anton looked around.

The truck bumped us again — oh, my precious car — and we spun. Anton corrected, and we zoomed south. Another police cruiser came at us from the left, from De Longpre Avenue. Anton turned and went behind the cop car and the pickup smashed into the cruiser's tail.

Anton took advantage of that slowdown and turned right onto Fountain. It was at that point I remembered a bad joke: How do you get to Hollywood. Take Fountain. It's terrible and it's oh so L.A. because it's a traffic joke.

Anton took a quick left onto a residential street, followed by another right.

The sirens quieted, but I started hearing the thumping of the helicopter. The LAPD were not going to give up on us that easy.

I looked out the back again. I didn't see Vaughn's truck.

Anton slammed on the brakes, bringing my car to a

complete stop and throwing me against the seat belt again.

"Are you done?" I asked, fumed.

"We have to ditch the car," Anton announced.

"What?"

He backed up to the front of a home and swung the car into the driveway. "Let's go," he said, giving no further explanation.

Moe followed him out of the car.

"We can't just leave my car," I shouted from the back seat.

Anton looked in through where the rear window had been. "The cops will *find* this car. We can't drive around in it anymore."

"But this is my baby," I pleaded.

Moe said simply, "Jimmy, it's time to go."

They were right, of course. I grabbed the Buddha and got out.

We walked away, heading toward Santa Monica Boulevard. Just three friends walking in the night, with a stolen, priceless artifact.

"We can't walk home," said Moe.

He was right, of course. But this was a world filled with solutions. I pulled out my cell phone.

Ten minutes later, a car pulled up to the corner where we stood.

A white guy in his sixties, wearing thick glasses and a blue-purple windbreaker, leaned toward an open window.

"Uber for Jimmy?"

I nodded to him. Anton and Moe took the back seat, leaving me up front, holding the literal bag.

The driver started up. "Hey, guys," he said to all of us, "how's your night going?"

I mumbled something about it being fine, that we had had dinner, and no, no, we weren't tourists, just didn't want to deal with driving. I kept my answers short so as not to encourage conversation. Eventually he got the hint and stopped talking.

I clutched the bag close to my chest, feeling relieved that it had survived intact. I couldn't believe it had worked. Well, mostly worked. If the goal was to have in my hands on the Buddha so we could turn it over to the police and ignoring all of the collateral damage, then, yeah, total win.

Maybe things were going to work out.

About thirty-five minutes later, we rolled up just past my mom's house. We got out of the car and I slung the backpack on my shoulder as the driver rolled away. I gave him five stars and a 20 percent tip. I did a quick look around, to ensure there was no one watching us on my mother's street. It looked all clear and we made our way up the driveway in silence. We hadn't said anything to each other on the drive, and we still didn't feel like talking. The adrenaline had worn off and I was hungry. Maybe there was still some takeout left.

I rang the doorbell.

Erika opened the front door, framed in the light from the entryway.

Not who I expected, nor had I been prepared to see her. Not after what I had said to her last night.

"Hi," I said.

She nodded. "Hi."

Awkward.

I peeked inside. "Where's mom?"

"She had an event."

"She had an event?"

"Yes. It was on her calendar."

As if I've been paying attention to calendars.

"People do things, Jimmy," she said. Then her eyes caught something behind us. She went pale.

I turned, as did Anton and Moe.

Walking up the driveway was Violet Ito, my cop girlfriend, her badge hung around her neck. "Hi, Jimmy."

30

WE WERE WAITING for someone to make a stupid mistake. Well, *I* was. Gordon was off doing something he didn't want me to know about. I sat quietly in my car watching Chad and Debi's house. Gordon thought music was a distraction, whereas I thought silence was a form of torture. But he had been doing this longer than I had, so maybe he knew better.

My car was close enough to keep my eyes on Chad and Debi, far enough to not be so obvious. The point, after all, was to give them enough space to let their guard down and do something stupid.

Gordon was a great believer in the stupidity of criminals. He felt they were criminals because they were inherently stupid. Even the well-educated ones. *Especially* the well-educated ones. He felt it was safer and easier to make money legally. "I'm not talking ethically," he said. "Go out and be a real estate asshole. You might not make as much, but then you're not risking a jail sentence either."

Me, on the other hand, I couldn't see these people as just stupid. People make choices for all kinds of reasons and reasoning. It wasn't because of stupidity that I turned to drugs and drinking, both of which I knew were "wrong." I needed something — anything — so I could take the edge off of the shit I was dealing with. And I was a bright kid. Precocious. Sharp as a tack (as the olds might say). And I knew that if I had handled my problems the "right way" — finding a grown-up who would believe me — I'd most likely have been labeled as difficult to work with, told that no one likes a tattletale, and pushed out of the industry. And then I'd lose everything.

And yes, the irony doesn't escape me.

So it wasn't stupidity that had driven me to my mistakes; it was fucking *pride*. My ego was at stake. My very sense of self. I *loved* being an actor, and I was good at it. I believed I could handle everything — the good and the bad — and get to keep everything. The problem was, when things started to go wrong, I doubled down on my plan of booze and pills. Things might've been OK if I had been able to let go of who I thought I needed to be— Jimmy Cooper, movie star — and face who I was: a kid in trouble.

Criminals aren't criminals because they're dumb. They're criminals because they think they're going to get away with it. Pride. Ego. And if Gordon understood that better —

Chad stormed out of his place, a gym bag over his shoulder, but he wasn't exactly dressed for the gym in his jeans, combat boots, and a sweatshirt. I grabbed my camera, zooming in on the action just as Debi came roaring out of the house, still in her jean shorts and bikini top. She had a few choice words for Chad. I could see how mad she was, but I couldn't hear what she was saying. He turned and yelled back. She reached for the bag and yanked it off his shoulder. The bag plopped on the ground, and because it wasn't zipped, bundles of cash spilled onto their front lawn.

OK, I was beginning to entertain the idea that stupidity did have a role to play. Why didn't you zip your bag, Chad?

I snapped more frames as he kneeled to scoop the money back into the bag while he and Debi continued to argue. She crossed her arms and shook her head as she yelled. He kept looking up at her, trying to get in a word. Once he had, he stood and beeped his car open.

As he was heading to his car, I finally heard her. "They will *kill* you, Chad!" she shouted before turning on her heel and flying back into the house, slamming the door shut behind her.

Oh, shit. Who was going to kill Chad? Why were they

going to kill Chad? And why was he going to people who were going to *kill him*? Chad, what are you doing?

His car started up, so I started mine and began following. I was sweating. This was the first time I had ever followed someone on my own. I tried to remember what Gordon had told me.

My phone started to ring. I glanced at the caller ID. Gordon Bixby.

I poked the phone and shouted at it. "Where are you, Gordon!?"

"Hey, hey, don't be snapping at me. I've been working," he replied, his voice tinny out of the speaker.

"Sure, sure," I said. What did he say about following? "Listen, I need to ask your advice about something." I said it quickly. Adrenaline was kicking in.

"Slow down, slow down. First I need to catch you up."

"What?"

"I have news," said Gordon. "It's important."

Chad stopped at a stop sign. I slowed down; I didn't want to stop right behind him.

"OK, yeah, but I really think I need — "

"Kemble called me."

Chad turned left.

"He wanted to meet," said Gordon.

"Meet? And you didn't bring me?" I paused at the stop sign and then kept after Chad. Was I doing this right? "I have a question — ”

"This is not the time to make this about you, Jimmy."

Not the time?

"It's not about *me*," I said. "Well, *it is*. But not in that way."

"Kemble's throwing Collins under the bus."

We were on Silver Lake Boulevard, heading south. Was he heading for the 101? OK, you can do this, Jimmy. "Gordon?" I said. "There's something you need to know."

"He's a good cop, Jimmy. Or, at least, good enough. Told me things about Collins that made him real uncomfortable. Collins has gotten a little more flashier in his spending recently."

"Oh?"

"Kemble also told me that Collins got real interested when he said something to him about Anton matching the description the witness gave. A little too interested."

"Uh-huh." I saw Chad going through the light and turning onto the 101, heading north. I gunned it to make sure I'd make it through, coming very close to the Subaru in front of me.

"Are you listening to me?" asked Gordon, annoyed.

"Yes, *but* — ”

"Jimmy, Kemble checked the evidence logs from when he arrested Anton. The cash is gone."

What did he say? I made it to the ramp just as Chad reached the top, ready to merge onto the highway. Traffic was thick as we were still in the middle of rush hour, so he wasn't going to get too far ahead of me.

"OK, so Kemble's going to the assistant DA, right?" I said, hoping I had heard him. "So I don't even have to do this thing with Chad."

"Kemble's not going to talk to anyone. He's stuck his neck out as far as he's going to on... *What* thing with Chad?"

"Chad's going somewhere with a bag full of money."

There was silence on my phone. I was five cars behind Chad. At least, I hoped I was. The sun was beginning to set and was in my eyes.

"He's going *where* with *what?*"

"He's got a bag of money. He's... I don't know. Paying someone off. Returning it. What does one do with a bag of money, Gordon?"

"Oh, shit."

"Yes, *shit.*"

It must've been bad. Gordon rarely cursed.

"Well, where is he now?"

I looked, trying to see past the cars in front of me. I saw an opportunity and darted into the lane to my left only to be greeted with a car horn. I moved a couple of cars ahead and darted back into the right lane.

"He's three cars ahead of me on the 101. We're heading north."

"You're following him?"

"I thought that was a good idea, Gordon. I'm trying to find out what stupid thing Chad is up to."

"Good man, Jimmy. Good man."

Was that… was that *praise*?

"Text me when he gets to wherever he's going. Just observe."

I promised I would. He hung up and I realized I had forgotten to ask how to tail someone. But by then, I decided I was doing a good enough job that I wasn't going to call Gordon back.

Chad put on his blinker. He was going to exit. I was glad he was a conscientious driver. I flipped on my blinker, too. He took the exit off the 101 toward Wilton Place. Only one car separated us, so I scrunched down in my seat, hoping that would work as a disguise if he looked back. He didn't.

Where was he *going*?

On Wilton, he turned left onto Sunset and then took a quick right into the parking lot of a Home Depot and I followed. Chad crossed the parking lot toward a ramp that led to more parking above the store.

As he headed up, I paused at the bottom of the ramp, wondering if he would be suspicious. I decided, no, Chad is the most unsuspicious criminal I have ever met, and headed on up.

Most of the cars were gathered closer to the elevators down to the store, but I saw Chad heading toward the western edge of the parking deck. I found a spot about halfway there, mixed in with the other cars. I grabbed my camera.

Chad parked. Empty spots were all around him. Four spots to the left and six spots to the right, two other cars were also parked. Out of the Mercedes on the left stepped Jerry Collins.

31

——

ITO SAT AT one end of my mother's dinning room table, just off the kitchen, in the spot where my mother usually sat. It had taken some convincing not to arrest us all right at the front door. She had refused to take off the coat I had given her, saying she wasn't planning on staying. That wasn't a great sign.

But the fact that she *hadn't* arrested us was *maybe* a good sign.

Erika had taken her normal seat, just to Ito's left. Moe was next to Erika. Anton sat at the other end of the table, as far as he could be from Ito. Well, not as far as me. I stood behind him. I didn't like the way Violet was glaring at me, arms crossed.

In between us sat the Buddha. I had taken it out of the bag, removing the bubble wrap Vaughn had swaddled the statue in. It was just under twelve inches high, and I wasn't sure if Louis LaFontaine was right about the glazes. They were... nice. Moe wasn't impressed, said he'd found better at World Market. But there the statue was, all priceless and shit, sitting crosslegged, eyes closed with the most serene smile on his face. I wished there was more of that vibe in the dining room.

My girlfriend broke the silence.

"Jimmy," said Ito, lacing her fingers together on the table, "I think it's best if I bring you, Anton and the Buddha in."

I pointed at my watch. "Technically, we're still in the 24 hours you gave me."

Her face twisted. "Mm. The car chase through Hollywood ruined that deal. You've escalated the situation. The DA is *pissed*. Collins wants to take charge of everything. You're lucky it was *me* who was outside your mother's house." She shook her head.

I put my hand to my chest and spoke honestly. "Listen, I would be touched if you were the one to arrest me."

Anton shook his head, exasperated.

Ito wagged her finger. "This isn't funny, Jimmy."

"Maybe not, but..." I started.

Ito leaned back, putting her hands in her lap. Her head tilted, and an eyebrow raised. This was her "get on with it" look. I got that look a lot. It meant I was testing her patience. I got it when I went on and on about a movie and its production or some such trivia. It meant I was running out of time before she was going to make a decision.

"I think you don't want to take us in."

Ito's head straightened. "Oh, no. I very much want to take you in."

"If you did, Violet, you would have," I said.

Erika looked at Ito, worried.

Ito put her hands on the table and stood. "You've made up my mind, Jimmy. I'm going to arrest you. All of you."

That's not how I thought this would go.

Moe pointed at himself, as if to say, "Me?"

"Yes, Moe, including you. You *did* break some laws tonight."

"What if I just said I was sorry?" he asked.

Ito snapped, "It doesn't work like that."

"Maybe," I suggested, "we ignore Moe's involvement in this."

"Ignore?" asked Ito. "I can't ignore that."

"He didn't do much," I said.

Moe shook his head. "I was a key player."

Erika gave him quizzical look. Moe nodded.

Ito wasn't having it, though. "He's involved now, Jimmy." She shook her head. "Maybe they won't prosecute. Maybe he can be a witness."

"I'm a great witness."

"Moe!" snapped Erika. He nodded again, locked his mouth, and threw away the key.

Ito looked at me. "If you had come to me — "

"I couldn't come to you — "

"As soon as this started — "

"You guys would've have arrested Anton."

She nodded. "If you had come to me when you *had* something."

"I have stuff. I have stuff now," I replied, pointing at the Buddha.

"This is the thing that was stolen. Do you have evidence of the other people involved?"

I looked at Anton. I looked back at her. "Not evidence evidence. Yes, we have the Buddha. But we don't have the people. And we can get them."

"Which people?" asked Ito.

I licked my lips. "I don't want to say. Yet. I *will*. Just... you know. Later."

"What?"

Given how this conversation was going, I wasn't sure I wanted to give up any names. Those names were my only leverage.

Anton looked at me. "Maybe the Buddha is enough. We got that back."

"No, *no*. That wasn't the plan, Anton," I said. My heart was thumping in my chest. I was sweating, and it was getting hard to breathe. I said to Ito, "I just want to do this right. I don't want them to get away with it." Again. I didn't say it, but it rattled around in my head. I didn't want these rich people to get away with it *again*. Like they had with Matty. I didn't want to blow the job this close to the end.

Ito looked to Erika and then to me. "Jimmy," she insisted. "Who?"

"I'm not going to tell you."

Erika cleared her throat. "What he means to say — "

"Don't do that," I said. "Don't *fix* what I said."

The room was beginning to narrow.

Erika put up a hand and said to Ito, "Jimmy has everything, but he wants to — "

"Erika. Stop it. I told her what I said."

"I'm just *clarifying*."

"I don't need you to."

Erika huffed. "I'm trying to protect you."

"I don't *need* it. I got this."

Ito shook her head. She said to me, "I don't think that you do."

I stared angrily at Violet. I took a sharp breath.

"Fuck it."

I turned on my heel and walked out of the dining room. I could hear Moe and Erika and Violet call after me, but I didn't stop. I stalked through the kitchen and then out into the backyard.

The air was cool and moist, and I took it in through my nose in great gulps and out through my mouth. The half moon lit the backyard, and I could make out Mom's landscaping. She took a lot of pride in it. If there was one thing she might call a hobby, it was her gardening.

I rubbed my hands together, pacing, trying to get myself under control. I was embarrassed and feeling stupid. What was I doing?

"Jimmy?" It was Erika. She had a glass of water in her hand, offering it to me.

I grabbed it and emptied it. I took another deep breath.

"That was some, uh, drama," she said.

"Was there? I hardly noticed as I stormed out." I handed her the empty glass.

She nodded, rubbing an arm. If I hadn't been freaking out, I would've noticed it was more than a little chilly outside.

"What happened in there?" she asked.

"Nothing *happened*," I replied. "I just... I needed some fresh air."

She nodded. "You know I can always tell when you're lying."

I gave her some side-eye. "It's the world's worst superpower."

"Yeah, well, it's a pretty good one right now." She paused. "What is going on with you, Jimmy?"

Rather than answering, I kicked up some grass. Mom would not like that.

"You haven't been you in, like… months."

"Oh, I know. You keep reminding me," I said, a bit of acid trickling into my tone.

She put a hand up. "OK, a bit aggressive. I was concerned. I'm not going to apologize for that."

"How about apologizing for putting me in this position?"

She crossed her arms. "You're gonna have to unpack that for me, Jimmy. What position are you talking about?"

"This one. This one right here."

She shook her head and shrugged. She still wasn't following me. I really needed to draw it out.

I groaned.

"Being responsible for Anton's *life*. For *anyone's* life. That shouldn't be me. Violet's right. I have fucked this all up from the beginning. I should've called you or Mom right away. I should've told the cops he was hiding in my car — "

"He was hiding in your car?"

"At the crime scene, yes." I nodded. "See! More evidence that I am not the guy!"

Erika shook her head. "You have your own ways of doing things. That's all, Jimmy."

"My girlfriend wants to arrest me."

"I will talk to her; she won't do it."

I groaned again, louder. "Stop. OK? Stop trying to fix the

situation. You've done enough."

"Me?" She pointed to herself. "What are you actually accusing me of?"

I put my hands on my hips. "You were the one who told me I could do this. That I *needed* to do this."

"Yeah..."

"You've set me up for failure."

Erika said nothing. "That's it? That's what you're accusing me of?"

"Well, yeah. Maybe I *did* get lucky on that first big case. And then... Matty... he got killed because of me."

She took a breath and shook her head. "He didn't get killed because of you."

"Well, sure, but the kid got away with it..." I closed my eyes and pinched my nose. "I know it's dumb. I know I'm wrong. But I can't help but think, if you hadn't convinced me that I was good at this, Matty would still be alive and Anton wouldn't be here."

"Jimmy, I didn't lie when I said you'd be good at this."

"I know." I rubbed my forehead and repeated, "I know. I just wonder how things would've turned out differently if I had just stayed in my lane."

Erika stepped closer. "I'm sorry it's been a shit time for you." I felt her arms around me. "I should've realized sooner something was going on. Maybe I didn't want to know. I'm sorry."

"I should've come to you. I just felt like such an imposter. Like I've been pretending to be a private investigator."

She held me for a long time.

"Do you think Dad left again because of me?" I asked.

Erika broke the hug. "What?"

"He left again, because of me."

"Our dad did not leave because of you."

"Sure feels like it," I said.

"He didn't."

I shook my head. "He did the first time."

Erika gripped my shoulders. "Our father, Paul Cooper, is an asshole. Who hides a whole family? We have a *sister*. What the fuck?"

I chuckled.

Erika shook her head. "He didn't leave the first time because of you. He didn't disappear the second time because of you. You needed help and he couldn't offer that. You're a good detective because you want to help when bad things happen to good people. You're the real deal, not a fraud like our dad."

My face squished. "Well, I feel like the fraud."

Erika shook her head while a neuron fired in my head.

"You're not a — "

I shushed her. I tried the word on again for size. "Fraud."

"Jimmy, you're not — "

I marched past her, heading back into the house.

"Jimmy?"

That stupid Buddha. That stupid fucking Buddha. It had been gnawing at my brain. The way Louis talked about it? Weird. The way that Horne was so desperate to have it back? And then, the DA... sending Collins after Anton? Like, that's fucked up.

In the kitchen, I looked through my mother's drawers, opening and closing them.

"Jimmy, what's going on?" asked Erika as she rejoined me inside.

I found what I was looking for: a meat tenderizer. I slammed the drawer closed and strode into the dining room.

Ito had been on the phone. She spotted me and covered it. "They arrested a Malcolm Vaughn, the man who was chasing a certain blue Toyota through Hollywood. Do you want to tell me about him?"

"Later, maybe," I replied.

She saw the metal hammer in my hand. "Are you OK?" She sounded worried.

"I'm great. Better than great." I reached for the Buddha, raising the tenderizer high into the air above it."

"Whoa, whoa, whoa!" Ito shouted.

Moe and Anton backed away. I lowered the tenderizer and looked at Violet.

Into the phone she said, "I'll call you back." She hung up. "What are you doing?" she demanded.

Breathing fast, I said, "I have a hunch."

She pointed at the ceramic piece. "That's evidence."

"Yeah."

"It's worth… millions."

"Is it?"

I raised the tenderizer again and before anyone could stop me, I smashed the Buddha right on top of his head. The piece cracked and crumbled. Moe put his fingers to his mouth. His eyebrows reached for the sky. Ito sat very still. Anton stopped breathing.

"Oh, Jimmy," said Erika shoulders collapsing in on themselves. "What did you do?"

Pushing through the pieces, I hoped I wasn't wrong. That would be embarrassing.

I found something that didn't belong. Picking it up, stuck to a piece of ceramic with putty, was a plastic film canister.

Anton frowned. "What's that?"

"Oh, sweet summer child," said Moe.

I pulled the canister away from the ceramic and opened it. A roll of developed film slipped out into my palm. "Guys, there's something not right about this ancient statue."

32

———

Three Years Ago

MAGIC HOUR IS prized in moviemaking. It's the twice-a-day moment when the sun is just at the horizon and the world looks magical. The sky is cool, the sun red, and everyone and every place looks compelling. Even the upper parking deck of a Home Depot.

But that moment is fleeting. Which makes it a nerve-racking choice to shoot during magic hour. You might only get a couple of useable takes, and if you don't get what you need, you have to come back the next day. And the next day costs money.

Such a waste of a magic hour watching Jerry Collins walk up to Chad Lane's car.

Chad got out and Jerry stopped. They stood about five feet apart. Chad seemed a little confused. I grabbed the camera and my phone. I texted Gordon where we were and added, *You wouldn't believe who else is here. Collins.*

I tossed the phone and started snapping pictures.

Collins seemed to be angry. Chad kept shaking his head. Collins took a step forward, and Chad took a step back.

From the other car, the one to the right Chad's, three guys in suits got out. Two white guys, one of them in his fifties, and a Black guy with dyed blond hair. From a distance, yeah, sure, that guy could've been Anton, if you had never met Anton before.

These were the guys Wyler, the witness in Silver Lake, had seen. I snapped pictures of them as they headed over to Collins and Lane. I zoomed in on their license plates. Nevada.

Collins saw them walking over and took a step back as Chad followed his look. He didn't look happy to see them.

I called Gordon. He answered right away.

"Jimmy, I'm, like, fifteen minutes away."

"I think the situation might be escalating," I said. "There are three guys with Nevada plates."

"Oh, shit."

"Yeah, and they look like they stepped off the set of *Casino*. You've seen that one, right?"

Gordon sighed. "Yes, Jimmy, I've seen — "

"Then you know."

"If things get out of hand, call the cops."

"Call the cops," I repeated.

"Stay in the car." He hung up.

Of course I was going to stay in the car. I wasn't a fool.

Chad was grabbed by the two younger guys in suits. The one holding up his right was a white guy whose suit was too small for his size and wore gold rings on all his fingers. On Chad's left was the Black guy, whose suit fit well, wearing it without a tie. His shoes were on point, black and shiny.

Collins took a step back, putting his hands up — trying to cool the situation, if I had to guess. The third man, the oldest one with thinning black hair and a nose that had been broken several times, pointed a finger at Collins, who took a few more steps back, shaking his head.

The third man turned to Chad. He started the conversation with a punch to his stomach. Chad's knees buckled, but the other two brought him back up. The man slapped Chad, grabbed him by the chin.

Collins said something. The third man snapped back at Collins, who was beginning to look very nervous. The man put a hand on Chad's shoulder and punched him in the side. Another. Another. The two men holding Chad had to work harder to keep him on his feet. A final punch to the nose sent Chad back to his knees as blood poured out.

The older man said something, and Chad nodded, his

head heavy. The man nodded to his partners and they let him go. Chad dropped to the ground. The older man, hands on his hips, leaned down and snapped at him. Chad put up a hand of surrender, nodding. He crawled to his car, used it to pull himself up, albeit wobbly, and opened the back seat as everyone watched.

He pulled out the gym bag and it fell to the ground. The older man shook his head in disappointment. Chad pushed the bag closer with his foot. The Black guy was close enough, so he leaned down to pick it up. I watched as Chad reached into the back seat again. Something caught the fleeting light. Oh, shit.

From the back seat of his car, Chad pulled out a katana.

Everyone reached for their concealed weapons as Chad wielded the sword.

I jumped out of the car, shouting, "Chad!"

All eyes turned to me. Confusion hung over the faces of the Las Vegas guys. Collins looked pissed. Chad squinted as he tried to make me out as his face began to swell.

I moved confidently toward the party. "My man, Chad! How are you, buddy?"

The older guy put his hand up. "Friend, I think you're making a big mistake. Best to turn right around."

I kept walking. "Oh, this won't take long. I just want a word with my man here," I said, pointing at Chad. His sword was beginning to waver. It must've felt pretty heavy after all the punching. "What you doing, Chad?"

"Stay out of this," said Chad, his voice coarse. He spit out a tooth.

"I think that's a good idea, friend," said the guy.

I looked at Collins, who suspiciously wasn't saying anything. I smiled at the older guy. "I really wish I could. This does look like a pretty serious conversation. I'm concerned people are going to get hurt." I looked at Chad. "More hurt."

Chad looked confused.

"This is business," the guy said. "As in none of yours."

My expression became one of worry. "Well, the thing is… it sort of is my business."

He shook his head, saying, "I don't think you want to make it yours."

Collins cleared his throat.

The guy looked at him. "What?"

"It's just…" He nodded toward me. "He might be harder to make disappear. He's famous."

"Oh?" The guy looked at me. "Is he?" He looked at his pals. "You guys know him?"

The Black guy shook his head, but the other one stared at me.

"I know him." The guy pointed at me, his gold rings looking every bit like brass knuckles. "He's funny."

I nodded and pointed back at him. "Yep. I'm famous for being funny. Lots of people have seen my movies. *Lots* of people. They recognize me."

Just keep talking, Jimmy. Gordon is on the way and he'll fix all of this.

The boss nodded. "Funny, huh? Tell me a joke."

"Huh?"

"Tell. Me. A joke." He brushed back his thinning hair. "You're funny. You should know jokes."

I licked my lips, feeling my throat get dry. "I don't tell jokes."

"You're known for being funny, but you don't tell jokes?" He shook his head, not understanding.

Gordon, where are you?

"It's my banter. I'm known for my banter. The trouble I get in. Observational stuff, you know? Like, I'm great on the talk shows."

The guy took this in.

"*Oh, yeah.*" The guy with the rings had recognized me. "He has a drug problem. Always in trouble for it. He once slow-crashed a car into a tree. It was hilarious."

Their boss raised an eyebrow, suddenly reassured in a way I found alarming. "Oh, a drug problem? That's unfortunate. Like, you could just disappear, and people would think it was the drugs."

I put up my hands. "To be factual, I'm clean. Sober. That's important to know."

"Relapses happen."

Collins cleared his throat again.

"What?" The guy turned.

Collins's eyes shifted around. He was nervous. "I'm not going to disappear anyone, OK?"

"Oh? You think you get to decide what you're going to do?"

Collins hadn't considered any pushback.

He got lucky. Gordon's car came roaring into the lot. Heads turned, and Collins pulled his weapon and aimed it at the three men. Gordon braked hard, and his car slid to a stop. He opened the door, drew his weapon, and stood behind the driver's-side door. Gordon was a badass.

"Get out of the way, Jimmy!" he shouted.

This time, I listened to him and backed away, hands up.

"This is how things are going to go," Collins told the Vegas contingent "Take your money. Chad and you are even, OK? I think it's best if you found someone else to hold your money. Chad here is... unreliable."

So this was about Mob money and Chad was their bag man. I guessed he hadn't been so careful with their money.

The boss guy thought about it for a moment. He looked at Gordon, looked at Collins. He nodded. "OK." He shrugged. "I might have let my temper get the best of me. It's something I'm working on." He nodded to his friends. They gathered the bag of money and headed to their car, which soon left the parking lot.

Chad lowered the sword, the tip banging on the blacktop. He breathed heavily as he wobbled on his feet.

Collins put up a hand as he slipped his weapon back into his holster with the other. He looked at us with that stupid face of his. "We cool, Gordo?"

"We are not." Gordon aimed his weapon at Collins. "You set up Anton to take a fall for Chad's shit. Now, I can't prove it, but I'm pretty sure you're on the take and those were your bosses. Were you paid to look the other way or clean up the mess?"

Collins just stood there saying nothing as the sun set behind him.

"I think it's best you go before I make a choice I don't like," said Gordon, lowering his weapon.

Collins nodded, eyed Chad, got in his car, and left.

Chad leaned against his car, breathing hard. I moved in.

He looked bad. The blood from his nose had stained his shirt and when he breathed he sounded awful.

"Hey, man," I said. "You're gonna be OK. But I would see a doctor."

He nodded, wiping blood from his nose as Gordon joined us. Chad swallowed and said, "You guys saved my life. Thank you. I'll do anything. You know?"

"Anything?" said Gordon.

I smiled at Chad. "How about telling the ADA the truth?"

33

ITO STOOD NEXT to me. She smelled great, like flowers in spring. However, she was all police-like at the moment. She pointed to the roll of film in my hand. "You did *not* know that was in there."

"Of course, I did," I lied.

Erika sighed.

Ito's eyebrows shot up.

"OK. I got lucky," I admitted. "Never underestimate luck in this business."

"Jimmy," said Ito, "that was evidence of a crime. Evidence in a murder investigation."

"Well, now it's a plot twist," I answered.

Ito shook her head, unsatisfied.

"This sort of changes things, right?" I asked the room. I looked at my girlfriend. "Are you going to arrest us now?"

Moe and Anton looked at her. She turned away from them and back to me. I couldn't tell what she was thinking, whether she was going to strangle me or kick me.

Erika asked the room, "Don't you want to know what's on it? It's a roll of film. You don't smuggle your vacation picture into the country." She paused, letting it sink in. "There's got to be something important on it."

I fingered the roll. "What's so juicy that Patricia Horne was going to spend millions to sneak it in? And why would it be dangerous for her to just carry it through customs?"

Ito put up her hands in surrender. "Fine. Let's see what's on it." She paused. "Then I'll make a decision about what to do."

I grinned. "Perfect." I pulled at the strip of film negatives. "How are we going to do that?"

Blank faces.

And it wasn't like we could get prints made somewhere right away. Who does film anymore?

An internet search turned up a solution. Erika put her iPad on the dining table, with a bright white screen. I changed a setting on my phone, inverting the colors; then I laid a bit of the negative across the iPad and opened the camera app. The negatives flipped to full on color. Everyone squeezed in to look.

"Guys? Can I get a little room?" I asked.

They leaned back, but Erika and Ito stayed close.

"Why didn't Horne just email the pictures to herself?" Erika asked. "Or just put it in the cloud?"

"Old school is the new school in hiding things," I said. "Paper and pen, film, they can't be hacked."

I looked at the image.

Two men were having what looked like a snack at a cafe. Given the lettering of the signs and the people around them, they were in China. The man on the left was Chinese, wearing large Gucci glasses, and, by the quality of his suit, was wealthy. The white guy on the right looked familiar.

"Oh, boy," I said, sitting up, my skin getting cold with recognition.

Erika and Ito bent down to look at the picture.

"That's the district attorney," mumbled Erika.

I nodded. Anton's eyes darted among us, wondering what that meant. It meant things really had taken a turn.

James Paul, the district attorney, was in his early fifties, his auburn hair puffed up and swept back, with longish sideburns (to get some cool cred with the kids, I guess). In the picture, he was in an upscale jean jacket, and his eyes were hidden behind sunglasses — his version of incognito. But it was clearly him.

Ito pointed at the other man. "That's Aaron Huang." By the sound of her voice, I guessed that was a bad thing. She filled us in. "Huang is a Chinese billionaire."

Billionaires.

"He's invested a lot of money in real estate in Southern California. Specifically, in the city of Los Angeles."

We waited for the other shoe to drop.

And Violet dropped it. "There were concerns that he was using his real estate holdings to wash and store his money. And that he's been bribing city council members to further construction projects." She paused and looked at Erika. "Allegedly."

"He's not my client. You can say he did it."

Ito smiled. "I had friends that were working on the case." She nodded toward the pictures. "Until they were called off. They were told they were needed on more important cases."

Erika and I exchanged looks.

Looking through the rest of the photos, they were all of Huang and Paul in conversation and smiling before ending their meeting with a handshake.

"This seems like a smoking gun," I said.

Ito sighed. "Patricia Horne endorsed the DA. Like, she's Team Paul. Why would she smuggle these photos into the country?"

I looked at the ceiling, thinking for a moment. "I don't know. I knew a producer that kept dirt on a certain movie star even though they were apparently good friends. No, not me. But he liked having leverage, just in case he needed a stick during shooting or negotiations. Maybe this is Horne's leverage."

"Ah, fuck," said Ito.

Erika shook her head. "This is bad."

"Really bad?" Anton asked, worried.

"International bad," said Ito.

Moe put his hands to his lips. "That is *bad*."

Anton sat back down, stunned.

"Hey, hey, hey," I said, looking around the room. "Guys, this isn't *bad*. This is pretty great, if you ask me."

"Jimmy," said Erika, "this isn't just about murder. This is corruption. On an international scale."

Feeling good, I said, "I know, right? It's perfect."

Ito crossed her arms. "How is this perfect?"

"It's perfect because we have everything we need," I said. I looked at Anton. "Hey. How you doing?"

Anton was looking into the middle distance. He snapped out of it and said, "Well, I'm involved in an international conspiracy; that sucks."

"Yes. It does." I said, cheerfully. I pointed at him. "But how would you like to get justice for Devon?"

Anton raised an eyebrow. "What do you mean?"

I pointed at my girlfriend. "She can take you in. We have some really great evidence. The pictures. And, of course, you could be a witness. And Patricia Horne might go to jail." I looked at her and nodded. "Right? He could get a deal...

with some assistant district attorney?"

"Sure," she said, not very convincingly.

"And we could take a chance on sending Patricia Horne to jail," I said. "But..."

"But?" Anton asked.

"But she could go free. She could claim she didn't know about the film."

"If I was her lawyer," said Erika, "it's what I would argue."

I pointed at her, nodding. "And then there's Richard Rivers. What actual proof do we *have* that he's involved?"

"Jimmy," groaned Ito. "Can you get to it?

"Or..." I said.

Anton frowned. "Or?"

"We run the table," I said. "We get them all. Horne. Rivers. Amini. Everyone who had a part of Devon's death."

Anton took a moment. "How do we run the table?"

I smiled. I had him.

"Jimmy..." warned Ito. "What are you doing?"

"I'm asking my client what he wants. Violet, this could work. You know Horne will get away with it. *Rivers* will get away with it. Unless we really do something."

She swallowed, shook her head. "What's your plan?"

I grinned. "I'm going to make them pay for it."

34

———

Three Years Ago

I HAD BEEN told that it would be best if I waited outside, so, I was relegated to a bench in the hallway as Mom, Gordon, Anton, and his mother spoke to the ADA. I didn't mind. I had company.

Sitting opposite me, also stuck in the hallway, were Collins and Kemble. They sat on opposite ends of the wooden bench, as far from each other as possible. Kemble sat, legs wide open, with his back to Collins, staring at his phone. I guess it was easier than being present.

Collins, on the other hand, only had eyes for me. Pretty intense. His resting empathy face had turned into "if looks could kill." He wore one of his best suits, I guessed, a dark blue pinstriped number, a crisp, collared shirt and a very red tie. His hands rested on his legs, but I could feel he was coiled, ready to spring.

I smiled as I tapped my paper cup of coffee with a finger, my legs crossed and my foot bouncing along. Waking up that morning, I had felt good. And why not? Everything had come up roses because of me. I had saved Anton. I had even saved *Chad*. I was the reason we were all here at this spot at this moment. And feeling so good — I thought, as I put on a cream-colored linen suit and a deep maroon shirt — I had to share it with the world. I gave Collins an even broader smile.

He nodded at me. "You think you got me?"

I shrugged. "Do you think I got you? Because *I* think I got you. I think Kemble over there thinks I got you, and he's *worried* that I got him."

"Leave me the fuck out of this," mumbled Kemble.

I pointed at the door behind me. "I'm betting my mom is arguing with the ADA that we got you. So I'm not sure why you're even wasting your time asking."

His face turned a shade redder. "You got a smart mouth."

"You're going to make me blush, Jerry."

His face twitched. He aimed a finger at the door. "I don't give a shit what your mom is saying in there. She's just another shitty lawyer — "

"Hey! My mom is a great lawyer."

"I don't give a fuck, *Jimmy Cooper*, because I'm a fucking

cop. A cop with *connections*." He shook his head and crossed his arms. "This is just a bump on the road for me."

I nodded. "Well, I hope you fastened your seat belt."

"What?"

My coffee cup swirled in the air. "It's a Bette Davis reference."

Collins looked confused.

"Admittedly, it's not a great one. She was saying it was a bumpy *night*; you said a bump in the *road*. Still. You know. It's devastating. You're devastated right now." I took a drink.

Collins looked at Kemble, and said, "You believe this asshole?"

Kemble didn't say anything; he didn't look up from his phone. Collins turned back to me, mouth open, ready to say something, but the ADA's office door opened. Holding the door was a man in his late forties, in a black tie, brown pants, a white shirt, and no jacket. Sweat beaded on his forehead. He spotted Collins, and his jaw set in a grim line.

Mrs. Greene led the group out, followed by Anton, then Gordon with Mom bringing up the rear. She paused. "Am I going to see you and your new wife at the fundraiser, Daniel?"

The ADA looked at her, lost for a second, and then said, "Yes, yes. We'll be there."

"I look forward to meeting her," said Mom with the polite smile she had mastered long ago. "Thank you." She led everyone out into the hallway.

"Collins," said the ADA flatly.

"Ooh, someone's in trouble," I sing-songed.

Mother darted her eyes to me.

Collins pushed on his knees, up to standing. He stepped closer to me. "I'll see you later, Jimmy. You won't know when, and that'll make it all the sweeter."

Gordon stepped in between us. "Don't talk to my partner like that."

Partner?

He continued. "You want him? You want *both* of us. You ready for that?"

Collins's eyes drifted from Gordon to me and back again. "Whatever, Gordo. You were a good cop once."

"Yeah, so were you."

"Burn!" I yelped.

"Collins, *now*," said the ADA. "Kemble, you're after him."

Collins slow-walked into the office and the ADA closed the door behind them. All eyes shifted to Kemble. He must've felt it and looked up from his phone. "Shit," he mumbled uncomfortably. He lumbered up. "Gotta piss anyway," he said and then strolled away.

I whirled to Mom. "So?"

"The charges are going to be dropped," she said.

I fist pumped. "Amazing. Fantastic." I felt like my movie had just opened at number one in the country. "Where are we celebrating?"

No one else was cheering. Mrs. Greene gripped her bag tighter. Even Anton wouldn't look at me.

"What's going on?" I was beginning to think my movie had bombed and they were trying to find the nicest way to tell me.

"While they are indeed dropping the charges," explained Mom, "they are only doing so because of a lack of evidence."

I frowned. This had to be a joke. But my mom wasn't funny.

"In other words, James, they aren't admitting they had the wrong person or that Anton is, in fact, innocent."

"What the fuck, Mother? You can't just let them — "

"James," she said, putting up a hand.

"No, *no*. Chad told me — "

She shook her head. "Chad is not talking right now. And Debi is only recanting her identification of Anton."

Gordon said, "She's saying she made a mistake because of the trauma of what happened."

"The trauma?" I said. "Her boyfriend let her get beaten up because he took the Mob's money!"

Mom shook her head, closing her eyes.

"I have *pictures*."

Gordon said, "You have pictures of Chad with money. You have pictures of Jerry Collins and men who may or may not be associated with the Mob — "

"They're *Mob* guys, Gordon."

"We don't know who they are. And Chad isn't talking." He pointed to the office. "Jerry isn't going to admit to any wrongdoing. He's in there covering his ass." He pointed in the direction of Kemble. "He's stuck his neck out as far as he's going to. He might've ruined his career. He's going to be lucky if he gets a decent partner." Gordon pointed to Anton. "But he gets to walk away."

"And Collins?" I asked.

"He'll be forced to retire," Gordon answered.

"*Retire*? That's it?" I couldn't believe it.

Mom put a hand on my arm. "Pushing him out is the best they can do. His union would fight hard and it would be a mess for everyone. This is the best we can do."

Not satisfied, I turned to Mrs. Greene. "You wanted us to prove he was innocent. Not some sort of legal shenanigans. You didn't want this hanging over him. This is not that."

She gripped her purse. "It's done, Jimmy. They've dropped the charges. I'm tired of all of this." I looked at Anton as he stared at the floor. "It's over. This world... well, it's not perfect. It's not going to wrap up all nice and perfect. Like your mother said, this is the best we can do."

And that was it. The three adults looked at me like I was now the problem. I had been here before. I'd been the problem one holding up something because I was high or drunk on set. Those were embarrassing memories. This, though… this stung. Because I knew I was right, but there wasn't anything I could do.

I looked at Anton, who looked away.

35
—

IT WAS LATE Thursday morning, and Anton and I were at the edge of the world. We sat in my mom's car, in a park high above the Pacific, between Santa Monica and the Pacific Palisades. When I had told her the plan this morning and that my car wasn't available, she tossed me the keys and told me to fill up the tank when I was done.

"The Fairest of the Seasons" by Nico played quietly as I stared out at the ocean. The morning fog had burned off, the blue sky was dotted with clouds, but the water still looked gray. We had arrived here early. We hadn't said much on the way over. The whole morning had been quiet. The end was near, and we weren't sure how it was going to turn out.

"Jimmy?"

"Hm?"

"I feel like this might be a bad idea."

I shook my head. "Hey, all the best ideas start out that way."

He frowned. "That doesn't make any sense."

I explained, "I'm saying, let's not judge the idea until we see how it turns out."

Anton snorted.

A voice whispered in our earpieces. "You don't have to do this, you know." Violet Ito sat in an unmarked van just around the corner, on the road leading up to this spot. "We can call it."

I looked at Anton, who was also looking out onto the water. "Nah. We're here."

It got quiet again.

"Devon was a good guy," said Anton.

"Yeah?"

Anton shrugged. "I mean, for a criminal. He was a good guy. You knew where you stood with him."

I smiled.

He went on. "He took me under his wing, you know? I didn't have a dad around. Mom was working. Devon looked out for me. In his way."

Anton ran out of words and stopped talking.

"We're doing what we can for him," I said.

Anton nodded.

"Are you guys ready?" said Ito in our ears. "A car just passed by. Heading your way."

I craned my neck around just as a black Mercedes came up the road and parked nearby. Mr. Darling stepped out of the driver's seat and went around to the passenger side, opening the door and Patricia Horne began wiggling out of the car. Darling offered a hand, but she slapped that away. Finally, on two feet, she got out, Jimmy Choo sunglasses in place.

I turned to Anton. "All right. Let's go."

He nodded and we got out of the car. Anton carried a bag as we crossed the parking lot.

"Jimmy!" said Horne with a rude twinkle in her voice. "I thought I hired you to find the Buddha for me. Imagine my disappointment when Mr. Darling told me you were going to *sell* it to me."

"Life is full of surprises, Patricia."

"Uh-huh," she said with a slight nod.

"I just thought, you know, why get a daily rate when I can get retirement money?"

She smiled grimly. "I appreciate your business sense, Jimmy."

"Jimmy, another car," said Ito.

I checked my watch.

"Are we keeping you from something?" asked Patricia.

I shook my head. "Oh, no. Just expecting more guests."

Her eyebrows disappeared behind her sunglasses as a familiar silver BMW rolled up. It stopped for a moment. I could see inside that Amini was at the wheel, with Rivers next to him, looking very unhappy.

Horne looked at Mr. Darling, who didn't know what was going on either.

She said to me, "What the hell is this, Jimmy?"

I put up my hands and put on a smile, "I promise you, it'll be worth your time."

"It better be," she warned.

Richard Rivers got out of his car, wearing a the same sort of casual white button down and jeans he had on yesterday. He brushed back his mane of hair before stomping over to us, keeping a respectful distance. Amini stood just behind him. Rivers took one look at Horne and asked, "What the actual *fuck*?"

"Classy," mumbled Horne.

Rivers turned to me. "You told me you have the Buddha."

"I do."

He pointed at Horne. "What is she doing here?"

Before I could answer, Ito interrupted. "Just spotted him, coming up the road. Collins is with him."

"Nice as always to see you, too, Richard," Horne said sarcastically.

"I'm going to explain everything, but we're waiting on one final guest." I turned, followed by Anton, as another car rolled up. Jerry Collins was at the wheel, and next to him was the district attorney himself, James Paul.

I looked at Horne and Rivers to see their reaction. Rivers didn't recognize him. Horne, on the other hand, took a step back and put a hand on Mr. Darling's arm.

Collins parked. Paul practically leapt out of the car and walked over to the group, with Collins catching up.

There were four groups of us, three of them facing Anton and me. A breeze off the ocean cooled the situation a little bit. That was nice.

"Now it's a party," I said.

"I don't know what you think you're doing — " started Collins but a hand from Paul shut him up.

"I got your call, Mr. Cooper." The DA said. He looked nice in his charcoal gray suit and black tie. It fit him well. He paid a lot for good tailoring. "I have to say, I thought it was pretty ballsy."

I curtsied.

"This is what I'm willing to offer you…" said Paul.

I waved him off. "Oh, no. You misunderstand." I looked at those assembled. "You all misunderstand. This isn't a negotiation between parties. This is an auction. Highest bidder gets the Buddha."

Anton slipped it out of the bag and held the statue in his hand. The Buddha sat there, resurrected, as serene as the day he was made.

Collins stepped forward, opening his jacket. His badge was clipped to his belt, and his service weapon could be seen. "Maybe I just come over there and take the Buddha from you."

Amini took a step forward. Mr. Darling scowled.

I shook my head. "I don't think you're going to do that. *We* all know why this piece is so important."

Of course, Rivers didn't, but Paul got my meaning. He called Collins off.

"Shall we begin the bidding?" I said. "Three million?"

"Three million?" scoffed Horne. "That's — "

"Three million," said Rivers, giving her the stink eye.

I nodded. "To connect with the universe, worth every penny."

"Four," said Horne, returning the look.

I looked at Paul. "I know the district attorney doesn't make a lot of money, but, you want to get in on this?"

"Four point five," he replied.

I gave an appreciative nod. "Mmm. Not too bold. I like that."

"Five," Horne countered.

Paul and Collins gave her a look.

"Ms. Horne, coming in with the deep pockets," I said.

I could see the wheels turning in both the men's heads. I pointed to Rivers. "I'll tell you what, I'll give you the Buddha, if your man here tells me who pulled the trigger first at the warehouse."

Rivers shot his man a look.

"That's *outrageous*," snapped Horne. "Darling, tell him that's *unfair*. I have the highest bid."

Mr. Darling opened his mouth, "Mr. Cooper — "

So did Paul. "No, no. You can't do *that* — "

Rivers said to Amini. "Tell him. Tell him *now*."

Amini, however, didn't want to tell. He stood there glaring at me. He gritted his teeth and drew his pistol from his shoulder holster. Amini aimed it at me.

Collins, every bit the cop, drew his and aimed it at Amini.

"Jimmy?" said Ito, watching from the van.

"It's OK," I mumbled. "We're OK. Just stay where you are."

Rivers took a step back, not wanting to get hit in the crossfire. "Hey, now." Things were spiraling in ways he did not like.

I asked again, "Who shot first?"

He said quietly, "Me. I did. I shot first."

"Great, great," said Rivers. "He answered. Let's put our guns down and give me the Buddha."

I shook my head. "He's lying. Why are you lying? Vaughn did the same thing. He said *he* shot first."

Rivers shrugged. "Who fucking cares?"

"I do," said Anton. "I care."

Rivers looked at Anton. "Who are you?"

I put up a hand and said to Amini, "You only lie to protect

yourself or someone else. So who are you and Vaughn protecting?" Then it occurred to me. "Jackson. You're protecting Jackson. You don't have to do that, he's dead." I paused. "Unless you're worried about his reputation. Are you worried about his reputation?"

Assim didn't answer, which was as good as a yes.

I nodded. "Even though it had gone wrong, you guys had gone to hell and back. You wanted to remember him for who he was. Not for what happened in the warehouse."

"He should've just been cool," Assim replied. "Everything would've been fine."

"Ah, well," I said, nodding. "He wanted to take care of his sister. He and Vaughn saw a possibility. Can you blame them?"

Amini lowered his weapon.

Rivers started to nod. "OK, he answered your question. I would like my Buddha now."

"Six million!" shouted Horne.

I shook my head. "I'm sorry." I took the Buddha from Anton's hands. "A deal is a deal." I turned back to Rivers. "Here."

I tossed it to him.

Friends, I was not what one would call "good" at athletics. At a certain point, I didn't have PE classes, and stunt men did all the really hard things.

The Buddha sailed toward Rivers in a high but short arc.

His eyes opened wide and he stumbled toward it.

But he didn't make it. The statue slipped through his fingers and shattered on the ground.

Rivers fell to his knees and stared at the rubble, devastated.

Horne and Paul stepped closer to see if *it* was inside.

"Don't worry," I said. "I got that Buddha at World Market this morning. But I know you two aren't really after the Buddha." Horne and Paul looked at me, daggers in their eyes. Rivers looked confused. I explained to him. "It wasn't real to begin with."

He picked up a piece of ceramic.

I held up the film canister. "Now, I think the bidding left off at six million dollars."

Rivers looked up and frowned. "What the fuck is *that*?"

"This is called evidence," I said. I looked at Horne. "Or leverage." I looked at Paul. "Leverage?"

Horne balled her fists.

Paul stared at me. "You're a real asshole, Mr. Cooper."

"Yeah," I admitted. "A lot of people have said that."

"Seven," said Horne.

I looked from her to Paul. "Wow, she really wants this leverage. What do you have?"

Paul licked his lips. "I'll drop the prosecution of your friend there."

I pointed to Anton. "Oh, so you'll drop any charges against my friend here... for this?" I shook the canister.

Collins wasn't thrilled.

Paul extended his hand. "Yes. Deal?"

"Deal," I said, smiling.

"Seven and a half *million* dollars," roared Patricia Horne.

Turning to her, I said, "Sometimes, it's not about the money." I walked over and put the roll of film into Paul's hands. I smirked at Collins. "Ok, now," I said.

Collins frowned. "OK? Now? What what you mean 'OK'?"

"Oh, I wasn't talking to you."

Sirens.

Cop cars and the van with Ito roared into the park. Rivers got up; he and Amini stepped back. Horne clung to Mr. Darling. Collins's eyes grew wide as Paul steamed. Ito stepped out of the side of the van, followed by a lumbering Kemble.

Police officers started slapping on the cuffs. Ito put the cuffs on Paul, who said nothing.

Kemble held his up as he stood in front of Collins.

"Kemble."

"Collins," said Kemble wearily.

"You're really going to slap the cuffs on your old partner?"

Kemble nodded. "Didn't give me much choice." He took a step forward.

Collins stepped back, stalling. "You know I know where all the bodies are buried. I'm going to destroy the LAPD."

"Sure, pal. Sure." Kemble turned him around and put on

the cuffs. Collins grunted. He made a point to not look at me as Kemble escorted him to a waiting police cruiser.

Anton and I stepped back and let the police do their work. We watched as Horne tried to sick Mr. Darling on the police, but they were having none of it as they stuffed the two into a police cruiser. I thought she was going to have an aneurysm.

Rivers kept looking at Amini, probably expecting him to do *something*. Amini had no more fight in him. He was disarmed and put in a squad car as was Richard Rivers.

Ito appeared beside me. The sun made her hair glisten. "What are you smirking about?" she asked, all business.

"I'm feeling good, honey. I got the bad guys." I nudged Anton. "I saved his ass."

"I also saved yours," said Anton.

I chuckled. I said to Ito, "I guess we're feeling good, honey."

She nodded, shook her head and grabbed my arm, spinning me around. I heard the cuffs come out.

"Hold on. What?" I asked. "Why?"

She clicked them tighter . "You *both* have committed crimes." She nodded to another officer who cuffed Anton. "And I don't get to decide whether you're prosecuted or not." She leaned in close to my ear and whispered, "But I'll put in a good word for you."

My knees buckled.

36

——

Three Years Ago

IT WAS IN the evening, two days after the hallway discussion, when there was a knock on my door. I rolled off my couch and paused *All About Eve*. Bette Davis looked like she was about to tear someone's head off. I had spent the past few days at home, in sweat pants and vintage T-shirts, avoiding work. My girlfriend, Rachel, had texted, wanting to accept my apology that I had never really given. I had replied and she replied back and we had made plans to see each other later.

I peeked through the window behind the TV to see who was out front. I wasn't expecting anyone. Especially Anton and Gordon, but there they were.

I had been avoiding work because I was mad about what had happened downtown and the deal that had been made with the ADA. It wasn't right. So, yeah, I was at home pouting.

I opened the door and said to Gordon, "Has Mom sent you to drag me back to work?"

"She has not. I think she's been happy with the peace and quiet."

Nodding, I replied, "You realize that's motivation for me to return, right?"

Gordon shrugged and I invited them in. Anton looked around my small living room. He was in a hoodie and his hair had been cut short, taking out all of the blond. "This is where you live?" he asked, questioning my choices.

"Yeah. This is where I live."

He said nothing, just nodded. "I thought you'd have, like, a mansion or something."

"Oh, my mansion? Yeah, it's not as good as this place. So I don't stay there," I replied.

Anton raised an eyebrow, not sure what to make of my joke.

Gordon, in a suit and tie, cleared his throat. "Anton wanted to stop by."

"Oh?" I said, looking at Anton.

"Yeah, man, I wanted to thank you. Personally, you know?" He nodded nervously.

I looked at Gordon, who watched Anton.

"Sure," I said. "You're welcome."

Anton swallowed. "You're the only one that believed me and that means a lot."

I blushed. He had really meant it. I looked at Gordon who was looking at me, which made this whole thing very uncomfortable. I found myself shifting from one foot to the other. If this had been the Emmys or the Nickelodeon's Kids Choice Awards — which I have *won* by the way — I would have known exactly what to say. I would have said something witty, charming, a lot devilish that would've gotten a laugh. But thanking me for something that really mattered? Oof.

"Well, Anton..." I struggled to find some words. "You stay out of trouble, OK?"

He nodded. I could see him working on something more to say, but nothing came out. "I will," he said and looked at Gordon.

"You good?" he asked.

Anton nodded.

Gordon said to me, "OK, your mother might like the silence, but there's work to be done. I expect you back at work tomorrow."

I agreed and opened the door for them. Anton was the first out, followed by Gordon. He paused and told Anton to head to the car. As he walked away, Gordon turned to me.

"Listen, Jimmy, there's something I've been thinking

about the past few days. I wanted to tell you before I told your mother."

I leaned against the door frame, frowning. "That sounds real ominous, Gordon."

He half-snorted. "It's not ominous. It's just I've been thinking about the future."

"OK."

He put a hand on his hip and scratched the back of his head with the other. "While I agreed to Anton's deal, I didn't like it."

I stood on both feet. "Why didn't you say anything at the time?"

"Because it wouldn't have mattered, Jimmy. I could've argued with the ADA all day long. He wasn't going to change his mind."

"But Collins — "

Gordon put up a hand. "He's off the streets. It's not much, but it's something. I don't want to talk about him. I want to talk about you and me."

"OK."

"Tomorrow I'm going to tell your mother that I'm retiring."

My head tilted. "Retiring? But you're so... well, you're not *old*."

He shook his head. "I'm not retiring immediately. I want out. I got a few more years left in me. In that time, I'm going to get you up to speed. Make you a real detective."

"Oh, Gordon, I don't know…"

He crossed his arms. "You don't know?"

I sighed and looked at the ground. "This is nice, what you're saying. But, I plan on getting my career back, you know? A few more months, a little more sobriety under my belt and I was planning on calling some agents."

"You're going to go back to acting?"

"Yeah, yeah. Nothing big, at first. Maybe some TV appearances. Build up some credibility. I want to show people that I'm ready and able to work."

Spoilers: it didn't work out.

Gordon looked at me right in the eyes and nodded. "Son, I won't stop you from doing what you want. I was really impressed with you on this case. And I think you have a real gift and it would be a shame if you didn't use it."

I nodded. "Sorry."

He nodded and looked toward his car.

"Does this mean you're not going to retire?"

He shook his head. "Oh, no. In a few years, I'm out of this town. Going some place with clean air. Maybe I'll start fishing or something."

I smiled. "Or something."

"Good night, Jimmy. I'll see you tomorrow." Gordon nodded and headed to his car.

I watched until he disappeared around the corner. Closing

the door, I went back to my couch and started the movie. And damn, Gordon. I didn't stop thinking about what he had said to me all night. I had a gift.

37

———

I WATCHED AS Mrs. Greene hugged her son in the hallway of the police station in downtown L.A. It had been three years since I had last seen her and she had gotten a little grayer. But next to Anton, she looked smaller. As they hugged, he lifted her up off her feet. Both of them smiled and both of them had tears in their eyes.

It was Erika Cooper that had gotten the charges dropped. It took her a day and a half, not that I was counting the hours. She had convinced the acting district attorney that it was in the best interest of justice to have Anton Greene and Jimmy Cooper as witnesses rather than defendants. After all, they had recovered the Buddha, had been responsible for the arrest of those who had committed the theft, and uncovered corruption in some of the highest seats of L.A. County government.

Corruption that allowed this very same acting district attorney to claim the office.

Also watching this reunion was Erika and a young Black woman in her twenties. She was about my height with long black hair, wearing a light gray hoodie and black leggings. She held her hands to her chest and beamed as she watch Anton and his mother.

"You're Janelle?" I asked.

She nodded. "You're Jimmy Cooper. I love your movies."

I smiled. "Those old things."

Erika rolled her eyes behind me.

Anton let go of his mother and moved to Janelle. They wrapped arms around each other and kissed. Anton dipped her slightly.

"Get a room," I shouted, laughing.

My sister poked me in the ribs.

Mrs. Greene put a hand on my shoulder and leaned in. "Thank you, Jimmy. I don't know what we would have done without you."

"He's a good kid." I paused. "When he's not being a pain in the ass."

She nodded. "Tell me about it. I'm happy right now to see him, but when I get him home I'm going to beat him for being such a dumb ass."

"And I'll help," said Janelle, pulling away from Anton. She looked at him, her hands cupping his face. "Really, baby, what were you thinking?"

Anton looked at me. "Help a brother out?"

I shook my head. "You are on your own."

He smiled, stepped to me, and gave me a hug, lifting me off the floor. "Jimmy. It's been fun."

Back on my feet, I said, "Yeah, fun. That's a word for it."

His smile dropped and he looked at me. "That Matty guy, he didn't die because of you. You save people, Jimmy. Sometimes you can't save everyone from themselves."

I took a breath. "Well, I got a second chance with you."

Anton chuckled. "Yeah, yeah, you did."

"You don't know what you did for me."

He looked at me, not quite understanding and I didn't have the words to explain it. His mother motioned for him and it was time for them to go.

"You should know there's press outside," said Erika. "You're news. You don't have to talk to them if you don't want to."

Janelle and Mrs. Greene looked at Anton. He shook his head. "If it's all right, I'd like to go home."

"Then go that way," advised Erika, pointing. "We can set up an interview with the press later."

Anton agreed to call another day. They left as Anton put his arms over the shoulders of the women in his life.

Erika turned to me. "I imagine you want to talk to the press."

I took a breath. "No."

"No?"

"I surprise myself," I admitted. "I just... I'm tired. I'd like to go home. I will be happy to talk to them another day."

She shook her head. "You have to pick up Mom's car from the impound lot."

I groaned.

"You told her you would be responsible for it when you borrowed it."

I had agreed to her terms, that was true.

"Tomorrow," I suggested.

Erika shrugged. "She's not going to reimburse the impound fees."

I rolled my eyes. Mother would not. "Fine. Can I get a ride?"

"Of course," she replied, smiling. She took my arm and we started to walk in the direction Erika had sent Anton and family.

I leaned to her and said, "Thank you for getting Anton's charges dropped."

She shrugged. "I'm a good lawyer."

"I'd tell you that you're better than Mom, but it would go to your head and there's only space enough for one self-involved person in this family."

She laughed.

Ito was waiting for us at the doors to the side entrance, leaning against the wall, arms crossed. Her badge hung around her neck on a chain. She was dressed more formally than I had seen before, wearing a dark blue blazer and slacks with a white button-down. Ito wasn't in her boots, but in dress shoes.

Our eyes locked. Erika let me go, saying, "I'll see you at the car." She nodded to Violet as she passed.

Ignoring the weirdness of Violet's clothing choices, I grinned and moved closer. I was feeling good and I was happy to see her. I leaned in for a kiss, but she put up a hand.

I bent back. "Right. At work," I said.

She glanced down the hall. "We need to talk."

My heart dropped. Why do people do that? We all know conversations like that never turn out well.

She took a breath and scratched her forehead. "I've just been in a very long meeting with the Chief of Police."

"Not fun, huh?"

She shook her head. "No, Jimmy, not fun. Especially when the subject is my relationship with you."

"What?" I scoffed. "Why does he care?"

"Because they think this" — her finger moved between me and her — "is compromising my ability to serve the LAPD."

I scoffed. "That's not true. You're a great cop. You just arrested — "

She wagged a finger. "It's not about arrests — "

I was getting worked up. "Not about arrests? That's your *job*. What else *is* there?"

"It's about loyalty, Jimmy."

That stopped me.

She went on, saying, "They want to know that I'm working for *them* and not for you."

That set me off. "Are they stupid? You don't work *for* me. We collaborate. That's it. That's all. Why should they have a problem with that?"

"Because you're not a cop, Jimmy. You're not on their side."

"Well, their side sucks."

She got quiet.

"Go fuck yourself, Jimmy Cooper."

"What?"

She looked at the floor and shook her head. "I need you to take this seriously. My job is on the line and you're making snide comments."

"It's not snide when I'm right."

She looked at me. "You know, you can stop digging yourself into a hole, right?"

Friends, to be honest, I often confused dying on a hill with digging myself into a hole. I said to her, "They can't tell you who you can date and who you can't. You should threaten to quit. You could go to the papers. They would love this story. You threaten, they'll back down."

She said nothing. "Unbelievable." Ito turned and headed back up the hallway.

"Where are you going?" I asked.

"I have work to do."

"You can't just leave it like this."

She paused and turned. "I have reports to do. Responsibilities."

I nodded. "Are you breaking up with me? Is *this* a break-up?"

Violet looked around the hall, hands on her hips. She shrugged. "I'll call you later." She turned and headed to the elevator.

Except that was a lie. She lied to me. She didn't intend to call me later. And she would know that I would know. I took a deep breath, watching her until she disappeared into an elevator, heading back to her desk.

Shit.

In the parking garage, Erika was waiting for me in her car.

As I got in, she could see something was wrong. Frowning, she asked, "What happened?"

I thought about what to tell her. What *did* happen? Did I just fuck something up? Finally, words bubbled up, "I might have been dumped."

Erika did a double take. "She *broke up* with you?"

"Maybe."

"Maybe? What does that mean, Jimmy? Why don't you know?"

My head wobbled. Why didn't I know? Because I hadn't stood there and listened. I kept moving my dumb mouth. I shook my head.

"I just don't. She and I will talk later." And I realized, it was going have to be me to make the call. "Can we just go?"

She stared at me for a moment. "You want to choose the music?"

I looked at her. "Always."

Erika started her car as I reached into my coat and dug out my phone. I connected it to her car and chose a song. With a sweaty guitar intro, Joe Walsh's "Life's Been Good" began.

Out of the parking garage, hit by the sunlight, I slipped on my sunglasses, and Erika did the same. After months, I felt like I was going to be all right, that I could hold onto the win of the last few days rather than the loss in the hallway. That I was, in fact, able to do the thing I was meant to do.

Taking a deep breath, I watched L.A. roll by, ready for whatever happened next.

THE END

Song List

Cher — Gypsys, Tramps and Thieves

Tones and I — Dance Monkey

Bleachers — Like A River Runs

Sweet — Fox On The Run

Eric Burdon — Spill The Wine

Styx — Come Sail Away

Linda Ronstadt — You're No Good

Clairo — Add Up My Love

The Velvet Underground — Oh! Sweet Nuthin

Spacehog — In the Meantime

Gladys Knight & The Pips — Midnight Train to Georgia

Miley Cyrus — Malibu

Hole — Celebrity Skin

Scissor Sisters — I Don't Feel Like Dancin'

The Beach Boys — Do It Again

Pet Shop Boys — All The Young Dudes

Indeep — Last Night a DJ Saved My Life

Electric Light Orchestra — Can't Get It Out of My Head

Thelma Houston — Don't Leave Me This Way

Nico — The Fairest of the Seasons

Joe Walsh — Life's Been Good

The playlist can be found at...
YouTube Music: https://bit.ly/GFYYouTube
Spotify: https://bit.ly/GFYSpotify

Special thanks to...

FIRST, I NEED to thank my editor, Jessica Hatch. She is generous with her thoughts, creativity, and support. My work would be a mess without her. With every book I learn something from her. In this case, my overuse of the comma.

One of the big reasons people have picked up this series are the covers, each done by the marvelous Enni Tuomisalo. She is a pro and a delight to work with.

Mindy Carlson helped unknot a problem I had early on in the writing of this book.

My son, who has been so patient with a bleary eyed father...

And, of course, a big thank you to Deepti Gupta. As I have said before, she is my biggest ally, my best partner, and my toughest fan. Hers is the last eye that sees the book before it gets to you, the reader.

This has been a difficult book to write. In May of 2024, my mother suffered a stroke and spent the next eight months in and out of healthcare facilities, before passing away this past March. The whole time I had been trying to write, believing it would be a way to take my mind off things. Friends, it did not.

My mother is the reason I'm a mystery writer. She introduced me to the genre by showing me the Jeremy Brett

Sherlock Holmes (still the best) on *Mystery!* here in America. And she was always reading mysteries, right up until she couldn't. So, a big thank you to my mom.

And thank you for picking up *Go F@!k Yourself!* I hope you enjoyed it and, if you did, tell your friends.

Until next time!

— LA

Jimmy Cooper will return in

F@!k Around and Find Out

—— ———————— ——

To stay up to date follow Lawrence Allan on social media
@WriteLarryWrite or join his newsletter:
bit.ly/LAWnewsletter
You can also find him at **LawrenceAllanWrites.com**

—— ———————— ——